The Hampton Affair

VINCENT LARDO

BERKLEY BOOKS, NEW YORK

This is a work of fiction. Names, characters, places, and incidents are either the product of the author's imagination or are used fictitiously, and any resemblance to actual persons, living or dead, business establishments, events, or locales is entirely coincidental.

THE HAMPTON AFFAIR

A Berkley Book / published by arrangement with
the author

PRINTING HISTORY
G. P. Putnam's Sons hardcover edition / May 1999
Berkley edition / June 2000

The Penguin Putnam Inc. World Wide Web site address is
http://www.penguinputnam.com

ISBN: 0-425-17482-4

BERKLEY®
Berkley Books are published by The Berkley Publishing Group,
a division of Penguin Putnam Inc.,
375 Hudson Street, New York, New York 10014.
BERKLEY and the "B" design are trademarks belonging to
Penguin Putnam Inc.

PRINTED IN THE UNITED STATES OF AMERICA

10 9 8 7 6 5 4 3 2 1

FOR
ROBERT BEAUMONT EVANS

Prologue

Wednesday—June 25

He followed the narrow path until it veered sharply to the left. Making the turn, he came to an abrupt halt, knowing that beyond the wall of vines and brambles he now faced, the ground dropped off precariously. He was standing at the edge of a precipice some twenty feet high. Clutching the binoculars, he cautiously parted the green curtain in the manner of an actor sneaking a look at his audience. There they were, seated on the narrow strip of gravel that surrounded the pond, the woman reclining on the dilapidated beach chair and the boy next to her, perched on a towel. They were both naked. Wondering if he was too early or too late, he brought the binoculars to his eyes and focused on the woman.

The first time he had viewed her through the glasses, he was surprised by the fact that she was much older than she appeared from a distance. The discovery did not diminish her appeal; she was tall, slim, fine-boned, and as graceful as a ballerina—attributes that had made him think she was a much younger woman. Her auburn hair, which she wore pulled back from her face and tied with a ribbon into a ponytail, was too pretty a shade to be anything but natural. In spite of her tan, or perhaps because of it, the fine lines beneath her eyes and around her unpainted lips were brought into sharp relief through the binocular's lenses. Her breasts were firm, the nipples as dark as the freckles that dotted her tanned flesh. She kept her legs modestly closed, revealing only a trace of pubic hair. Forty, he thought, give or take a few years.

He moved his gaze to the boy and once again found himself staring at freckles. These on the bridge of a slightly tilted nose. Bright blue eyes, a toothy smile, and blond hair, fashionably layered. The boy could easily have been the woman's son, appearing to be in his late teens. The thought aroused the spy and he began to move the glasses down the masculine torso, whose shape exercise machines promise but seldom deliver. The couple, he concluded, looked as serene and content as their surroundings. He was too late.

He shrugged, lowered the glasses, and took in the entire scene, amazed as always that life here imitated calendar art. The placid pond was surrounded by tall pines, and the old, flat-bottomed boat beached at the pond's rim could boast a provenance of Maine or the Canadian Rockies. The naked couple offered a note of prurient mystery to the scene. What they did here every Wednesday, weather permitting, was obvious: they sunbathed and screwed. Who they were and where they came from was the enigma.

The boy rose and stretched. The woman appeared not to notice. Bad sign. Like an old married couple, they had become used to each other's nakedness. The boy took a few short steps to the pond's perimeter, and as his toes touched the water the Peeping Tom shivered in empathy.

Pausing, the boy turned to the woman and beckoned. Seeing his intention, she shook her head. Then, as if spontaneously, the boy walked to the boat, whose parched gray wood frame was dotted with wormholes, and pushed it partway into the pond. Again he turned to the woman, this time bowing from the waist, like a chauffeur at the door of a limousine.

Laughing, she rose and walked to him. Yes, gracefully, like a dancer. He helped her into the boat, then pushed it into the pond before hopping aboard. Balancing herself with outstretched arms, again the ballerina, she moved to the prow of the craft and gingerly lowered her bare bottom to the wood seat. From the boat's floor her gondolier picked up an oar—or rather half an oar, judging from its handle, which was shorter than the boy's arm—and took the seat opposite.

"The Owl and the Pussycat went to sea in an ancient flat-bottomed boat," their hidden observer thought as the boy paddled around the pond's perimeter and then to its center, where he raised the oar and allowed the boat to drift aimlessly. The woman, trailing one hand in the cool water, closed her eyes and tilted her face to the warm June sun. The boy, as if out of boredom, began to rock the boat, gently. She opened her eyes and appeared to scold him, reinforcing the image of mother and son.

The boy, laughing, increased his effort and his passenger, not amused, gripped the wood railing and shouted at her antagonist. Her fear served only to increase her tormentor's enthusiasm for the game and he continued to rock the boat precariously until—with one final push—it capsized, tossing them both into the pond.

A childish prank. Well, he thought, what else did she expect from a teenage paramour?

The boat, now bottom up, continued to float. After what seemed like a minute but was probably half that time, the pair did not surface and he grew apprehensive. He looked at his watch but since he did not know when they went over, the gesture was moot. What were they doing down there, arguing?

Finally, the blond head appeared. The observer drew a deep breath. Moving with the proficiency of a seal, the boy approached the boat, turned it on its side, and deliberately allowed it to fill with water. With surprising strength, he righted the cumbersome craft, which rode so low in the water only the railing was visible. Now, he had only to tilt the boat slightly to accomplish his goal.

All that remained afloat was the oar, which the boy grabbed as he made for the shore. Reaching the shallow bank, he walked the short distance to land, his behind shiny white between tanned back and legs. Still holding the oar, he gathered their belongings with his free hand, stuffed them into a brown leather tote bag, hoisted it by the strap over his naked shoulder, and without a backward glance, disappeared into the woods.

The beach chair, its green and white webbing in tatters, was the only prop not cleared from the set of this macabre drama enacted on Two Holes of Water Road in East Hampton, on a warm Wednesday afternoon in June.

Michael Anthony Reo

One

The discovery of the second hole of water, my witnessing a murder, and the events that followed were all a result of the heart attack suffered by my father-in-law, Joseph Kirkpatrick.

When that name is dropped in conversation, the usual response is, *"The* Joseph Kirkpatrick?" The answer is yes, *the* Joseph Kirkpatrick. When appearing in print, the name is inevitably followed by the epithet "media mogul." I think "prick" would more aptly delineate Joseph Kirkpatrick, but no one has ever sought my opinion.

The seizure occurred a few minutes after midnight, New Year's Eve, at the Kirkpatrick home on Dunemere Lane in East Hampton. Kirk, as he is known to intimates, traditionally celebrated the holiday with a gala black-tie dinner at his beach house. Renowned names in politics, high society, and show business vied for invitations. One hundred, exactly, were chosen. "The party of the years," as one columnist dubbed it, survived the austere thirties, a world war, a cold war, the twist, rock 'n' roll, and punk rock.

But about the time a B-movie cowboy moved into the White House, Joseph Kirkpatrick's empire was the victim of a hostile takeover by a Japanese conglomerate, making him five hundred million dollars richer while transforming the charismatic entrepreneur and womanizer into a cantankerous old recluse.

Thereafter, the gala became less of an event and more of a command performance, until this year, when a much smaller cast—of exactly five, including the host—greeted the new year.

At midnight there was the obligatory champagne toast. Those of the opposite sex kissed; the gentlemen shook hands. The ladies, of course, are allowed to touch cheeks and purse their lips like guppies in a bowl. We sat down to dinner prepared by Maddy, the housekeeper, and served by John, her jack-of-all-trades husband, who this evening donned his butler's hat. John had just finished ladling out the turtle soup when Kirk, seated at the head of the table, turned the bilious color of the broth and began gasping for air. The lawyer, Mark Barrett, seated at Kirk's left, shoved his chair back, retreating as if Kirk had exhibited signs of a contagious disease. Barrett's wife, Milly, seated next to her husband, lifted her damask napkin to her lips daintily although she had not yet tasted the soup. Kirk's daughter, Victoria, seated at her father's right, screamed and I think muttered, "His heart."

I, Michael Anthony Reo, Victoria's husband, was startled by the fact that Joseph Kirkpatrick *had* a heart.

John called 911 and in less than ten minutes an ambulance rounded the circular drive of the Dunemere Lane house, lights flashing and siren wailing. John, to be sure, had broadcast the victim's name, because John could not carry on a conversation—even a cry for help—without telling his listener that he'd been, for forty consecutive years, Mr. Kirkpatrick's valet, chief bottle washer, and (if need be, on occasion) pimp. Every volunteer in town seemed to have piled into the ambulance, thoughtfully leaving just enough room for the patient.

Vicky and I followed in the Land Rover, which John had brought around to the front door for our use. Notice, please, that I said Land Rover. Michael is not allowed to drive the Rolls, because Michael is accident-prone. His most disastrous mishap was, I admit, marrying into this family.

The ambulance went screaming back up Dunemere Lane, which disturbed no one because no one in their right mind was in residence on Dunemere Lane on a frigid December night. Vicky sobbed all the way to Southampton Hospital. Keeping my eyes on the flashing blue and red lights, I thought of an argument I'd had with Kirk—one of many—that ended with the bastard postulating, "Whoever dies first loses."

Had I won? Not that night. The next morning a prestigious specialist was flown in from New York City. Southampton Hospital's intensive care staff was chagrined, but contemplating the largesse of the Kirkpatrick Foundation, they welcomed the man with open arms. The specialist did exactly what the intern on duty had done the previous evening—watched and waited.

The news of Joseph Kirkpatrick's heart attack hit the wire services on January 2; his Bachrach photo did not have to compete with a shot of Times Square at midnight. Timing had always been Joseph Kirkpatrick's long suit. Two weeks later, Kirk was discharged from the hospital into the care of a nurse supervised by the hospital's heart man, who, in turn, answered to the New York specialist.

One private telephone line was kept open at the Dunemere Lane house. All inquiries regarding Kirk's condition were handled by the public relations staff of WMET, the independent network founded by Joseph Kirkpatrick, where he still retained the honorary title of chairman of the board and an office in the MET Tower building he hadn't occupied in over ten years.

Vicky was determined to remain at her father's bedside. I could do as I wished. "I'll stay," I announced, feigning concern. She wasn't fooled for a moment but welcomed the company. The Dunemere Lane house contains two master bedroom suites, four guest bedrooms, breakfast room, dining room, sunroom, great room, den, and eight servants' warrens on the third floor. (Not the ideal place to wait for the grim reaper in the middle of winter.) The only thing more boring than waiting for someone to be born is waiting for someone to die. You can be coaxed in, it seemed, but not out.

Every night the nurse—cheeks like apples and gray hair cut as short as a man's—announced that Mr. Kirkpatrick was nearing the end of his journey, and every morning the traveler ate a hearty breakfast. By March, I had gained one inch around my waist—totally unacceptable for a vain man, especially one who has good reason for his vanity. Six foot one, a hundred and seventy pounds, a full head of hair which—at forty plus a few years—shows no signs of leaving my head. The result of an Italian–Irish marriage, I was blessed with the best features of each and spared the worst.

The afternoons having finally turned warm enough to make the outdoors enjoyable, I decided on bicycling as a means of exercise. The activity also offered the added incentive of getting me out of the house and away from Operation Death Watch for as long as my legs would hold out. John produced a handsome ten-speed from wherever such things are kept, and handed it over to me like a father bestowing an expensive gift upon an unworthy son. I hope John will do the right thing when Kirk dies and fling himself into his master's grave.

An ancient privet hedge separates the Dunemere Lane house from the back nine holes of the Maidstone Club's golf course. The prestigious club's front yard is the Atlantic Ocean. Every American town of substance has such a club, but few can claim this location as well as a membership comprised of old-guard names and new-guard money. I avoided this route because the old and new were already swarming over the fairways and, if spotted, I would be obliged to assume the demeanor of an undertaker and report on the mogul. Cycling in the opposite direction, away from the ocean, I began to explore uncharted territory. This is how I chanced upon Two Holes of Water Road.

Intrigued by its name, I traversed it from one end to the other in search of the holes of water. The area was dense with tall pines and brush, but thanks to the winter landscape, some very impressive houses could be gleaned from the newly paved road that meandered like a snake through a series of hills and dales. Vicky would no doubt call their inhabitants the nouveau riche—the Kirkpatrick fortune went back all of fifty years.

Besides the houses, I discovered one of the water holes at once. It was what I would call a large pond, some hundred feet off the northern end of the country road. The second hole of water eluded me, and since I had nothing better to occupy my time, searching for it became something of a game. After a week, however, the game became more work than play and I decided that the second hole of water had dried up either by dint of nature or through the efforts of one of the new rich.

One afternoon, in the local bookstore, I chanced upon a rack filled with maps of the area. I found one that contained a blowup of my cycling route, and spotted the blue dot that I knew to be the hole of water I was familiar with and, not far from it, a smaller blue dot that I assumed was the second hole of water. I purchased the map. Utilizing its scale, I calculated the elusive hole of water to be about a half-mile below, or south, of its visible counterpart.

Starting at the north end of Two Holes of Water Road, I cycled south and—estimating the distance—abandoned the bike at what I hoped was the half-mile mark. Walking and scanning the woods as I imagine hunters would when stalking deer, I discovered the path. Hardly wide enough to accommodate two people walking side by side, it would easily go unnoticed by a passing driver and be completely obliterated by foliage in the summer.

Timidly, I ventured onto the path and followed it for some fifty feet, where it turned sharply to the left and terminated abruptly at the edge of a cliff some twenty or thirty feet high. Below me, at the bottom of a dell or ravine, I discovered the second hole of water. The small pond, almost circular, was bordered by a narrow gravel beach and surrounded by tall pines. It could have been the primeval forest if not for the fact that standing on the gravelly bank was a beach chair, green and white webbing in tatters, and not far from it, a decaying flat-bottomed boat.

Feeling like Robinson Crusoe on the trail of Friday, I returned to the spot almost daily. Sometime in April I was rewarded with the appearance of a young man—a boy actually—seated in the chair wearing only his underpants, sunning himself. How he got there, short of dropping out of the sky, was a mystery. Given his sudden appearance and the day not being Friday, I dubbed him Adam. In the following weeks he appeared sporadically in various stages of undress until, in late May, Eve appeared, and judging from what they were up to, I would say the apple had been plucked, devoured, and forgotten. Paradise lost or found—take your choice.

I didn't purposely buy the binoculars and I know this fact doesn't excuse using them, but it tempers the guilt. I recalled the pair I'd seen in the pigeonhole of a fall-front desk in the den—a room Vicky insists on calling the drawing room—and borrowed them. Employing the binoculars, I discovered that madam was a hell of a lot older than Adam. Teacher and student? A thought I found persuasively erotic.

After the murder, I never returned to my observation post. Why? Because I was scared. Would she, in time, float to the surface, bloated and half eaten by whatever aquatic life inhabited the pond? Would I see him, in his briefs, sunning himself? Either was possible, and both frightening. I became paranoid, was certain that he had seen me and, having committed one murder for no apparent reason, would not hesitate to commit another to keep his secret safe. There were even moments when I could talk myself into believing that I had imagined it all, including finding the pond.

Why didn't I go to the police? How could I explain my presence? Bird-watching? Yes, of course, that's why I carried the binoculars. The tabloids would have a field day. "MEDIA MOGUL'S SON-IN-LAW POUNDS PUD IN BUSHES OF POSH RESORT." Shit.

Friday evening, two days after this event, Joseph Kirk-patrick reached the end of his journey. It is said that there is never a second without a third. Who, I wondered, would be next?

Two

"Private. Just the family. A mass, of course, and the interment will be here, next to Mother, so there's no need to go to the city."

Vicky, brandishing an unlit cigarette and functioning in the highest possible gear, delivered this pronouncement in a tone that said her mind was made up and nothing short of Kirk's resurrection could change it. It was an inflection learned and perfected early in life when dealing with a series of nannies who usually resigned in tears after a short-lived career in the care and feeding of the Golden Princess.

I was stunned. More to the point, I was packed. Ready to flee the wide-open spaces of Dunemere Lane for the comforts and safety of our brick and mortar castle on Fifth Avenue. We didn't have a moat, but we did have a doorman, a concierge, and an elevator attendant to protect us from brash young men with unique methods for breaking off love affairs. Vicky had worshiped her father and the sentiment, believe me, was reciprocated. I had imagined Kirk's last hoorah would be orchestrated with slightly more pomp and circumstance than the laying to rest of a pharaoh beneath his pyramid. Instead, this humble approach to death was uncharacteristic and therefore suspect.

Vicky, naturally, knew nothing of my predicament, and quite frankly, I didn't trust her with the gruesome details. Having no idea what the future held now that Kirk was gone, I didn't want to put any rash ideas into my wife's head. Divorce, after all, is messy and expensive.

She was aware of my bicycling afternoons, however, so I did tell her of my discovery of the second hole of water. My efforts were rewarded with, "Really, darling, such a fuss over a hole of water. You could have asked John, he knows the area quite well, or Mark. The Barretts were here before Columbus."

Vicky talks as if her life were scripted by Miss Manners. John wouldn't know where Two Holes of Water Road was because no one who interested John boasted that address. Like all servants, our John was a snob. That I should have consulted Mark Barrett derived from the fact that since Kirk blew the cover on his immortality, the lawyer and Vicky were in constant communication, no doubt discussing money.

One can imagine Vicky's reaction to my tale of the goings-on around and under that hole of water: "Really, darling, such a fuss over a murder. You should have gone directly to the police. It's their business, not ours."

And, I admit, she would have been correct. I should have gone directly to the police, but it was too late for that now. I can just imagine the conversation I might have with our local men in blue.

"Why, Mr. Reo, did you wait so long to report this incident?"

"Well, sir, my father-in-law dropped dead between then and now."

"My, my, Mr. Reo. Your path seems to be strewn with the newly departed."

No, that would never do. Besides, it was the boy's word against mine. I couldn't prove a thing. And worse, if they failed to locate the boy from my description, I would become the chief suspect because who but the murderer would know where to find the body and the boat?

But the boy didn't see me. I was sure of that. Why the paranoia? And why, lately, the disquieting feeling that I had witnessed a similar crime? Déjà vu, it's called. Nerves? Guilt? Why should I be guilty over another's crime? It was all very disconcerting. And now this startling news about Kirk's funeral.

"Later, September perhaps, we'll have a memorial service in one of the Broadway houses or the auditorium of the MET Tower building." Vicky was still discussing the arrangements and trying to keep from lighting her cigarette. Drawing on an unlit cigarette was her latest ploy in a two-year attempt to withdraw from the weed.

"I thought about putting together a short documentary on Father's life for the occasion. It could also be given a public viewing on one of our news specials."

If you include footage of all his mistresses, you could turn it into a miniseries.

"Not the rags-to-riches approach," Vicky said with distaste. "Father wasn't a pauper before he founded the network."

Indeed not. He struck gold at the altar when he married your mother. The former Victoria Aimsworth was a Philadelphia heiress—it was the late Mrs. Kirkpatrick's money that bought the local radio station Kirk parlayed into a mega communications network. He repaid this kindness by being the most unfaithful husband since Bluebeard. The bastard even bought a minor movie studio in the 1930s to ensure himself a harem of peroxide blondes. One of his starlets actually became a top box office attraction, who, if she were still alive, would surely lament his passing. When the lady hit on hard times she blackmailed Kirk periodically for thousands. Her ace in the hole was a reel of "home movies" shot aboard the Hearst yacht on a fun weekend cruise between Santa Barbara and San Diego. I imagine this film clip would be excluded from Vicky's testimonial.

"We would stress his contribution to broadcasting and his participation in the war," Vicky intoned.

The Second World War, that is. It's the only one Vicky acknowledges. The army commissioned Kirk a major. On the home front he aired Sousa marches between readings by Broadway and film stars on a series called "A Letter from an Unknown Soldier." On the war front he took on Tokyo Rose, lost every skirmish in the battle of the ratings, but as history will bear out, won the war.

These arrangements, short- and long-term, were unlike my Vicky. She just didn't think this way. In fact, Vicky seldom thought at all. Her father had done it for her. Her marriage to me twenty years ago (how time flies when you're having fun!), believed by many, including the bride, to be a bold and defiant statement, was in fact playing right into the old codger's hand. Even I was fooled, but I soon learned that Joseph Kirkpatrick was more diabolical than his enemies imagined.

Here I began to detect—or should I say smell—the Machiavellian hand of the family solicitor in Kirk's unpretentious burial and elaborate future commemoration.

Kirk's final appearance in the *New York Times* was accompanied by Bachrach's official portrait. The *Times* used the more polite "media giant" to explain Kirk's positioning on its front page and a good three-quarters of the obit section. The paper called him "the last of a pioneering triumvirate," his cohorts none other than William Paley and Robert (General) Sarnoff. Kirk would have been pleased.

The announcement that the funeral would be private precipitated hundreds of condolences, prompted no doubt by relief that those obligated wouldn't have to make the tedious journey to the East End of Long Island. Vicky somehow managed to retain the nurse, Ms. Johnson, to handle and record the avalanche of paper. Leave it to the rich to get the most out of the hired help. Also, taking on a secretary for the job would open the sacred portals of the Dunemere Lane house to yet another stranger. Nurse was a necessity, so let her double as chief clerk in retaliation for her unavoidable intrusion. The kind woman was better able to deal with the sick and dying than Federal Express and a fax machine, and after her first day on the job looked ready to take her place next to Vicky's long-forgotten nannies.

The obit notice having failed to direct donations to charities, the house and grounds soon took on the appearance of a humongous float in the Tournament of Roses pageant. Ms. Johnson was told to call every florist in the Hamptons to head off the flow, and ordered to dispose of the ridiculous number of wreaths that had already gotten through. The poor woman had them taken to the small country church, probably causing mourners and clergy to wish that gas masks were provided along with the Sunday missals.

Just family, Vicky had trumpeted. Vicky and I had not

produced an heir, and the Kirkpatrick and Aimsworth clans not being prolific, I thought Kirk would be accompanied to eternal rest by his daughter, his son-in-law, and, as de facto relations, John and Maddy. As in everything else connected with this interment, I was wrong. The Barretts, Mark and Milly, became instant kin.

The lawyer had now insinuated himself into the family. What next? I wondered, giving up all thoughts of going back to the city the minute the last shovelful of dirt came between the mortal remains of Joseph Kirkpatrick and this vale of tears. Not even a murderer on the prowl was going to force me to usurp my position next to the heir apparent with the likes of Mark Barrett waiting in the wings. But waiting for what?

Could my father-in-law, with Barrett's help, have written a will that would make it impossible for me to get my hands on even a fraction of that half-billion? I have a recurrent nightmare—a judge, hammering his gavel so that it echoes throughout a cold and impersonal chamber as he shouts, "IRREVOCABLE TRUST." I awake, shivering and sweating and thankful that it is only a dream. But dreams—if they're nightmares—very often come true.

I doubt if anyone attending a requiem mass ever follows the liturgy while praying for the repose of the deceased's soul. The mind, on these occasions, tends to dwell on frivolities, mostly to keep from reminding us that before very long we'll be the one reclining in the box being doused with holy water.

I began by contemplating Vicky, who never seemed to be able to get her act together, no matter who was consulted and how much money was spent in the effort. Having six months to prepare for the inevitable, she had neglected to contact Bergdorf's or our housekeeper in the city, to send her something more appropriate than the dress she wore at the New Year's Eve gala. Thank God it was black, but even so, it looked more winter than spring and more festive than funereal.

Vicky's blond hair also seemed to mock the solemnity of the occasion. Parted on the left and cascading in soft waves to just above her shoulders, her hair was her trademark in our social set. Hence she used a lemon rinse to highlight its presence. Her green eyes competed with mascara and liner and lost. Vicky used makeup as a shield rather than to enhance. Beneath the foundation and blush was a lovely complexion, however. I thought it prudent not to criticize but often imagined that if the clever mask were removed all her features would disappear, challenging the master painter to try again.

Mark Barrett, on the other hand, was always appropriately dressed, groomed, and at ease, whether his venue was a boardroom, the golf course, or, we now saw, a Catholic church. To see him stand, sit, kneel, and execute a sign of the cross, always one beat behind us Romans, made one forget that his ancestors had most likely supported good King Henry in his bid to oust the Pope and take in Anne Boleyn.

Mark's wife, Milly, my friend and confidante, had better sense than to pretend to be what she was not. Milly sat in the soft glow of the dappled light, which filtered through the church's modest stained-glass windows, suppressing the nausea aroused by the conflicting aromas of flowers and incense locked in mortal combat for domination in the stifling atmosphere. Milly was, as always, smartly dressed and coiffured, with hands serenely folded on her lap in the manner taught—and never forgotten—in Miss Porter's classes. Milly came from old Boston money and good breeding. Mark came from old East Hampton money, which tended to be, like Texas money, a little rough around the edges. My money came from Vicky and hers from the guy in the coffin, which was too close for comfort.

If God was not blinded by the black smoke His high priest was wafting His way, I doubt if He looked upon this *cage aux folles* gathering with love and benevolence. Nor, I suspected, did the lone girl sitting in the rear of the church, who I guessed was a reporter from the *East Hampton Star.* John and Maddy, sitting directly behind us four principals, sobbed throughout the service. Crocodile tears I assume, as Kirk had often boasted—in their presence—that upon his death dear John and Maddy would be pensioned off for life. And what of the blue-eyed, raven-haired hunk of a pirate who had run off with the Golden Princess? Would he be pensioned off too? Over my dead body. Or should that be her dead body? Mark Barrett's body? The options, it seemed, were endless.

Otherwise engaged, I was not aware the mass had ended until I heard our meager congregation reciting the Lord's Prayer. Here was something our Protestant brethren could be at home with, and like minor players whose cues do not come until the final curtain, Mark and Milly delivered their lines with gusto. I joined in the refrain.

"And forgive us our trespasses as we forgive those who trespass against us," I prayed, not believing it for one fucking instant.

Three

A small crowd had gathered outside the church, thanks to WMET's television van, parked directly across the street from the hearse and our Rolls. The network had deigned to send a mobile unit to record their founder's last moment above ground. As we walked to our car, I saw what's her name, the popular anchorperson, gesturing with her mike to several young men who pranced to the beat of her electronic baton.

Our caravan was led by the hearse, followed by our Rolls with John at the wheel, Maddy beside him, and Vicky and me in the rear. Behind us, Mark and Milly were in their Jaguar, and at a not very respectable distance behind them rolled the white van bearing the network's logo and call letters in black. The van—like a magnet—led an odd assortment of vehicles to the cemetery, picking up, I imagine, some curious passersby who had no idea where they were going.

The weather, along with Vicky's dress and hair, was at odds with the solemn occasion. Blue sky, bright sun, dogwood in full bloom, and an air of expectation peculiar to a beach resort a few days before the Fourth of July holiday conspired to produce a setting more conducive to a wedding than a funeral.

Arriving at the Kirkpatrick plot, I discovered why the rich are different from you and me. They're cheap. The piece of real estate was so small that I wondered if there would be room enough for Vicky and me to be laid to rest side by side. If so, I hope I'm planted as far from my father-in-law as possible. Eternity is a long time.

As we waited those disconcerting moments for the coffin to be put in place, poised for descent soon after we mourners had departed, I forced myself not to gawk back at the onlookers crowding the narrow path opposite the grave site. However, they appeared more interested in what's her name, the anchorperson, than in poor Kirk.

The men manipulating the coffin and the priest perusing his Bible held no interest for me, which left our party fair game for my scrutiny:

Vicky in her black New Year's Eve dress, her blond hair set in motion by the gentle breeze; Milly in a perfect, navy blue Chanel suit, sunlight causing the gold threads in her brown hair to twinkle, her pretty face and faultless complexion revealing not a trace of makeup; Maddy, in a black and white print dress, accessorized with black vinyl pumps, a black vinyl purse, and a black hat too bizarre to describe, so I won't try. Her pained expression was, I'm sure, more a result of the pumps than of the reason for our gathering.

And John, his ruddy cheeks looking strangely rouged in the merciless high-noon light and his paunch ready to burst out of the black suit that was his chauffeur's uniform, while Barrett, in a small blue suit, looked like a white Anglo-Saxon Protestant. At fifty and slightly over six feet tall, his skin is unlined and his hair, perhaps a tad long for his age, a distinguished salt-and-pepper. Trim, he resembles an ex-athlete, still in good form. I report this begrudgingly.

Finally, yours truly stood by in a custom-made, banker's-gray, three-buttoned job, looking the part I had been engaged to play twenty years ago: consort to the Golden Princess.

The funeral director beckoned and Mark Barrett reached for Vicky's arm and a second later withdrew it and took Milly's. The faux pas was so spontaneous, so swift, that had I not been staring at Barrett, I would have missed it. It was at this moment, precisely, that I knew Mark Barrett was after my wife and her money and wouldn't stop for a red light in pursuit of his goal. While digesting this fact and moving into position under the canopy set up adjacent to the grave, I was forced to face the onlookers, and found myself staring at freckles dotting a slightly tilted nose. Jesus Christ! The murderer!

Four

Two weeks since we buried the old man and nothing has been resolved. I'm a general being stalked by an elusive enemy in a war of nerves, who suddenly discovers insurrection in his own camp. For twenty years I thought that Joseph Kirkpatrick's demise would provide the launching pad for my resurrection. With the Golden Princess at my side and the Kirkpatrick Foundation in her pocket, we would resurrect the power and glory of the Kirkpatrick name. Others, it seems, had the same idea.

Whoever dies first gets a good night's rest. My slumber would be forever fitful thanks to the scene in the cemetery.

Before me, that gaping grave. Behind me, Mark Barrett. Vicky on my left, and to my right, the boy, my eyes drawn to him like a tongue worrying a sore tooth as the priest recited, "Let not your heart be troubled. You believe in God, believe also in me."

All I could believe was that Joseph Kirkpatrick, beneath the lid of that pretentiously expensive box, was grinning at me. He was gone, but look what had taken his place. A designing lawyer and a murderer who looked like a refugee from a Norman Rockwell magazine cover.

"In my Father's house there are many mansions. Were it not so, I would have told you, because I go to prepare a place for you."

For weeks I had rehearsed a variety of scenarios germane to this moment. True, I didn't expect the meeting to take place in a cemetery, complete with corpse, priest, and television camera to record the event. My romantic mind runs more to waterfronts at midnight, foghorns, and streetlamps casting pools of yellow light over the confrontation arena. And there we were, under a blue sky, surrounded by family, friends, rubbernecking spectators, and the word of God.

"And if I go and prepare a place for you, I am coming again, and I will take you to myself; that where I am, there you also may be."

Score one for God.

My own plots had me ignoring the boy, running from him, confronting him—the gamut of emotions, except the one that struck at the moment of truth. Shame. That's right, I was embarrassed. It was as if his presence flaunted my indiscretion in the bright light of day, to be witnessed by this multitude; and my indiscretion was proving more appalling than his murder. It was me people would whisper about should the truth be known, not him. Anyone who owns a television, reads a newspaper, or buys a ticket to the films has become impervious to murder. Fear of our secret lives going into the public domain, not murder, is the basic instinct.

Intimacy breeds contempt because the heart is a gateway to the soul. So it's intimacy we fear more than death or dying; intimacy we flee from and avoid at all costs. And I was as intimate with that boy as if he were my lover. No, more so. Lovers are subjective. I had observed him, almost literally, under a microscope and derived a good deal of erotic pleasure from my snooping.

I felt my skin flush under the warm sun as I stole glances at my silent partner in crime. Silent partner. Very apropos indeed.

"Jesus said to him, 'Have I been so long a time with you, and you have not known me?' "

I knew him, all right, as if endowed with X-ray vision. Under the white T-shirt that fit like a potato sack was a beautifully defined and hairless chest, a stomach hard and taut. Under the jeans, the Fruit of the Loom briefs. Which pair? The ones with the hole, like a moth bite, over the left buttock? The ones so frayed from wear that colored threads hung, like fringe, around the elastic waistband? And beneath them, a dick of heroic proportions, whether flaccid or otherwise engaged.

He made love coyly, half shy, half afraid, exuding a boyish coquettishness of which he was fully aware. She led, teased, cajoled until he forgot his ineptness, real or pretended, and went at it like a rapist, seeking only to please himself, and in doing so, became the stud she fancied. Once, he withdrew at the crucial moment, anointing her with his passion. The sin of Onan, I thought at the time. I now knew that it was his first, audacious attempt to get her into the pond. The ploy had not worked. She made him dampen a towel and used that to wash clean her dancer's body. Surely they had discussed her fear of water or abhorrence of that particular watering hole. Hence, his use of the boat.

Again, there in the cemetery, I had that eerie feeling of having witnessed the crime before, in some remote and forgotten past. And that feeling was triggered by what? The ejaculating penis? The flat-bottomed boat? The murder? My forehead was uncomfortably moist. I refused to mop it in his presence.

"But he comes that the world may know that I love the Father, and that I do as the Father has commanded me. Arise, let us go from here."

And we did.

When we returned from the cemetery, Vicky moved out of our bedroom and into her father's master suite.

"You understand, darling."

What I understood was that I was being informed in the most morbid of gestures that the king was dead; long live the queen. Christ, his body was still warm and so too, I imagine, was his bed. Was this fodder for Sigmund Freud or Edgar Allan Poe? Even Ms. Johnson, our medical secretary, looked askance as Maddy and Vicky scurried from south wing to north wing toting dresses, shoes, and lingerie into her former patient's bedroom. This wasn't going to be a one-night stand with Papa's ghost.

When I was a boy, we moved from an apartment in the North Bronx to our own home in Paramus, New Jersey—this thanks to a zero down payment and FHA financing for veterans of the Second World War, of which my father was one. We owned a brown and white beagle, who reacted to the movers carting away the furniture with bewilderment, fear, and an attack of the runs. The only world he knew was being dismantled, his place in it uncertain. I held him on my lap, stroked his neck, and described Paramus in terms I thought a dog would understand. A backyard, squirrels, rabbits, and no more leash. He was fine as long as he remained in my arms; the physical bond conveyed the assurance words could not communicate. So I cradled him from the Bronx to New Jersey and we both survived the transition.

Bereft of a pair of loving arms, I would have to survive this passage by my wits. The thorn had been removed from my side and the empty hole was proving more painful than the barb. Not wishing to watch the charade or Ms. Johnson watching me, I moped about the den until I spotted John through the French doors, puttering around in the backyard. Whatever he was doing was totally unnecessary as we employed a lawn and gardening service.

"Maddy and me will stay as long as we're needed, Miss Vicky," John had announced as we were leaving for the church that morning. What he meant, I imagine, was that they would stay until the will was read and the promised pension a reality. No hardship, really. When Kirk's position at WMET was deemed superfluous by the Japanese conglomerate, he had designated the Dunemere Lane house his permanent residence, moving John and Maddy into the two-bedroom, two-bath apartment over the garage. Kirk had wintered in Palm Beach, in an apartment he owned at The Breakers, where he had all the help he needed, leaving John and Maddy poshly unemployed—but salaried—for a good six months of the year.

I walked out the French doors and stood for a moment on the concrete patio abutting the back lawn. John waved when he saw me, a gesture which took me totally by surprise. There had never been any love lost between John and me. Kirk had never made a secret of his animosity toward me, and John followed suit because thinking like the boss was part of the job description. This attempt at camaraderie made me think that John was also embarrassed by Vicky's antics. Perhaps he became fearful of his future as he watched her pull rank in a way that was unpleasantly reminiscent of ol' Kirk. Show and don't tell.

Forty years with Joseph Kirkpatrick must have afforded John a multitude of opportunities to see the mogul lie, cheat, and devour people he no longer needed with all the aplomb of a python swallowing a rat. Was the much discussed pension at the end of the rainbow a pot of fool's gold? Was John looking for a compassionate ally or a comrade in arms?

Stepping onto the lawn, I noticed that the weather—like the atmosphere in my home—had gone from sunny to bleak. Black clouds were rolling in from over the ocean, the sound of the surf ominous, and a fine mist threatened to become a deluge by nightfall.

Rising from a circular patch of pachysandra around an ancient elm and rubbing the palms of his hands on his trouser legs, John greeted me with the statement, "No funeral meats."

I knew what he meant, but I had never heard it expressed so graphically.

"Always a big spread for friends and family after a burial in the old country."

What old country he was talking about, I had no idea. Vicky had once told me that both John and Maddy had been born and raised in the Yorkville section of Manhattan. An amalgam of German, Irish, and Middle-European cultures, it provided the city with some of the best and most unpretentious restaurants and delicatessens in the five boroughs. Judging from the style and excellence of Maddy's cooking, I would say Vicky's contention regarding their origins was correct.

John's hands were once again in motion as he removed the baseball cap from his head and pressed the crook of his arm against his forehead. The black suit and chauffeur's cap had been replaced with baggy canvas pants, white collarless shirt, and waterproof Docksiders. "The Barretts should have put on a spread for us," he declared.

Was this a backhanded swipe at Mark Barrett? Did John know something I didn't? Servants usually did. Or was it that John too believed the lawyer was insinuating himself too deeply into our domestic arrangements? A paid employee exerting undue influence on the lady of the house. We had all heard stories of rich old men who made promises they forgot to put into writing. If John needed witnesses I was certainly on his list, but I wasn't going to commit myself before the sun had set on Kirk's grave.

Sorry, John, but it's too soon to take sides. I have my suspicions of Barrett but proof of nothing, so I'll just wait and see, thank you. Besides, before this damn will is read and settled we might both be in need of a good lawyer. The first rule of living by your wits: Don't burn any bridges.

"Mrs. Barrett did invite us to lunch, as a matter of fact, but Miss Vicky wasn't up to it," I answered.

John shot a glance at Kirk's bedroom windows, where the new orphan was busy setting up headquarters. "No matter. The missus is planning a special treat for dinner." Not getting any gossip out of me, John sank back to his knees in search of weeds among the pachysandra. I turned and walked back to the French doors, the mist just turning to a fine drizzle.

Dinner. Now here was something I hadn't thought about until John uttered the word. Purposely? It was the only meal in the Dunemere Lane house we always sat down to as a family. Not exactly formal, but Kirk, like a retired general who refused to forsake his uniform, always wore a suit and tie. Vicky changed into a smart dress and I—happy to play along—donned slacks, jacket, and shirt, if not always a tie in the height of the summer. But never shorts or jeans. Cocktails in the den—or drawing room as Vicky would have it—at seven and dinner, of course, at eight.

It was, however, the seating arrangements that interested me at that moment. The inlaid mahogany table sat fourteen—six on either side and two Chippendale armchairs, like thrones, for the host and hostess. In the old days, when dinner parties were the norm several evenings a week in the summer and most weekends off-season, Kirk and his wife occupied the throne chairs. When Victoria senior died after a short but distressing illness, Vicky, still in her teens, inherited her mother's place at the table.

For our more modest gatherings we occupied the end of the table closest to the butler's pantry, to save Maddy and John steps. Kirk at the head, Vicky to his right, and I to his left. How would the table be set this evening? More show and don't tell? As it turned out, it was more "no show" than anything else.

"I have no appetite, Michael, you understand? I'll just take a tray in my room, if you don't mind. Please forgive me."

Did I have a choice?

Several months earlier, we had watched a television documentary on Her Royal Highness Queen Elizabeth II in which Her Majesty admitted she often took a tray in her room after a hard day at the palace. Since then, whenever indisposed, Vicky followed suit.

Well, it had been a hard day at the cemetery and I was

hungry. I showered at six, dressed in a pair of chinos, a new striped button-down shirt, sans tie, and a light cord jacket. I arrived in the den at seven and mixed myself a very dry, stand-up, gin martini into which I dropped an olive, sipped it with satisfaction, and lit a cigarette. I am an occasional smoker, a fact that drives Vicky crazy. I could enjoy one with a drink or after an exceptionally good meal, and not light another for a week or a month or a year. I wondered if, upstairs, Vicky was lighting the one she had been toting around for a week.

At eight I entered the dining room and found the table set for one. My usual place, to the left of Kirk's empty chair. Enter Maddy with the promised funeral meats. A loin of pork surrounded by perfectly roasted potatoes. John followed with a healthy-looking tossed green salad. After placing it within my reach, he withdrew from the sideboard a rare vintage of chardonnay that had been cooling in a bucket of ice, awaiting my arrival. He removed my empty martini glass and filled the crystal goblet. Satisfied, the pair retreated to the butler's pantry, the food, wine, and gently swinging door the only evidence of their silent and faultless service. I was being treated with great respect. And I imagine the lady in the master bedroom suite was being similarly honored. Maddy, I guess, had gotten as much out of Vicky as John had pried out of me. Comparing notes, the two had obviously decided not to play favorites with the surviving members of the household.

I raised my wineglass in salute to the empty throne chair and whispered, "Gone but not forgotten, you son of a bitch."

Five

After dinner, I enjoyed another cigarette, a snifter of fine brandy, and the ten o'clock news on WMET. The network Joseph Kirkpatrick had sired and nurtured for fifty years laid him to rest in exactly seventy-five seconds.

Vicky, from a distance, looked rather smart, her blond hair shimmering in the bright sun, her black dress testimony to her grief. I, as always, looked like the ideal husband in spite of the anguish I was suffering at the time, testimony to my peasant lineage. The Barretts and John and Maddy were identified as friends of the family. Really! The priest got the best coverage with a big fat close-up as he read the word of God.

Life in instant replay. Imagine if I had had a camera to record the antics of my Two Holes of Water lovers and their subsequent parting.

As we filed past the coffin, the camera panned the scene and there he was, in the forefront of our audience, the boy I had dubbed Adam. My silent partner in crime. I must say he looked every bit as good on camera as off. And when the anchorperson, what's her name, wound up the segment in ten seconds, clutching the stem of her microphone in a vaguely erotic fashion, guess who was beaming into the camera over the newswoman's shoulder? I shuddered.

Only an idiot, and I was certain the boy was not one, would go out of his way to be televised while in the process of stalking a potential victim. That worry was laid to rest. He was in the cemetery for the same reason the other strangers were there: follow the leader, with Ms. Anchor in the role of the Pied Piper. This fact and the brandy helped me relax and rationalize my position.

I could not have prevented what happened, because I didn't know it was happening. What with two naked bodies tumbling into the water, I imagined a little hanky-panky of a rather kinky nature taking place below the surface.

Should I have reported the incident in the name of justice? Justice for whom? A dead woman who couldn't care less or her champion who would be labeled a Peeping Tom—or worse—by the press. That I had happened upon the scene—taking a path all but invisible from the road and hardly accessible—just as the murder occurred was unacceptable. Given who my wife and late father-in-law are, the trial would be a circus.

I still maintained that my original gut feeling regarding my involvement in the crime was correct. I knew I could not prove any accusations aside from the fact of knowing where to find the body, and the boat. And who but the murderer would know that?

Finally, I'll admit that in the darkest corner of my mind, one vexing thought occurred again and again: Perhaps the lady deserved what she got.

My conscience was clear. Finis the Two Holes of Water affair. I would erase Adam from my mind as fastidiously as the editor of WMET's ten o'clock news had erased Adam's face from the screen. I would concentrate on my own problems, which, I would soon discover, were more acute than I knew.

Built at a time when ostentation was considered good taste and live-in servants outnumbered members of the family, the Dunemere Lane house had back stairs that rose from the kitchen to the second-floor bedrooms and continued up to the deserted servants' quarters above. I deposited my glass and ashtray in the kitchen and made my way upstairs. The afternoon drizzle had fulfilled its promise of a heavy downpour, accompanied by lightning and salvos of thunder. Kirk not getting his way in the celestial hereafter? I felt the tiny hairs on my arms rise as I mounted the dark and narrow staircase and suddenly remembered that Vicky and I were alone in this grandiose mausoleum.

John and Maddy had retired to their digs over the garage directly after dinner, no doubt to catch themselves on the telly. Ms. Johnson no longer lived in, but judging from the speed with which she was cataloging the condolence messages and responses, she would be on our doorstep every morning at nine for weeks to come.

When I reached the first landing and opened the door to the upstairs hall, I was relieved to see the hall lit. The atmosphere, however, was still chillingly eerie as I made my soundless way over the plush carpeting toward Kirk's old room. I paused outside the door. After twenty years I knew how to beguile Vicky, if not to come back to our room, then to get myself invited to spend the night in the master suite and, once ensconced, return with my gear on the morrow. This marriage wasn't over by a long shot. I was raising my hand to knock, when I heard the muted but distinguishable sound of a telephone ringing once. Kirk's private line. Who but Mark Barrett knew the number and would dare to call at this late hour on the day of Kirk's funeral? I resisted the impulse to put my ear to the door and instead fled, like a rejected lover, to the south wing and my bachelor digs.

Shaking with anger, I undressed, hanging each garment neatly in the dressing room in an effort to instill some order in a life gone haywire. When I shed my T-shirt and shorts, I wrapped myself in a light flannel robe and settled into one of a pair of comfortable club chairs. Here, I began to think logically. (A good point to remember: Anger is a debilitating emotion.)

Unless Barrett was attempting to contact the dead, he knew damn well who was now occupying Kirk's room. And if he did, it was because Vicky had advised him of her move or, more probably, because he had engineered it. So, Barrett segues from funeral director to marriage counselor. It was quite clear the lawyer was taking Kirk's place in Vicky's life, with the added attraction of not being blood kin and all that implied.

As the rain pelted my bedroom windows, the reason for my wife's quick and rather macabre change of bedrooms became overwhelmingly clear. If Vicky wanted to establish her independence now that Kirk was gone, she would have to begin by breaking the tie that binds: the marital bed. Sex wasn't merely an adjunct to our union, it was the sole reason for it. To understand this phenomenon, one must go back to the beginning, when Vicky and I met at a party, as she likes to tell it. What she chooses to omit is that she attended as an invited guest while I was a member of the catering service.

At that moment, bartending for a smart catering service was the first step to stardom. I wasn't enrolled in the Actors Studio because I had neither the money nor the talent. What I did have was a face and body that prompted people, starting when I was twelve, to brush the dark bangs from my forehead and exclaim, "You oughta be in pictures, kid."

Unfortunately, I believed them.

After two years at a community college, I crossed the George Washington Bridge with a bankroll of fifteen hundred dollars. I promised my parents that if I didn't attract the attention of a viable producer in one year, I would return to school and, pooling all the Reos' finances, emerge a doctor, dentist, or lawyer. This was the dream of a first-generation Italian father who drove a yellow cab in New York City, and a first-generation Irish mother who sincerely believed housewifery was an honorable profession.

What I attracted was the daughter of the king of producers. The Golden Princess, as she had been christened by one society editor, was already famous (or infamous—take your pick), at the tender age of eighteen. The gossip columnists preferred "vivacious," "enfant terrible," and "devil-may-care" to describe the daughter of the CEO of radio and television station WMET. Across the damask tablecloths where ladies lunch, more vicious characteristics were attributed to the Golden Princess—crude, cheap, fast, and "like father like daughter," to name a few.

Were Vicky a male heir, Kirk would have been proud of the comparison. But a daughter with a ravenous sexual appetite is an embarrassment to a man who has spent most of his life exploiting other daughters with similar tendencies.

I knew who the girl hanging around my makeshift bar

was. Victoria Kirkpatrick was not a classic beauty, but her lovely blond hair, green eyes, and flawless complexion went a long way in softening a somewhat prominent nose and perhaps overgenerous smile. A trim figure and a pair of shapely legs added to her appeal to the opposite sex. If not beautiful, Victoria Kirkpatrick was indeed striking.

The hired help was not permitted to pass the time of day with those we served, but no such restriction could be imposed on the guests. Vicky made no pretense of hiding her interest and before the evening ended invited me to escort her to the theater the following evening.

"Two tickets and my friend can't make it," she lied.

"I can," I assured her.

"I thought you might." She handed me her glass, which I filled with rye over ice. "Thank you . . ." A studied pause.

"Michael. Michael Anthony Reo."

"Thank you, Michael. I'm Victoria Kirkpatrick."

I, the Don Juan of Paramus High, was a virgin. Vicky taught me everything she knew, which was considerable, given her age. To say we were sexually compatible would be a gross understatement. We were extraordinary, the answer to a sex therapist's prayer. Why? I have no idea. You look for answers when something is wrong, and for us, everything was right.

Kirk loathed me before he met me. Gigolo was his assessment. A rather passé word popular in his youth. If the Prince of Wales was out of the question, Kirk would settle for a Mellon or Astor or Du Pont for his princess. But Reo was the knight in shining armor who possessed the lance that rang the princess's chimes. Vicky went from bitch in heat to contented cow, from vivacious to poised, from enfant terrible to Daddy's little girl. The gossips and society editors noted it, and her father—with a sigh of relief—noted it. Being a levelheaded businessman who knew a good trade-off when he saw one, Kirk relented.

However, as with everything else Joseph Kirkpatrick did, even when bestowing largesse, the match suited his purpose: to keep his daughter's name and reputation above suspicion. I was the lesser of two evils, the other being Vicky on the loose.

Did I love her? I was twenty-two and poor, a combination that makes blond hair cascading over the collar of a sable coat irresistible. Not to mention the headwaiters who bowed to us, the celebrated names who fawned over us, and the little voice in my head repeating, like the chug-chug of the wheels of a rapidly moving train, "You're going to be a star." How could I miss? I was engaged to the daughter of the man who could make it possible with one small wave of his magic wand.

The wedding was posh and small. My parents were impressed and intimidated. Vicky treated them, on the few occasions they met, the same way she treated John and Maddy: with reserved respect. A week after the honeymoon, Kirk invited me to lunch in the boardroom of the MET Tower building. He ordered the duck flambé for two before reading me the terms of my indenture.

Being Victoria Kirkpatrick's husband and Joseph Kirkpatrick's son-in-law was a full-time job. Acting was out of the question; it would put Vicky on a par with the people her father employed, usually with much disagreement over remuneration and artistic license.

Vicky didn't have a cent of her own (this accompanied by a sneer of satisfaction). She was totally dependent on her father and would be until the day he died. (Whoever dies first loses.)

If I divorced Vicky, I wouldn't get a penny and he would see to it that I was blackballed from the acting profession for the remainder of his lifetime. (Note how much hinged on Kirk's death.)

If Vicky divorced me, I could go my way and do as I wished.

Dessert was tiramisù.

Was it all bad? Of course not. Headwaiters still bowed. Celebrated names still fawned. The view from the Fifth Avenue triplex dazzled. And, like the Duke and Duchess of Windsor, we didn't stay in one place long enough to become bored. We were members in good standing of the international set, all carte blanche, thanks to Father Christmas. After the famous New Year's Eve galas in East Hampton, our crowd continued the party by way of limousines and chartered jet to Jamaica. We arrived, still in formal dress and without sleep, to be greeted by Noël Coward pouring champagne in the VIP lounge.

If Vicky was unfaithful to me, and I seriously doubt it, I never knew it.

Me? Look, I was surrounded by the most appealing, charismatic, talented, and—sometimes—the most intelligent men and women of our time, most of whom made their availability obvious. When I strayed, I did so with the utmost discretion. If Vicky knew, she never complained.

Given the success and frequency of our mating, the fact that Vicky never conceived puzzled me, albeit not for long. Were she pregnant, I had no doubt that Kirk would be the first to know. I wondered if my father-in-law, fearing the leverage a grandson and heir would give me in my tug-of-war with him, would advise her to abort—or had he already advised her to take precautions to avoid the problem? Would an incipient grandfather do such a thing? If he was Joseph Kirkpatrick, he would.

Kirk tolerated me because the alternative was Vicky once again on the prowl. I tolerated Kirk because I liked the lifestyle his wallet made possible. Vicky played us one against the other as suited her fancy. Like a good parliamentary government, we functioned via a system of checks and balances.

Most important, no major disagreement survived a night in our bedroom—until now, the reason for my solitary musing on this dark and rainy night. Had she found in Mark Barrett a replacement not only for Kirk but for me? The best of all possible worlds: a father she could fuck.

While I could see Vicky plunging headlong into such a relationship, I wondered at the motives of the lawyer. Here was a handsome and rich man, married to a charming and rich woman. Vicky was certainly attractive, but too often a colossal pain in the butt. If Mark wanted a mistress or an occasional fling outside the Barrett home, there were enough pretty young ladies in East Hampton who would be happy to accommodate him. If neither money nor passion fueled Barrett's ardor, what did?

Also, how much did Milly know, suspect, or care?

I spent the night in that chair: speculating, nodding, waking. When the sky grew light over the Atlantic, I went down to the kitchen and brewed myself a pot of coffee. I carried a cup back to my room and stood by the window, weary but too unsettled to crawl into bed. The rain had stopped but an early-morning fog now shrouded the grounds like a steaming cauldron. The Dunemere Lane house had become the House of Usher, but which of its surviving denizens would be buried alive was still to be determined.

I had put in my time. Stuck to my part of the bargain and in the process become accustomed to a life I was not ready to relinquish in return for a generous settlement. No amount of money would compensate for being severed from the aura of the Kirkpatrick name. Like a prisoner grown smug and secure in his cell, I refused to return to the real world.

Man is capable of the most horrendous acts when someone threatens his creature comforts. Yes, perhaps the lady deserved to be pushed overboard.

Six

Barrett House, c. 1890, was erected on the site of the Barrett cottage, c. 1692. So when Vicky says the Barretts were here before Columbus, she's off the mark by some two hundred years.

"Really, darling. Such a fuss over two hundred years. Besides, it's a figure of speech, not a historic fact."

Well, my dear, the Shinnecock Indians were here a thousand years before Columbus, and that is a historic fact.

Located on Main Street, west of East Hampton's small business district, Barrett House stands at a respectable distance from similar mansions of that period. Using the house as a fixed point and circumscribing an arc of 180 degrees, local landmarks would include the clothier Mark, Fore & Strike, the Palm restaurant, the Maidstone Club, and the old town cemetery where dozens of Barretts (not enough to suit me) are buried. So, if one is lucky enough to be born a Barrett, one can be outfitted, dine, play eighteen holes of golf, and get buried all within walking distance of one's front door.

The offices of Barrett and Barrett are located in what was once the carriage house of the Barrett mansion. The house itself, a huge colonial, is barely visible from the street. A vast lawn is fronted by a brick wall along Main Street; the house, sitting on a slight rise, peeks out from behind ancient oaks and willows strategically placed to ensure privacy. A curving driveway leads past the law office and continues to the mansion's front steps before terminating at a four-car garage toward the rear of the property. On most days, spring and summer, a team of men work the property: planting, trimming, raking, watering, and weeding. Thanks to the mistress of the house, the result is more affable than manicured perfection.

"Sorry I've been so long, Michael," Milly greeted me, as she entered her living room with the panache of an actress in a long-running hit who is confident of the audience's warm reception. In lieu of applauding I stood, and Milly acknowledged the gesture with a smile. Our relationship is far less formal than this implies, but in our set observing the customs is more habit than obligatory.

"When MJ calls he's all business. When it's my dime he's nothing less than verbose," she said.

MJ is Mark junior, who would soon return from Cambridge with his law degree ready for framing and hanging in the carriage house. Mark and MJ would be the third and fourth generations of Barrett solicitors to represent the family firm.

"Don't worry about me, Milly. I'm so used to being ignored I wouldn't know what to answer if someone asked me the way to the loo."

"Poor Michael," Milly sighed, sounding like a mother consoling a child who is often misunderstood. The voice and sentiment suited the woman whose figure was more matronly than the popular anorexic look of the haut monde. Her skin radiated the delicate color and texture that bespeak expensive face creams. Tonight her hair was pulled straight back from her forehead, accentuating her blue eyes and flawless skin, terminating in an elegant chignon. Milly's brown hair showed no traces of gray and I had no doubts that nature alone was responsible.

"Are they still at it?" she asked.

"They" and "it" were Mark and Vicky conferring in Mark's office. We had been invited for drinks at seven followed by dinner, and Vicky had seized the opportunity to pop in to see Mark before coming up to the house.

"It's art appreciation night," I explained.

"I thought Kirk left the entire collection to museums."

"He did," I answered. "The Met and the Modern. Each got what they craved. But the museums have generously agreed to put on loan to Vicky any or all of the collection for an indefinite period, so our walls will not go suddenly bare. It's business as usual and Uncle Sam gets the proverbial finger. Your husband is a very clever man, Milly."

"And late, as usual. I see no reason to wait. I'll have a vodka, Michael, and toss in an olive for appearance sake."

The Barrett home is a harmonious blending of American and English antiques, a bit of modern and a lot of comfortable if undistinguished furnishings. A lovely Peale oil hangs over the marble fireplace, dominating the great room whose proportions more than justify its name. Philadelphia side tables, a gracious tall clock, and a Bokhara carpet reside in perfect compatibility with pieces that boast no provenance other than good taste.

I moved to the bar and fixed drinks for my hostess and myself. "When does the new lawyer arrive?" I asked his mother.

"A week, give or take. And he asked me to tell you to reserve a court for next Saturday. Says he's been practicing."

"I haven't touched a tennis racket in months." I gave Milly her drink and raised mine in salute. "*Cent'anni,* my dear."

"I'm halfway there, Michael."

Milly and I enjoyed a rapport often found between those born to great wealth and privilege and those born with nothing but the will to survive and the wit to achieve that goal. Vicky, of course, could not understand this mutual attraction and attributed it to what she called Milly's roving eye. Milly couldn't care less what Vicky thought, and therein lay the basis of their relationship.

We sat in our usual places: Milly in a wing chair adjacent to the fireplace and I in a settee facing it, all part of a cozy grouping around the Peale. "Tell me, Milly," I said. "Is my wife your husband's only client?"

"No, but she's his richest."

"If he charges by the hour, he's well on his way to owning WMET."

Milly sipped her vodka before answering. "That's a lot of hours."

"Who's counting?"

"You, obviously. Tell me, Michael, what nettles you more, Mark's fee or the amount of time he spends with Vicky?"

Leave it to Milly to come directly to the point after two slugs of her white lightning. If Vicky had spent an unreasonable amount of time with Mark Barrett during her father's illness, she was now practically living in the guy's back pocket. I was not invited to participate and learned only what Vicky elected to tell me—which was very little—regarding disbursement and our future now that our ménage à trois had been reduced to a pas de deux, replete with boxing gloves.

I was not mentioned in Kirk's will, a fact that caused some embarrassment for all present at the reading: Vicky, myself, John, Maddy, and the reader, Mark Barrett. The slight was made more conspicuous by the largesse the old man had showered upon John and Maddy. Barrett did his best to avoid contact with me for the remainder of the meeting, which, as intended, accentuated the slight.

"Time is something I'm in great supply of. And in case you haven't heard, we now occupy his-and-her bedrooms." What the hell, let it all hang out and see where it goes.

"Oh, but I have heard."

I raised an eyebrow. "Really? Mark?"

"No, Annie."

"Good God, your cook."

Milly nodded happily. She enjoyed good gossip. "She got it from Maddy. They shop together at Dreesen's." With a shrug I conveyed my ignorance, and she explained, "A market on Newtown Lane. Good meat selection if you can afford the prices. It's popular with the touristas who patronize it for their coffee and doughnuts, sipping and munching as they window-shop or take advantage of the public-accommodation benches."

"You mean Annie and Maddy sip coffee alfresco and discuss my sex life?"

"Or lack of it," Milly corrected cheerfully.

I was tempted to toss back the bourbon and water I had been toying with, but refrained. Instead, I tossed Milly's volley back into her court. "What about you? Do you think the money Mark is going to make from this justifies their daily conclaves and the nightly telephone chatter? Jesus, Milly, the only thing they don't have is those ridiculous beepers."

An ex-smoker, Milly looked longingly at a crystal ashtray displayed on the table next to her chair. "As Margaret Mitchell so bluntly put it, 'My dear, I don't give a damn.' As I expect you and everyone from Southampton to Montauk knows, Mark and I agreed to disagree some years back and since then retreated to our separate corners. This house, in case you haven't noticed, is very large."

Well, well, it wasn't Halloween but the skeletons were certainly rattling in the Barrett House closets. Their quarrel concerned MJ's older sister, Sarah, who, like a mad wife locked in the attic of a Victorian novel, was a taboo subject. A hellion from the age of two, Sarah overdosed on boys, booze, drugs, and radical politics while at prep school. Banished to a similar institution in Switzerland, she learned to ski while indulging her passion for boys, booze, drugs, and radical politics. Sarah followed a handsome young ski instructor to California, where they were busted for possession and trafficking of illegal substances.

Her father came to her rescue and vowed it was for the last time. Her mother, who had been opposed to the Swiss school, once again wanted her daughter home where she could be given the help she so desperately needed. Mark, against his wife's wishes, offered Sarah a generous monthly allowance if she promised never to set foot east of the Hudson River. When the girl accepted, Milly felt betrayed by both husband and daughter. It was a bitter defeat.

Milly and her future husband had met when he was a student at Harvard and a member in good standing of debutante ball stag lines. Millicent Hull Stiles was usually at the receiving end of such lines. The marriage was looked upon favorably by both Boston and East Hampton society.

"Why didn't you leave?" I asked.

"MJ," she replied before sipping more vodka. "I wouldn't go without him and I had no right to take him away from his heritage. The Barretts roots run very deep in East Hampton and MJ has the right to all the privileges of his birth. If he wants to leave now that he's an adult and established, that's his right, too. But he was a child then and I wouldn't make the decision for him." She spoke with a conviction that made me wonder if the day of reckoning had come. Was this why she was telling all? It no longer mattered?

"And you, Michael." She gently lobbed the ball back. "Why don't you leave?"

"Because I'm a coward, Milly."

"Afraid of the big bad wolf?"

"Afraid of life without a Titian over the fireplace. Wouldn't you miss your Peale?"

"Oh, it would come with me. It's mine. So is a lot of what you see in Barrett House. I'm not dependent on Mark. My father had the good sense to set up a generous trust for my brother and me. I'm a rich bitch, Michael."

"And I'm a poor stud whose services are no longer required, it seems."

"You're in your prime," Milly assured me, "and better-looking than any film star I've ever seen. Do you know what Mark said the first time Vicky took you to the Club? He said Michael Reo makes every woman in the room regret her marital vows and every man question his heterosexuality."

I brushed the compliment aside with a wave of my glass, but she knew it pleased me. "Did you ever hear the sage of my film debut, Milly? . . . No? Indulge me, it does have a point."

I would have lit a cigarette in the time-honored tradition of the reconteur but resisted in deference to Milly. "We were in Italy the year it was thought Rome would replace Hollywood as the film capital of the world. Orson Welles, of course, was very much on the scene then. The paparazzi loved to photograph this whale of a man eating pasta. He was already a has-been and everyone knew it, but still a genius to be reckoned with. He told anyone who would listen that he had completed a shooting script for *Wuthering Heights* that would make Cathy and Heathcliff more memorable than Scarlett and Rhett. One night, at a dinner party, he asked me to test for Heathcliff.

"It was all very hush-hush, which made it all the more exciting. Orson managed to borrow a soundstage at Cinecittà and a crew to go with it. They loved him over there, you see, and he was a great con artist to boot. I was costumed in something left over from an eighteenth-century swashbuckler. According to Orson, I was a sensation and the search for Heathcliff ended. I was so excited I was ready to do battle with Kirk over the offer and I was sure Vicky would back me.

"Immediately, using me as bait, Orson went to Kirk for financing. What a fucking joke. The fool was probably the only person in Rome who didn't know Kirk would pay to keep me off the silver screen. Kirk couldn't wait to pass on the juicy details to me, saying with glee that Welles would sign Frankenstein's monster for the role if he thought someone would back it, and that was probably a true assessment. My self-confidence, Milly, has never recovered."

"How do you know Mr. Welles wouldn't have used you if he had gotten backing from some other source?"

"I don't. And I never will. Maybe Orson and Kirk are up there, or down there, having a good laugh over my screen test."

Milly finished her vodka and thought a moment before asking, "Do you like Italy, Michael?"

I nodded. "In my blood, I guess, or fifty percent of it."

"We have a small villa on Lake Como. My brother and I, that is. I'm thinking of going over in the fall. Best time of year in Italy, I think. I wouldn't mind company."

The invitation lingered in the air like the cigarette smoke of yore Milly still craved.

Seven

If you can believe two impossible things before dinner, you've either followed Alice down the rabbit hole or you've tarried too long in East Hampton.

First: Milly's invitation. The kind offer of a port in a storm or a blatant immodest proposal?

Second: Mark Barrett's fly was open.

Let me take it from the top. I was rescued from responding to Milly's bid by Carol, a young gal Milly employs to help around the house. Enter Carol.

"Excuse me, Mrs. Barrett, but Annie wants to know if she should hold dinner." Carol spoke slowly, with an almost imperceptible pause between each word, reminiscent of a reformed stutterer. Carol was not the victim of a speech impediment, but what educators politely refer to as a slow learner. Local girls like Carol were Milly Barrett's charity. She had made it her mission to employ, train, and encourage them to extend themselves to the height of their ability. Carol would never enter the world of private secretaries or steno pools, but after Milly worked her magic, Carol would have as positive an image of herself as any computer whiz kid. There were those who thought this calling was a displacement for

Milly's wayward daughter. I always believed Milly's kind heart was equally accountable.

"Absolutely not," Milly answered. "Eight-thirty as planned. If the others aren't here, they get cold pickin's."

"Roast beef?" I asked Carol, who looked very prim and proper in a navy blue skirt and white blouse. The schoolgirl outfit was regulation dress for Milly's girls, a uniform they wore with great pride.

"Yes, Mr. Reo. Just the way you like it."

"Ask Annie if she'll marry me."

"Oh, she's much too old for you, Mr. Reo," Carol protested quite seriously.

"And you, alas, are too young."

"That will be all, Carol," Milly broke in, and poor Carol made a hasty if reluctant retreat.

"You've got all the young wives at the Club acting like teenagers, but I'll be damned if you start turning the heads of my staff," Milly lectured.

"Moi?"

"Yes, *moi.* Or rather, you. How do you do it, Michael?"

"Do what?"

"Charm the young. And it's not only women. You have a rapport with MJ that his father envies, and you didn't hear it from me. Last year he asked me if he could have you instead of his father as a partner for the Father and Son Tennis Tournament."

"That's because he wanted to win." Relief induced my cockiness. I didn't want to think about MJ at the moment, as I had more than enough on my plate and dinner was still an hour away. Reserve a court, indeed. The kid was a great wit, not to mention cheeky. Knowing Milly could chat forever if MJ was the topic, I quickly headed her off.

"I take it Annie will report to Maddy tomorrow morning, over their coffee break, that my wife and your husband were locked up in the office till after dark," I complained.

Milly nodded. "I'm sure. And Annie gets it from her husband, who helps around the grounds and pops into the kitchen for a cuppa every few hours to exchange his outdoor news for her indoor observations. Nothing is sacred, Michael."

The tall clock struck the quarter hour: fifteen to eight. "What are those two up to, Milly?"

"Art. Isn't that what you said?"

"Bullshit. I'm talking about the cabal that's been going on since day one of the new year."

"I would imagine Mark is trying to talk Vicky into investing in one of his get-rich-quick schemes."

I winced. "My wife got very rich the moment Kirk closed his eyes for good. Money, she doesn't need."

"But Mark does. It's his passion. There was the retirement village in Georgia. I think the slogan was, 'Retirement with a Difference.' The difference turned out to be that no one retired there. Then came strip malls all over Long Island that irked the environmentalists and those who value their sanity. The only thing that got stripped was Mark's bank balance."

"Motel conversions from Amagansett to Montauk," I joined in. "He owns a lot of beachfront property, Milly."

"The banks own a lot of beachfront property," she corrected.

So, Barrett's wallet was bleeding, and guess who could stop the flow? "Why does he do it?" I wondered aloud.

"The same reason the Rockefellers go into politics and

banking. To prove that being born rich isn't a detriment to achievement."

"You think he's preaching that bit of crap to Vicky? She's smitten, Milly."

"She won't be the first. Mark used to keep an apartment in town. *Pied-à-terre* was the polite term for a multitude of sins. Mark's weakness was chorus girls and models."

"No wonder he got along so well with Kirk. The old man must have died happy, comparing notes with his lawyer. You do know Kirk didn't mention me in his will."

Milly twirled the ice cubes in her empty glass. "But John and Maddy are set for life."

"'Maddy and me will stay on as long as we're needed,'" I quoted John. "They'll stay on with room, board, salary, and Kirk's pension. I'm sure those two could teach Mark a thing or two about getting rich quick."

"Is there such a thing as a happy marriage, Michael?"

Now I twirled the ice in my empty glass. "There are marriages that work and marriages that don't. Happiness has nothing to do with either."

Enter Mark and Vicky, giggling like newlyweds who think everyone knows why they're late for dinner.

"Sorry, people," Mark exploded, "but my lady client insists on business before pleasure."

I stood to greet Vicky as she walked to me and turned her cheek for me to peck.

Mark advanced to Milly's chair, bending as she turned her cheek for him to peck.

Vicky got in line behind Mark and when he was done, poor Milly got pecked again, this one leaving behind a trace of lip rouge.

Mark and I shook hands as if we meant it. "Long time no see, Mark."

Not long enough, prick.

It was all so staged you could vomit.

"Don't apologize," Vicky said, sitting in her usual place to Milly's left. "These two are never happier than when they're alone together. Milly and Mike. Sounds like a vaudeville team, but they don't sing or dance. They gossip and tell dirty jokes."

"I'm shocked," Mark emoted.

"You'd be catatonic if you really knew what we talk about," I said.

"Not about us, I hope," Vicky answered.

"No, dear," Milly assured her. "Our gossip runs more to the sublime than the ridiculous."

Vicky, while wondering if she'd been trashed, lit a cigarette. Yes, she had once again succumbed. I imagine the rigors of great wealth and adultery, in tandem, were too much for her fragile nature. Milly gingerly moved the crystal ashtray toward Vicky. I looked at the two women, who were both rich enough to have anything money could buy, and couldn't imagine two more divergent souls. Milly, in a black dress that was probably twenty years old but looked as if it had just floated off a Paris runway. Vicky, in a striped summer frock by Versace that would have fared better on a younger woman.

Mark, with courtroom tact, deflected his wife's barb. "Have we time for a drink?"

"Just," Milly told him. "We sit at eight-thirty sharp. It's roast beef, the way Mr. Reo likes it."

"Medium rare," Vicky said from behind a cloud of smoke.

"Martini for you, Vicky. Milly, that's vodka with an

olive to deceive and bourbon for Mike." Seated once again, I held up my glass as Mark Barrett walked past on his way to the bar, and noticed that his fly was open.

Stunned? "Paralyzed" would better describe my reaction. To suspect some bastard's putting the horns on you is humiliating. To peer into the culprit's unzipped grotto is as mesmerizing as peering into a crystal ball. Given the circumstances, I saw not the future but the past.

"Before I forget, Mark, Galen Miller called," Milly said.

"Did he now," Mark stated.

This chatter whirled about me like conversations gleaned while elbowing your way across a crowded room. I was staring at a *tableau erotique,* which is what the curator of a renowned museum in New York called his celebrated collection.

"Galen. What a lovely name. A man or a woman?" Vicky asked.

"A boy," Mark said as he served his wife and Vicky their drinks. "A boy with a big pair of balls."

A tall, slim man, meticulously dressed in a business suit, poses beside a gleaming mahogany desk. A woman, also fully clothed, kneels before him, her lips gripped about the head of his erection, which juts out of his open fly.

"Mark, really," Milly chided. "He said he called your office twice this week and left messages with your secretary. He wondered if you got them."

"I got them and I told Susan to ignore any more calls from Galen Miller."

"Why?" This from Vicky.

"He's probably shopping for a lawyer for his father, a world-class drunk and troublemaker. He's been through every lawyer in town and God knows what makes the boy think I'd be interested in representing Lester Miller."

The incongruity of a carefully dressed and poised couple engaged in a lewd act heightened its erotic appeal and put the curator's *tableau* a cut above porn. To my dismay, I was becoming aroused. Uncomfortably so. Of all nights to be wearing Jockey shorts. But then, one never knows.

"Galen's mother worked for us. Remember, Mark? Lester would come around, usually on payday, drunk, and make a fuss. Finally, I had to let her go. Poor thing died when Galen was a boy," Milly explained.

"Here you are, Mike."

I took my drink, once again forced to stare into the parted zipper of Barrett's lightweight summer trousers. Beneath, I now knew, were pale blue boxer shorts. Paul Stuart. Thirty-five dollars a pop. What were the chances that Mark Barrett forgot to zip up after using the john? Nil. The act is as instinctive as breathing. The barn door, no doubt, had been left open after the stallion had leaped out and limped back in.

Annie's roast beef and the Barretts' wine cellar shifted my focus from crotch to belly and put me in a reflective mood. By dessert I was ready to give the affair of the ventilated fly the benefit of the doubt. Our dinner conversation was amiable, nonthreatening, and dull. From the weather—not too humid, yet, for July—to indignation over the fact that Choate was now called Choate–Rosemary Hall. I was happy to report that Paramus High was still called Paramus High, which got a giggle from Milly and a frown from my wife. We were four people in a state of terminal denial. I heard a perfectly modulated electronic voice announcing, "Your life will self-destruct in ten seconds. Have a nice day."

My wife had left my bed and I pretended not to notice. This prompted her to flaunt the fact. After twenty years the honeymoon was over and the game of brinkmanship had begun. Vicky all but flaunted her clandestine phone calls at all hours of the day and night and made a point of extolling the virtues of her lawyer. After each meeting I learned that Mark was a genius and a dear who had gently removed yet another weight from her overburdened shoulders. I think I was supposed to ask pertinent questions for which pertinent answers had been scripted and perhaps rehearsed. Or, I was to flee back to New York in disgust, which in lawyer parlance is called desertion. But two could play the game, and remember, I had learned the art of brinkmanship at the knee of the guy who invented it, Joseph Kirkpatrick.

I answered Vicky, constantly, with the two most galling words in the marriage lexicon: "Yes, dear." I drove the Rolls without asking permission and lunched at the Club daily, flirting with the pretty wives openly and with their husbands covertly. Dining room and locker room became erogenous zones; healthy tans were tinged with crimson and a good time was being had by all. This was not to be the summer of their discontent.

"My real estate news," Milly informed us, "is that the Beaumont estate has been sold."

"That white elephant?" Mark countered.

Strange comment for a man who specialized in the genre.

"I remember Daddy talking about the Beaumont estate," Vicky broke in triumphantly. "I think he and Mommy dined there years and years ago. He said it was enormous."

"Thirty acres on Gardiners Bay," Mark said. "Twenty

bedrooms and as many baths. I think it was the baths everyone envied. We used to go there when I was a child. Old Beaumont was still alive then and gave a big Fourth of July party every year. All the cake and ice cream you could eat and rides for the kids. In the evening there were fireworks on the bay from a barge anchored directly in front of the house. One year during the war, the air raid sirens went off in the middle of the ruckus and everyone thought the Germans had finally made it to Long Island."

"The place must be a ruin," Vicky said.

"It is," Mark answered. "After the old man died the children and grandchildren took the money—there was plenty of it—and ran. That was twenty years ago, when big estates were more an embarrassing liability than an asset. It's been on the market ever since and I can't imagine anyone wanting to own it."

"Well, someone does," Milly said. "I can't remember his name, but they say he's worth billions, and he's going to restore the place to its former glory, according to Gilda Farmington, our real estate agent to the stars."

"Stephen Fletcher," I enlightened them, and all eyes were on me. "It was topic number one at the Club this afternoon."

Mark wrinkled his nose and squinted in an effort to place the name. "Wall Street or computers?" he guessed wrongly.

"Show business," I told them. "He started as an actor, went on to produce a game show on the telly that's been running for over twenty years, and added a few sitcoms, just as successful, to his list. From there to hotels in Las Vegas, Hawaii, Hong Kong, and London, with several cruise liners to cart you from port to port. I also think he does a brisk trade in polo ponies, art, and starlets."

"Well," Vicky exclaimed, "what's his background? Maybe Daddy knew him or his family."

"I doubt it," I told my wife, pausing just long enough to give the final wrench to the turn of the screw. "His parents were sharecroppers in Mississippi. Stephen Fletcher is black."

The silence was delightfully rewarding. Vicky lit a cigarette. Mark unwrinkled his nose. Milly saved the moment by proclaiming, "It's going to be one hell of a summer, ain't it?"

I had parked the Rolls on the drive just outside the Barretts' front door. When we left, Milly walked Vicky to the car, Mark and I behind them. A three-quarter moon lit a sky bright with stars. The air was cool, the night so still one could hear the pounding surf almost a mile south of Main Street. The kind of summer night that justified the ever-skyrocketing cost of owning or renting a home in the Hamptons.

With the women a good distance ahead, Mark paused and touched my elbow. "A minute, Mike."

This is it, I thought. "Yes?"

"You know MJ will be home in a few days," he began.

MJ? "So Milly told me."

"He'll be working with me while he preps for the bar exam," Mark went on, a bit hesitantly.

"Yes?"

"I know you two get along very well and I appreciate the time you take with him, but I was hoping you would cool it this summer."

"Cool what?" I asked.

"You know. Hanging out together, if you will. The more work and less play, the better his chances of passing the bar on his first shot. Distractions, he doesn't need."

"You think I'm a distraction?" I asked, annoyed and not hiding the fact.

"As a matter of fact, yes," he replied in kind.

First my wife and now MJ. I was no longer inconvenient, I was the fucking plague and this son of a bitch was going too far too fast. Kneeing the guy in the groin would be crude, so I vented my frustration by poking him in the ribs and confiding, "Your fly is open."

Galen Miller

Eight

My oasis on Two Holes of Water Road went from love nest to graveyard in six fucking months, thanks to a deal between a hotshot lawyer and my father, Lester Miller.

When that name is mentioned in conversation, the usual response is, "The town drunk?" The answers is yes, the town drunk. When appearing in print, the words "Driving While Intoxicated" usually follow the name. All the nasty rumors regarding the life and times of Les Miller are true, and proof of this fact can be found by checking the East Hampton police blotter. This source provides a blow-by-blow account of the life and times of Les the Mess, as he is not affectionately known on the East End of Long Island.

We live, Les and me (Les and I?) in a run-down farmhouse with four bedrooms, one bath, a leaky roof, and a refrigerator that was one of the marvels of the 1939 World's Fair. This pile of termite fodder and rotting shingles sits on ten acres of the meanest land on Long Island, a home to tick-infested deer, field mice, rabbits, and moles, all happily tear-assing through weeds as thick as bamboo, crabgrass, and poison ivy. The Miller estate at Cedar Point, an environmentalist's Eden.

In the summer, Les & Son mow lawns and drink beer, our capital being a twenty-year-old Chevy pickup truck and two mowers, a weeder, several rakes, and a pair of rusty clippers. In the winter, we do odd jobs—like hauling garbage to the town dump—and drink beer. I have a little sideline, which nets me some cash that goes into a nest egg with the word "escape" written all over it.

So why am I still hanging around? Why is a woman dead and presumed missing? Why is Les bugging the police instead of vice versa? Why is that shit-face lawyer Mark Barrett ignoring my calls? Because last Christmas the lawyer gave Les a hundred bucks and the promise of more to come, that's why.

Last December. Fucking freezing. The ancient radiators are delivering more noise than heat. Colder in than out. The snow is frozen solid on the roof, so for the moment the house is bone-dry. Frigid, but dry. I came downstairs, my breath visible with each step like a locomotive puffing down a mountain.

Les sat at the round kitchen table nursing a beer, his back to a curtainless window framing a frozen landscape in the early-winter twilight. "I talked to Mark Barrett today," he announced.

"Forget it," I told him. "Unless the lawn needs mowing or the trash needs hauling, Barrett doesn't want to know you. Get one of your ambulance chasers or represent yourself, Christ knows you've got the experience." I didn't bother asking him why he needed a lawyer. That would be like asking your lungs why they need air. Instead, I opened the refrigerator and gazed at thirteen cans of beer and a bottle of Stoli. Where did he get the money for Stoli, and was that why he needed a lawyer?

"What were you planning for supper, besides Stoli and beer chasers?" I asked.

"I'm taking you out for a burger."

In spite of the antifreeze in his blood, the water on his brain must have frozen. The few bucks I made that month went for the necessities of life, like electricity, fuel, telephone, and an occasional hot meal. Les blew his on booze and lottery tickets. Before I could remind him of this fact, he pulled some bills out of his shirt pocket and laid them on the table. "If you think your father is poor, you don't know nothin'."

Four twenties. Throw in one for the Stoli and he had gotten his hands on a hundred bucks. "You hit the numbers?"

He grinned with his lips pressed tightly together, a grimace he picked up when his teeth started to rot. Though only forty-five, he looks sixty. People who grew up with Les tell me I'm the spittin' image of my ol' man twenty-five years ago. Now all we have in common is hair the color of sand and blue eyes. Surprisingly, Les still has a tall, lean body that has somehow avoided showing the effects of twenty years of hard drinking. Poor Les—his face has taken the brunt of this abuse, like it was battered by every whiskey bottle he emptied. Barroom talk has it that Lester Miller possesses the biggest dick in East Hampton, if not all of Long Island or North America. I have seen my father drunk and naked, so, I know for a fact that this is not raunchy bullshit. So—Les and me have more in common than blond hair and blue eyes.

I helped myself to a beer and repeated, "You hit the numbers?"

"I told you. I seen Mark Barrett."

"And he gave you a hundred bucks? What did you do, blow him?"

"You know, kid, you got a fucking lip problem." Les waved a threatening fist at me and tried to stand to drive home the point, but didn't quite make it. He wasn't used to the designer vodka, cheap gin being his drink of choice. "And don't forget, I'm your father."

"Forget? Forget? I've been trying to forget for nineteen years, but the cops keep reminding me. 'Hello, Galen, we got your father in the cooler.' You spend so much time in the cooler you look like a fucking Eskimo."

He grinned, this time baring his teeth, maybe hoping to frighten me. "That's why I'm thinking of spending some time in the heater." He looked at me with eyes wide, if a bit bleary, and waited for me to take the bait. When I didn't, he continued. "Florida. Arizona. Mexico. Hot tamales and hot women. What do you say, kid?" He began strumming an imaginary guitar. "How would I look in a sombrero, kid?"

"I think a straitjacket is more your style."

"There you go again, with that lip. But you better be nice to your father, because he can make all your dreams come true."

I clapped my hands. "You're going to drop dead? Oh, Daddy, thank you."

"Don't sass me, Gay. Don't sass me tonight or you'll be sorry for the rest of your life."

I've been dealing with this man for so long I know his mind and moods almost as well as I know my own; the drunk talk had ended. I sat down opposite him and unzipped my leather jacket, a bonus I had paid myself after a very bountiful summer. I pointed at the twenties. "Where did you get them?"

"I told you—Mark Barrett." Like most professional drunks, he could talk and appear cold sober when necessary. This frightened me more than his drunken blabbering. "There's gonna be more. This is a down payment. A . . . a . . ." His hand shook as he raised the can of beer to his lips. "A show of good faith."

"I don't get it."

He leaned across the table and took my hand. His was cold and trembling. I held it in a tight grip. "There's gonna be more, Gay. A million. Maybe more."

"What the fuck are you talking about?"

"Mark Barrett is gonna buy the farm."

I yanked my hand free and stood, toppling the chair behind me. "You bastard!" I shouted. "I believed you. I fucking believed you. Mark Barrett wants to buy this place." I walked around the kitchen, looking at the ceiling. "What for, Les? A second home? Or maybe he's got a fancy lady he wants to set up in style? Eh? Is that it, Les?" I made a grab for the money and he caught hold of my wrist, pulling me across the table until my nose was pressed against the twenties.

He was kissing the top of my head, nibbling on my hair and talking all at the same time. "You shut your mouth and listen to me, you hear?" He spit the words out like an orgasm he'd been holding back for forty-five years. "You listen good, you hear?"

"Okay, I hear."

He let go. I stood up and righted the chair. Sitting, I ran my fingers through my hair. It was damp from his saliva. "So, I'm listening."

What I heard was that Mark Barrett had paid a visit to Les Miller. This was like hearing the Pope had dropped in on Madonna. Barrett, it seemed, was shopping. "He's looking to pick up bargains north of the highway," Les told me.

For those not familiar with the Hamptons, the "highway" is Route 27, which doubles as Main Street for every Hampton village east of Southampton. South of the highway is the Atlantic Ocean and, naturally, the most expensive real estate in the villages that make up the town of East Hampton. North of the highway is the bay side of East Hampton, which includes Gardiners Bay, Northwest Harbor, and Sag Harbor. The Miller patch in Cedar Point is a short walk from Northwest Harbor. Barrett, it was well known, had invested heavily in oceanfront motel conversions to condos and time-shares. Now he was interested in developing a community of condos especially suited to boat lovers, which would include a marina on Northwest Harbor.

"The hundred-thousand-dollar Chris Craft set," Les boasted, no doubt having heard it from the lawyer. Les is a quick study.

In spite of the cold, I could feel the sweat breaking out on my forehead and under my armpits. My T-shirt was damp, sticking to my skin like it did when I cut a lawn in the July sun. I stared at Les's beat-up face, looking for signs of insanity. Once, when I was a boy, he told me we were going away where nobody knew us—I wouldn't have to be afraid and ashamed anymore. I was so happy and excited I couldn't eat for days. When I realized it was all a drunken dream, I cried myself to sleep for weeks. Sometimes, I still do.

"Then he laid the hundred on me," Les finished. " 'Have a nice Christmas. You and that boy of yours. In good faith.' That's what Barrett said. 'In good faith.' "

My sweat turned cold. "You didn't sell the place for a bottle of Stoli and four fucking twenties?" I cried.

"I didn't sell the place, period. Not yet. You think I'm fucking stupid?"

I'll never forget the moment. It was like holding a lottery ticket in your hand and watching the balls fall into place on the television screen. The first five numbers matched. One more. One more. I felt like an elephant had planted his ass on my chest. "How much?"

"Seventy-five, maybe a hundred thousand an acre."

Click! The ball dropped and I was a fucking millionaire.

"When?" I said. "When?"

"Take it easy, kid." Les was enjoying this. A visit from Mark Barrett and now a conversation with his son that wasn't an argument. But not for long. "These things take time," Les said. "First he's got to line up the parcels. Then he's got to get the town board to make some concessions. Variances. Zoning changes."

"What the wheelers and dealers do every day of the week," I informed him. "For a Barrett it's as easy as falling down stairs. When?"

"Early spring. Maybe a little longer. But definitely before the summer."

"A hundred thousand an acre," I said, for no other reason than because I liked hearing it. "A million bucks." Then I did something I had never done before. I went to the refrigerator, took out the Stoli, and downed a slug straight from the bottle. It burned my gut and the tears of joy I was holding back started flowing. "A hundred thousand an acre." I banged the bottle down on the table. "A million fucking bucks."

Les grabbed the bottle. "You're not used to this stuff.

It'll make you sick." What he meant, of course, was that he didn't want me guzzling his share of Barrett's good faith.

"Half of it's mine," I announced.

"Says who?" He wrapped his arms around the Stoli and held it against his chest.

"I mean the house, not the vodka."

"I know what you mean. And the house is mine, same as the vodka. You're greedy, kid. You might wait till you're offered a share before you shoot off your mouth."

"I'm entitled," I said.

"To what?"

"To half of whatever you get. It's my mother's house."

And that was the truth. It belonged, originally, to my grandparents, my mother's folks, who ran it as a working farm. When they died, my mother was sole heir and some asshole lawyer talked her into putting the deed into joint tenantship. This made Les sole heir when she died. My grandparents barely made a living off the land, and when Farmer Les took over he drank up the meager profits before letting the land go fallow. Les should have gone into fertilizer, because everything he touches turns to shit.

My mother worked to support us. Cleaning houses mostly, because that's all she was educated to do. She died at the ripe old age of thirty, when I was five years old. Breast cancer, they say. Misery would be nearer the truth. I remember a frail, blond woman who cried more often than she smiled. After that we had a parade of live-in bimbos who seemed to vie for the privilege of supporting Les Miller. Those sex manuals that tell you size doesn't matter don't know dick about dick.

"Was, kid, was. It *was* your mother's house. Now it's mine."

"You can't cut me out," I told him.

"I can do whatever the fuck I want." He took a swig from the Stoli and wiped his mouth with the back of his hand. "You ever hear the expression, you can catch more flies with honey?" Les lays this on me like I'm hearing it for the first time. Christ!

"You ever hear the expression, you cheat me out of my half and you get your knees nailed to the floorboards?"

"You know what your problem is, kid?"

"No, tell me."

"You watch too many movies on that video machine. You're starting to talk like them."

"And I'll act like them if I don't get my fair share."

"Half a mil," Leo said. "What would you do with half a mil?"

"Put as much space between me and you and this fucking town as this country is wide, that's what."

"Los Angeles," Les sneered, "where they make the movies. You wouldn't do well out there, kid, you know why? You ain't got balls, that's why."

"Try me," I told him.

"Why are we fighting, Gay?"

"Because you won't give me what's mine."

"I don't have anything, yet," Les said. "Mine *or* yours, so why don't you cool it until the deal is made and we know what's in the kitty. Okay?"

"You won't fuck me?"

"I don't fuck pretty boys. I don't even fuck ugly boys." Les laughed at this great show of wit. He shoved two twenties across the table. "Go get your burger."

The kitchen was almost dark now but I didn't turn on the light. Les was slumping in his chair thanks to the Stoli.

"You're not coming?"

He shook his head. "Don't want to spoil your appetite."

"What does that mean?"

"You're ashamed to be seen with me."

"When did I ever say that?"

"Every time you look at me."

"Shit." I grabbed the twenties and stuffed them in the pocket of my leather jacket. "I'm taking the truck."

"I didn't expect you to walk."

"You sure you don't want to come?"

"Get out of here."

"I'll bring you a hero. Or a pizza."

"Beat it."

Outside, it was snowing. We were going to have a white Christmas.

Nine

We spent the winter, Les and I (Les and me?), like bears in a cave, laying low and living off the fat of my escape fund. Hell, why not? I could afford to be generous now that I had expectations. I even bought Les a bottle of Stoli every few weeks just to keep his right hand steady for signing on the dotted line. He never asked where the money came from. A good Christian, Les trusts in God to give him this day his daily bread, booze, and broads. Amazingly, he's seldom disappointed.

I would awake at first light, shivering in spite of the thermal long johns and several layers of blankets. Before Barrett's visit I usually pulled the covers over my head and went back to sleep. Now, as soon as I opened my eyes I told myself, "A million bucks. Early spring, maybe a little later, but definitely before the summer." I was so hypnotized by that million I even neglected my early-morning hard-on. Hell, with that kind of money I could hire someone to do it for me.

While waiting for payday I stuck close to home, which for me is my retreat on the second floor of Barrett's future condo for the boat set. On a clear day I have a view of Northwest Harbor, a long, thin strip of blue on the western horizon. Entering from the upstairs hall of "*my* house," as Les refers to our pot of gold, I feel like Dorothy leaving drab old black-and-white Kansas and stepping into the Technicolor land of Oz.

I've covered the walls with grass cloth, a tip from a decorator client two summers back. But even that tough fabric is beginning to lose the battle against the damp, peeling plaster walls and breaking out in mildew like zits on a thirteen-year-old. My four-poster bed—which is a three-poster because one post, so the story goes, went the way of firewood one harsh winter during the Great Depression—belonged to my grandparents. Maybe it's an antique—a question I posed to one of my antique-dealer clients, who told me the missing post made it worth shit. But it's big and roomy and comfortable. I gathered the best pieces of furniture from around the house, bypassing those that would even be rejected by the discriminating East Hamptonites who shop exclusively at the town dump. A chest of drawers, a desk, and ladder-back chair, all sanded down to the natural wood and left that way. Not painted, which is gauche, a word I learned from my decorator client. When I described my collection he said it all sounded like Grand Rapids, c. 1920, and rolled his eyes toward heaven. "It's a look," he conceded, "but don't paint it, boy. That would be gauche." Well, fuck him, which is a lousy comeback because he would love it.

I couldn't find "gauche" in the dictionary, mostly because the first two letters aren't G-O as they fucking should be, but G-A. I tossed in the towel after a week and took the problem to my teacher, chief guru, and sometime girlfriend who holds forth at the video shop on Main Street. Helen's parents own the shop and she's on duty every day, Sunday included, from ten to four, dispensing scene-by-scene descriptions, memorized reviews, and personal opinions regarding the visual arts under her care. Helen is a living book of knowledge on film lore and other subjects relating to the human condition. A lady came in one day when I was there, and asked Helen for a film, naming the star. Helen looked at her customer as if she was a refugee from a loony bin. "That, miss, is the television version. What you want is the 1938 classic starring Constance Bennett."

The old broad stared down Helen and said, "What I want, miss, is what I asked for."

Helen does not take rejection well. Her shoulders sagged and her eyes watered as she reluctantly handed over the inferior television version of a classic. Unable to help herself, Helen shouted to the woman's retreating back, "The Bennett sisters, Constance and Joan, were two of many sister actresses in Hollywood during the golden years. The Lane sisters, the Young sisters, and Joan Fontaine and Olivia de Havilland—even though they have different names and hated each other." The lady banged the door closed on Helen's voice like she fucking hated Helen.

But then, that's Helen Weaver. Teaching, she says, is a displacement for passion. She's been telling me this since we met, in the first grade. Helen's schoolgirl crush on little Galen Miller has matured into womanly passion in the form of lectures on the dramatic use of blacklighting in the films of Ernst Lubitsch. I tell her, instead of displacing it, why not indulge it? Sex with Helen is boring unless necrophilia is your thing. Maybe we've been at it too long. We started petting in the sixth grade. Before we graduated from the middle school, Helen showed me my circumcision scar. I didn't even know I had one. We did it the first time on the bank of a secluded hole of water that was my secret hiding place, just off Two Holes of Water Road. This—and Helen's passion for movies—was to change the course of my life, as you will soon see.

When we graduated from high school, we joined the family firms, Helen and me (Helen and I?). She went with Main Street Video and I went with Les & Son, a position I'd been training for every summer since I was ten. At this time Helen saw an ad in the Sunday paper that displayed dozens of books, spread out like an accordion, stating that reading all these books was the equivalent of a college education. Helen, shrewd as ever, noted that every one of those books had been made into a film, as were a hundred more masterpieces that weren't even pictured. Here we enrolled in a visual home-study course, Helen playing Mr. Chips to my preppie.

A Tale of Two Cities; Hamlet; Oliver Twist (with and without music); *The Rise and Fall of the Roman Empire; I, Claudius; Pride and Prejudice* by Jane Austen. A-U-S-T-E-N. Not I-N like she's from fucking Texas. I learned this just from the titles, so I guess Helen is right. I've watched so many masterpieces I'm heading straight for a Ph.D.

Helen, by the way, is pretty like a movie star. Dark hair, straight as sticks, that falls to her shoulders, except when she's got it done up in a ponytail. Her eyes are brown in sunlight and gray at night. Her figure, day and night, is the main attraction of Main Street Video. Her problem is that her life has become a movie. All hot and bothered until it's time for the volcano to pop, then fade and cut to vine-covered cottage with tricycle blocking the front door. No thanks, Helen. I've got plans. Big plans, and marriage, diapers, and East Hampton ain't among them. Like some guy said, "Go west, young man. Go west." And if you don't believe I'm going, just count the days I'm gone.

What I should do, but won't, is give up Helen so her most ardent suitor can stake his claim. That would be Eddy Evans. You like that name? His mother, Helen claims, must have read a lot of detective fiction to come up with that. And guess what? Eddy Evans is a detective. A real one. One of East Hampton's finest. He's also twenty-fucking-nine years old, which makes him old enough to be Helen's father, if he'd had her when he was ten. So Eddy, wild for Helen, is a dick, and just to remind himself of the fact, he spends hours of the taxpayers' time and money in Main Street Video, pressing the real article against the wall of the counter that separates him from Helen Weaver, as they chat one on one. She's extolling the genius of D. W. Griffith while Eddy is bemoaning the tightness of his Jockey shorts.

Eddy doesn't know anyone is wise to his sexual relations with Mr. Weaver's counter, least of all me. So when I catch him at it, I quietly sneak up behind him, tap his shoulder, and shout, "Hi, Eddy, how's it hanging?" Eddy takes great pleasure in calling me every time they put Les in the cooler.

Helen dates Eddy whenever I'm busy elsewhere. A fact Eddy knows and for which I am unfairly despised by the dick. Can I help it if I'm fucking good-looking? He takes her on dinner dates, as Helen calls these freebies. On his salary, he can afford it. When I take Helen out, we go—where else?—to the movies. Dutch, you understand, because I don't want any sexist gestures coming between us.

I think Eddy is onto my summer moonlighting. Does

Helen know? I suspect she does, just because Helen knows everything and what she doesn't know she goes to the library and researches. And if the library can't help her, Helen has a unique backup: a fucking psychic. This crystal ball lady is new in town and word has it that business is booming. I don't know what she tells Helen and this worries me. What I know, I can deal with. What I don't know scares me. So, when Les went missing for seven days, I was fucking scared.

Ten

Les disappeared somewhere between Delray Beach, Florida, and East Hampton, New York. Obvious question: What was Les Miller doing in Delray Beach? Not so obvious answer: Attending to the only steady job he's held for the past five years. For all those years, on the Saturday after Thanksgiving, Les drives a Mercedes to Delray Beach and flies home. In the early spring, when summoned, Les flies to Delray Beach and drives the Mercedes back to East Hampton. The car's owners, of course, fly both ways. Upon arrival, north and south, they rent a car at the airport and drive it to their home, keeping it until Les delivers their Mercedes.

Obvious question: Who in their right mind would trust the champ of drunk drivers to chauffeur their upscale auto some fifteen hundred miles twice a year? Not so obvious answer: An old, kind, sincere retired couple. When the MacAlisters—who must be a hundred because they got grandchildren in college—retired out here, they saw Les's ad in the local paper and hired him to care for their lawn. "Les and Son. It sounds so respectable and family-like," old Mrs. MacAlister said. Respectable? Les & Son have been called a lot of names, but "respectable" has got to be an all-time first.

Many of our customers are those who rent for one summer, never to return for whatever reason. We seldom get repeat business. But ol' Les, like all professional drunks, knows a mark when he sees one, and the MacAlisters, who have never dealt with low-life, snap at the bait. He mows their lawn, does a little trimming—"No extra charge, ma'am." Next he fixes a dripping faucet, repairs a fence, takes the Mercedes in for its oil change, and in short, acts like a handyman on retainer, only it's always, "No extra charge, ma'am."

One rainy afternoon, he hauls their trash to the dump and that becomes a weekly chore for good ol' Les. The "no extra charge" line is waved aside by the old man and after each trip to the dump a ten-dollar bill is slipped into Les's shirt pocket. Soon the MacAlisters come to depend on Les like he's the fucking family doctor. And soon a lot of ten-dollar bills are slipped into Les's shirt pocket for chores that aren't worth ten cents. When the old couple's children visit, they thank Les and tell him how secure they feel with him in charge of Mom and Pop. "Anything goes wrong, we just call Les," Mrs. MacAlister brags.

The MacAlisters must have heard of Les's addiction to booze and broads, but he has made himself as necessary to them as running water and indoor plumbing, so they turn a deaf ear to the gossip and a blind eye to the police blotter, published weekly in the *East Hampton Star.* It's called denial. The poor old things need Les Miller. In Les's favor, I'll say he has never fucked up getting the MacAlisters' Mercedes to and from Delray Beach each year. And why should he? The MacAlisters are his chief source of revenue, especially the cash bonus for ferrying the car, plus there's the prestige of spending one day, twice a year, in Delray Beach.

So where is he?

He got a note from the MacAlisters, along with a one-way plane ticket to Delray Beach, early in March. I drove him to the airport and the MacAlisters told me he arrived as scheduled and they departed as scheduled, turning over the keys to the Mercedes and cash for expenses to Les, as usual. He drove them to the airport that Sunday morning and—they assumed—headed north. The usual timing for these trips is two days on the road, arriving, in either direction, on the afternoon of the third day. Based on this, we expected Les would be in East Hampton sometime on Tuesday. He wasn't. No big deal. Any-thing—from heavy traffic to a flat—could have caused the delay.

"But he should have called," moaned Mrs. MacAlister, sounding worried. You see, she can't deny the fact that a rented Honda Civic has replaced the Mercedes in her garage. I wasn't worried because Les wouldn't have the common sense to call.

When the sun rose and set on Wednesday with still no sign of Les, I got uneasy. By Friday the MacAlisters were frantic. "We must notify the police," Mr. MacAlister preached, and rightly so. "We want our car," he de-manded.

"And I want my father," I demanded back. That did it. They didn't give me any lip when I insisted on going to the police and reporting back to them. It was a stall for time and that's all I wanted. You see, I thought I knew the whereabouts of Les.

The MacAlisters always gave Les his expenses in cash and his pay for the job on arrival. Les never had extra cash for dallying on the job. Remembering how I'd been foolishly supporting him this past winter due to my expectations, I thought that he must have stashed away a few bucks in anticipation of playing the big-time spender while tooling around in someone else's Mercedes. Les, I was sure, was in a motel with some bimbo, drunk, and would remain in that mode until the money ran out, which wouldn't take long, and the dame had drained both his dick and his wallet dry. So, instead of going to the police, I went to Helen.

"You should go to the police," Helen advised.

"I don't want that Eddy Evans laughing at me. 'Your ol' man finally screwed up his meal ticket.' That's what he'll say. The dickhead."

"What do you want from me, then?" she asked.

"Go see the crystal ball lady and ask her if she can locate Les."

"You're kidding?"

"Me, kidding? You give her seventy-five bucks a visit and you think I'm kidding for asking her to put up or shut up. What the fuck does she see in that crystal ball, besides a steady income?"

"She does not use a crystal ball and she sees, mentally, the other side, not who's shacked up at the Holiday Inn."

"The other side of what? The moon?"

"The other side. Where we go when we leave here."

"You mean . . ."

"You know what I mean."

"Well," I said, "maybe Les is on the other side."

And this, I swear, was the first time I thought of the possibility of Les's demise, as lawyers call passing over to the other side. But even then, I swear, I didn't make the connection between Les's death and Barrett's offer until Helen blurted, "If he bought the farm, you own one."

"He's not dead," I answered. "Not Les. They would reject him on the other side and send him back." I should say here that neither Helen nor anyone else, so I thought, knew about Barrett's offer for the farm. Barrett had cautioned Les to keep it quiet until he presented his case to the planning board, and Les passed the warning on to me. This secrecy made the expectation so much sweeter. Helen's comment, I knew, was offered more in pity than joy. The farm, as far as she knew, was no prize.

There was one customer in Main Street Video as we spoke—an old man who moved slowly down the row of displayed videos, bending for a closer look, poking at the boxes, selecting, rejecting, and all the time, like a cat stalking a mouse, moving closer and closer to a bin over which hung a sign: "ADULT VIDEOS. BE TWENTY-ONE OR BE GONE." In case you've never noticed, no one walks into a video shop and goes straight for the porn. That would be gauche. First they check out the new arrivals, then they browse around the nostalgia like they knew who Alan Ladd was. Next they scan the musicals and hum a few tunes, and as if to atone for their sins, past and future, they read the hype on the flip side of at least one Disney presentation.

Arriving at their destination as if by accident, they condescend to flip through the flattened cardboard jackets, trying to remember which ones they've already seen because they're all fucking alike, while keeping a sharp eye on the front door, ready to abandon the operation should someone they know enter. When they think no one is looking, they peel off the tag that bears the number corresponding to the desired work of art and present it to the clerk, who couldn't care less what they rent as long as their money is green.

"You're going to love this one," Helen told the old man, who didn't appreciate the recommendation.

Once my stake in Les's demise found its way into my head, I couldn't shake it. Not a half-million, if Les was willing to part with that, but the whole million. And Mark Barrett would have to deal with me, and maybe I would want more than a hundred thousand an acre. Maybe I would look the deal over and see just how much Barrett stood to make on it. Maybe I would want the million and a piece of the action. Maybe a lot of things, all dependent upon what side Les was currently guzzling his gin.

A million. Plus holding Barrett by the short and curlies. Six months in New York to polish my act. Drama school, speech, poise, some designer clothes. Lessons, to learn French or Italian. One of my clients told me Italian was in. In what, I haven't got a fucking clue. But I'll learn. I'll learn what I have to learn to make all the people in this fucking town who spit on me and my father squirm at the sight of me. And the number one pricks, Mark Barrett and guys like him, will fund my revenge. Did I say it was sweet? Man, it's like jacking off after wearing boxing gloves for a year.

Helen was looking at me like she knew what I was thinking, which she usually does. Helen could teach the crystal ball lady a trick or two, let me tell you. Maybe my eyeballs were suddenly shaped like dollar signs. Or was it the way I kept looking at the big blowup of this punk superstar and thinking I look better than him when I wake up in the morning? Last year I had a client who told me I could make it big in the movies. No bullshit. He gave me his card and said to call him if I ever decided to go west. Andrew Moody, with an address on Mulholland Drive in Los Angeles. I checked it out and learned a lot of important people live on Mulholland Drive in L.A. Stupidly, I told Helen about this. I covered myself by telling her Moody was a housguest where I was mowing the lawn. Did she believe it?

"What does he do out there?" Helen asked when I showed her the card.

"He's an agent."

She tossed it back to me like we're playing stud poker. "Which means he's a pimp."

Helen, you see, is jealous of anyone who threatens to separate us. "So where does it say that?"

"I can read between the lines. All he wants is your body. When he's had enough of it, he'll pass you on to the legion of perverts who infest Mulholland Drive."

"You're sick, Helen."

"Not as sick as Moody." Then she didn't speak to me for a week and accepted three dinner dates with Eddy Evans. If those two ever marry, they'll look like fucking elephants in six months.

"Corpus delicti," Helen announced, abruptly bringing me back to the problem of my father's latest fuckup.

"A delicious corpse?"

"No, Gay. A missing corpse."

"Les is not a missing corpse. He's just missing."

"But if he never turns up alive, you have to have a corpse to prove he's dead. No corpse, no farm."

No farm, no million. Things were going from bad to worse and I still had the MacAlisters to deal with. "So what do I tell the MacAlisters?" I asked, figuring a corpus delicti could wait, seeing as it wasn't going anywhere.

"Tell them the police are putting out an APB on Les."

"What's an APB?" old man MacAlister shouted into the phone, because he's a little deaf and thinks shouting will help him hear better.

"An all-points bulletin." Shit, don't they watch television? "I gave them Les's picture. They'll make copies and send one to every motel along Interstate 95. They'll even send one to every tollbooth collector between here and Delray Beach." When I start tossing the bull I don't know when to stop. "They got this well in hand, Mr. MacAlister, believe me."

"They don't have to check every car," he bellowed. "Just any black Mercedes heading north."

"I'm sure they know that, Mr. MacAlister."

"Hold on, Galen." Then I heard him talking to Mrs. MacAlister. When he came back on the line he said, "Mrs. MacAlister has a question, son."

"Put her on."

"Galen?" she asked, like who the fuck does she think her husband's been talking to?

"Yes, ma'am."

"Suppose he uses the exact-change lanes, they'll never catch him."

Give me a fucking break.

They didn't bother me on Saturday. Too soon. Sunday morning the phone rang at a respectable nine sharp. I fled and hung around Main Street until ten, when Helen opens Main Street Video. Early March and the tourists are already strolling up and down Main and Newtown Lane.

Spring is in the air and East Hampton is alive with the sound of money changing hands. Please God, let some come my way. A million to be exact.

"I've got news for you," Helen greeted me.

"From the crystal ball lady?"

"No, you fool. From a lawyer."

I didn't like this. "What lawyer?"

"Mark Barrett. He stops in on occasion. Never rents. Just likes to chat."

And look at your tits, I thought, before the name settled in like an unwanted guest carrying a very large valise. "Christ, you didn't tell him about Les?" That's all I needed. If Les was on the other side, I wanted to be the one to tell Barrett. I didn't want to give him time to think of some way to fuck me out of my due.

"No, Gay, but if Les doesn't show up soon, everyone in town will know he's gone missing. What I did was pose a hypothetical question to Mr. Barrett. I said, suppose a man goes on safari to darkest Africa and is never heard of again?"

"Helen, it sounds like a Tarzan movie."

"This man," she continued, paying no attention to me, "has one heir. Does the heir collect?"

Now I'm listening. "Well, does he?"

"It depends," Helen answered in her maddening way. You must also remember that the shop was filling up. We were constantly interrupted by people renting videos and returning videos, and kids asking for change to play the damn game machines.

"Depends on what?" My heart was beating so fast I thought I was going to have some kind of fit in Main Street Video.

"The will, if there is one. How the estate is set up for

tax purposes. But there's always a waiting period, so the courts have to give the heir power of attorney to act for the guy in the jungle. Sign checks, make deposits, pay bills."

What the fuck was she talking about? There is no will. The estate is the farm. We have no bank accounts. There's nothing to deposit and the bills seldom get paid.

"After the waiting period the guy is presumed dead and the heir collects." Typical Helen, she ended the story with a smile like the reel is running out on a Doris Day movie.

"How long is the waiting period?" My heart was about to explode.

"It varies, but in most states it's seven years."

"What!" I yelled. Everyone in the shop turned and stared.

"Take it easy, Gay. We don't even know if he's dead."

"Seven more years in this town, Helen, and I'll be dead."

I drove back to the farm late that afternoon, and in the rapidly fading sunlight I spotted a shiny black object parked out front. The Mercedes, I thought with more joy than disappointment, I hope. It was a Lincoln Town Car. Barrett? Had he heard about Les and come to check on the facts? Helen? I'll kill her if she lied. Maybe he was just looking over the house with his architect, measuring the square footage, or maybe he was interested in making an offer for a three-poster bed. I didn't know, so I was scared. So scared I never even noticed the Lincoln's plates.

I went in the front door and headed straight down the hall to the kitchen. And there, sitting at the round table, sipping a beer and framed by the curtainless window, was my father, Lester Miller.

I was so relieved I could have kissed him. Instead I ranted, "Where the fuck have you been?"

"That's a nice welcome home if ever I heard one."

"Where's the Mercedes? How the fuck did a Mercedes become a Lincoln? You are in the deepest shit of your career."

"You got a lip problem, kid."

"Where's the Mercedes?" I repeated.

"Where it belongs. In the MacAlisters' garage."

"Did you take their rental back to Hertz?"

"Don't I always?"

"So how did you get from Hertz to here?"

"In the Lincoln."

"I didn't know you could rent a Lincoln Town Car at Hertz."

"It ain't a rental."

"So who owns it?"

Eleven

"You must be Galen."

The voice was deep, sexy, and unmistakably female. It caught me off guard, like a tap on the shoulder just when you think you've gotten away with pocketing a candy bar at the checkout counter. When I turned I saw its source standing by our ancient refrigerator. She was wearing a white silk blouse that showed a lot of cleavage and a black skirt that hugged a pair of slim hips. Below, a great pair of legs standing on towering high heels; above, a face that could sell an icebox to a couple moving into an igloo.

"And whom must you be?" I asked.

"Betty. Not short for Elizabeth." She raised her hand like she's showing off her manicure. Her fingernails were painted a pale pink and buffed to a glossy shine.

What else could I do? I took her hand in mine, not knowing if I was expected to shake it or kiss it. It was ice-cold, so I let it go without doing either.

"Cold hands, warm heart," she said, like she knows she's got the body temperature of a barracuda.

"So what are you? Some kind of fucking nurse?"

"Keep a civil tongue in your head." This came from

Les, who didn't seem the least surprised at the presence of this gorgeous creature in our humble abode. I didn't like the smell of this one fucking bit. Smell? She was saturated in a perfume they don't sell in drugstores. The kind of scent that gives little boys big ideas. Christ, if she didn't look right at my crotch when I'm thinking this.

"Who is she?" I asked Les. "A genie that popped out of one of your gin bottles?"

Betty laughed, tossing back her head—reddish-brown hair just grazing the shoulders of her white blouse, red lips parting to reveal a set of caps that must have set her back ten grand, and eyes like two shiny black mirrors.

"Tell him," Les cackled. I knew the sound well. Les had had a few belts of gin before the beer he was nursing, or maybe Stoli, compliments of Miss Frigidaire.

"Tell me? Tell me what? That she owns the Lincoln?"

"Yes. Is it in your way? I don't want to impose."

"Then disappear."

"I'm afraid I can't do that, Galen." She moved away from her supporting prop and sat at the round table, crossing her legs. Her nylons, I couldn't help noticing, were a shade lighter than her eyes. "I peeked into your room. I hope you don't mind. My, my, it's like a theater. I never saw such a huge television screen."

"What were you doing upstairs? Who are you?" I looked at Les sitting across from the woman and staring at her with a shit-eating grin on his wino puss. Over the years, living with Les, I'd seen a lot of women come and go but never one with the class and brass of this Betty, not short for Elizabeth. "Okay," I sighed. "What did he promise you?"

"To love, honor, and obey," Betty answered.

"Tell him. Tell him." Les started pounding the table

with the palm of his hand, causing it to tremble on its unsteady legs.

The lady, the Lincoln, Les acting crazy. Love, honor, and obey. My stomach started making funny noises and everything went out of focus except those bloodred lips purring, "Your father and I were married yesterday."

Twelve

It was true. They tied the knot (around my neck) in some burg on the fringes of Baltimore. I wouldn't take her word for it. Not the word of Betty—not short for Elizabeth, but just long enough for bitch—if she was wearing ten gold bands and not just the one she kept waving at me like she was giving me the finger.

"That doesn't mean shit," I told her. A bit gauche, but when I'm in a rage I remember my roots: white trash. So she showed me the marriage license. Lester Miller to Betty Zabriskie. Fucking foreigner.

They were joined in the office of a justice of the peace, which was also the office of the motel where the two were shacked up, waiting for the results of the mandatory blood test. Blood test? Taking blood from Les is like draining a distillery. What on this planet can thrive in pure alcohol? And a motel with a built-in justice of the peace. Convenient? Everything about this marriage was convenient, like the smooth assembling of a do-it-yourself letter bomb addressed to Galen Miller.

Based on past experience, I mentally reconstructed the courtship of Les and his blushing bride of twenty-four hours, like a dying man whose life flashes before his eyes as he sinks into the abyss. She's sitting on a bar stool in some watering hole along Route 95, wearing her black nylons and expensive perfume, and sipping a drink that cost five bucks, only it's on the house because she's the joint's main attraction. She's waiting for some traveling salesman with time to kill and money in his pocket to make her an offer she can't refuse. Along comes poor Les with his tongue hanging out, and him she can refuse with a look that's designed to take the starch out of any guy's hard-on. Only Les isn't any guy. The panting tongue turns into a silver harp and the lady is at first amused, then listening, and finally hooked. He told her about his million-dollar iron in the fire, I knew that, and she believed him. Why not? What's she got to lose?

Only she's not going to settle for any promises. Not this Betty, not short for Elizabeth. She wants the whole enchilada, this one. No wedding, no nookie, sweet man. Did this bother Les? Hell, no. It's the best offer he's had since he won my mother and the farm that went with her. Betty's kind travels light. If he's a four-flusher, she leaves him faster than she attached herself to him. If he's telling the truth, she's in on the kill. For Betty it's a no-lose situation. For me it's the fucking kiss of death.

I lost my cool and, naturally, made all the wrong moves. First, I read her my standard welcoming speech like Marlon Brando in *Julius Caesar*—that's a movie by Shakespeare. "Betty," I ranted, "lend me your ear. This is where we keep the plunger for the toilet which seldom works without encouragement. I hope you take baths, because using the shower in this house is like being pissed on by a guy who needs a catheter. If I'd known about this match made in hell, I would have had a wedding present waiting for you, but tomorrow, I promise, I'll pick up a ten-year supply of Prozac, which you will soon realize, living with Les, is more usable than a silver tea service from fucking Tiffany."

Betty laughed, looking at me as if I was some stand-up comic. That didn't help my cause. "Look around, Betty, because what you see is what you fucking get."

This bitch looked me straight in the eye, lowered her gaze to the bulge in my jeans, and announced, "What I see, Galen, is what I want." Balls? Jesus.

Les was jumping up and down, clapping his hands, thinking maybe this is his fucking bachelor party. I never saw him so drunk, so out of it, but too much was going on for me to focus in on what I later suspected was happening to Les. Getting nowhere with her, I turned on him. "You told her, didn't you? You fucking told her after you made me promise to keep my mouth shut. After you told Mr. Barrett it wouldn't go beyond this house. In good faith, Barrett said. So where is your fucking good faith?"

"He didn't tell me," Betty said. She didn't shout. She never shouts. She spoke calmly, quietly, and with an authority that made me certain she was telling the truth. The words, the way she said them, sent a chill down my spine. What did this mean? I didn't know, so I was scared.

"Help me put your father to bed," she said.

"He's your husband, lady."

"Then he can sleep with his head on the kitchen table."

"He's done it before," I told her.

She walked past me into the parlor. When she came back she was wearing a fur coat. "Good night," she said.

"Where are you going?"

"To Gurney's. You don't think I'm going to sleep in this dump." She turned and was gone. Next thing I heard, above Les's snoring, was the Lincoln's motor turning over.

Man, I was scared. I was fucking scared.

The next morning, I found Les where we had left him the night before. As usual, he's sipping a beer, but I think it's the same one he was nursing when he passed out. Warm beer. Just the thing for a groom's wedding breakfast.

"Where's Betty?" he asked.

"In the bridal suite of Gurney's Inn," I told him. "She sends her regards." Then I was history.

Straight to Helen, where I unloaded my troubles in Main Street Video. Naturally, I had to tell her about Barrett's offer so she would understand why I was in a shit fit over Les's marriage. Mr. Barrett will be happy to know that our little secret is now known to enough people to fill Madison Square Garden on a good night. I was hoping Helen could recommend a film that would tell me how to proceed. Unfortunately, she did—but I don't want to get ahead of myself. That's my trouble, I leap before I look and shoot off my mouth before I think.

Helen listened to what I had to say and then tore into me. "You leap before you look and you shoot off your mouth before you think."

"I know," I said. "But they're married. My half goes to her."

"Galen," she reminded me, "the spread belongs to Les and Les alone. You don't have any half."

"I know, but he agreed," I half lied, "to splitting with me."

"Well, now there's another interested party, with a legal claim I think, so little Galen can't go running off to Hollywood and take the movie world by storm," she gloated.

"What's my legal position?"

"I don't think you have one. If Les wants to share with you or give you something, he can, but I don't think he has to."

"That bitch won't give me dick. She left Les passed out in the kitchen last night and went off to Gurney's."

"Les has passed out in the kitchen almost every night for the past twenty years. So what does that prove?"

"She has no heart, that's what."

"But she's beautiful?"

I agreed she was.

"Good figure?"

"Like Miss America."

"And she owns a Lincoln Town Car?"

"Brand-new."

"Galen, think. What does this lady want with your father?"

"His money."

"He doesn't have any money. Not yet. Barrett's offer is speculation, at best. She must know this. And from what you tell me, it looks like she already has a million bucks, or near to it. Not everyone is as hard up as you, Gay. So I repeat, what does she want with Les?"

I had no answer.

"Think, Gay. Think. A lady like this wouldn't look at your father twice. He charmed her, you say. Gay, a woman like you're describing wouldn't let the likes of Les Miller near enough to light her cigarette, let alone charm her. And she said he didn't tell her about the Barrett deal."

I nodded. "That's what she said. I believe her, Helen. I can't say exactly why, but I believe her."

"Conclusion. She went after Les, not the other way round, because she knows something."

"What?" I pleaded. "And how did she know where he was, to go after him? And who told her whatever the hell she knows?"

"That, Watson, is what we have to find out."

"Oh, great. How?"

"Charm her."

"How do you charm a cobra?"

"With a little music and a big flute."

"You got a dirty mind, Helen."

"I find you irresistible and you haven't compromised me in weeks."

"I have a lot on my mind."

"It's getting to be spring. Some days are almost warm enough to sunbathe. I can get time off, pack a lunch, and we can slip away to our private pond on Two Holes of Water. Like tomorrow."

"I'll think about it."

"Don't play hard to get, Gay, it's not appealing."

"You don't have any sympathy for my situation."

"Your father got married—so what?"

"To a gold digger, that's what."

"Maybe there's no gold in them hills, Gay."

"Oh, but there is. I know there is and I want my share."

"Go see Mr. Barrett."

"Helen, don't tell him about this. Don't tell anyone about this. I know, it'll be all over town soon enough, but I want time to think. Promise?"

"You know me. Mum's the word."

"Thanks, Helen."

"What about tomorrow?"

"We'll see."

Thirteen

We were like a dog and a cat sharing a cage, Stepmama and me (and I?). We circled each other but never crossed paths, thanks to a daily routine you could set your clock by. I left the house early each morning and returned just before dark. I knew that she was there when I wasn't by the changes taking place in our kitchen and in her husband. This amazing lady actually set up a bar on the kitchen counter. Rye, scotch, gin, vodka, mixers, and by God, swizzle sticks. Les, when he's not guzzling his mate's beverages, sits at the kitchen table, framed by the curtainless window, and stares at the bottles thinking, I'm sure, that he died and went to heaven. "Jesus, Jesus, you are one hell of a host."

But can Les think? This lady had him on what recovering alcoholics call a maintenance level. This I learned from reading A.A. pamphlets given to Les over the years by well-meaning friends. It means ingesting enough booze to keep the addict from going into a withdrawal seizure. In this case, it meant keeping Les perpetually sedated and out of Betty's lovely hair.

Is Les enjoying the fringe benefits of his marriage? A quickie on a lazy Tuesday afternoon? I really don't know and neither, I'm sure, does Les. She has made it her business to keep Les happy and uncomplaining. He doesn't even know she's not living with him, because he's usually passed out, on his bed, when I get home. I figure she helps him upstairs while he can still walk. And has a look in my room? Here's where I go on the offensive.

Employing a technique favored by James Bond (a superspy created by Ian Fleming), I moistened a six-inch length of black thread and stuck one end to the jamb and the other to my closed bedroom door, creating an almost invisible seal which, if broken, would tell me for certain what I only suspected.

That night I found a note on my bedroom door. "Dear Galen, The spittle dried and the thread fell. Have you considered installing a lock?"

Give me a fucking break.

To her credit I will say that in addition to the bar, she brought food into our home. Bread, cold cuts, cans of soup, and salad. If she is going to kill him with booze, it won't be without the homey touches of the caring wife. At the autopsy they will not discover a man who suffered from malnutrition. Clever? My stepmother makes Cinderella's stepmother look like Mother Teresa.

During this time, I was not idle. I visited some of last year's customers, hoping for repeat business, which we seldom get. I'm thinking, business as usual. I don't want anyone to suspect the Millers are coming into money. The only thing bigger than people's ears in this town is their mouths. I especially wanted to keep Mark Barrett from learning of Betty's stake in the land deal. Like Helen said, we've got to find out what Betty knows, what she's up to, before we send a wedding notice to the *East Hampton Star*.

Helen also learned the following from one of her lawyer customers—not Barrett, she swore.

In the state of New York, if a man dies intestate, which means without a will, his wife is entitled to one half his assets and any surviving children the remainder. If Les lives to close the deal, I'm at their mercy and Betty will see to it that Les doesn't give me the time of day. If Les dies before Barrett comes through, I split with Stepmama whether she likes it or not. So if Les wants to OD on his wife's thoughtful liquid diet, who am I to interfere? Cruel? Hey, this guy shit on me for nineteen years and what goes around comes around. Right? And to ensure that this woman does not bury a husband and stepson in rapid succession, I vowed not to turn my back on the charming Betty Zabriskie for one fucking second.

Everything was happening too fast, like I'm doing drugs or some shit like that. From dirt-poor to millionaire with wicked stepmother snapping at my ass in less time than it takes Less to toss back a case of Bud.

I went to the MacAlisters' and did a little spring tidying up. I told them Les was down with the flu, and they didn't seem the least disturbed by the news. After the scare he gave them—thanks to Betty, not short for Elizabeth—I think the MacAlisters are having second thoughts about employing Les for long-distance hauling. And not a word to them about Les's marriage. Strange, but I have the feeling that Betty is just as anxious to keep this marriage a secret as I am, and the reason for this would soon become very clear.

But most of the time, I spent sunning and plotting at my secret hideaway off Two Holes of Water Road. I discovered the spot years ago when I used to wander off by myself to get away from Les, his current girlfriend, and

the sympathetic gaze of teachers, schoolmates, and their
parents who whispered, just loud enough for me to hear,
"He's Les Miller's boy, poor little thing."

Two Holes of Water Road runs north and south, beginning at Stephen Hands Path to the south and ending at
Swamp Road going north. I remember roaming through
the woods off Swamp Road, just before it meets Two
Holes of Water, and suddenly coming upon a pond surrounded by tall pines, shrubs, and tangled brambles. A
narrow ring of pebbles made a sort of beach around the
oval of water and somebody had even abandoned an old
flat-bottomed boat at the site. It was so isolated I could
have been on another planet.

I never saw another soul near the pond. The spot became my spot and I went there every chance I got, which
was almost every day after school. In the summer I swam
bare-ass and even got up the nerve to drag the boat into
the water and paddle it around with the bottom half of an
oar I found in the dump.

In the winter I never went near the town pond because
I didn't have skates like the other kids, but I had my own
hunk of frozen water, so what did I care? I glided across
my ice on a lid from a garbage can and didn't have to
worry about disturbing the fancy figure skaters and
would-be hockey champs.

I didn't tell anyone, not even Helen, about my hole of
water, and back then I thought I was the only person on
earth who knew it was there. Now I know that the spot is
pictured on every map of East Hampton, there for anyone
who wants to go look for it. What kept it free of the hik-
ers and bikers was its location. The pond sits in a dell.
The route I discovered, through the woods off Swamp
Road, is a good half-mile to the oasis. There is no path

and if it's a bitch of a tramp in winter it's near impossible in July and August, when I literally had to hack a path through the wild brush to get to my pond. As far as I know, my route via Swamp Road is the only way to reach it. If there was a path off Two Holes of Water Road you would have a drop of some twenty or thirty feet to reach the spot.

Tarzan had Jane and Galen had Helen Weaver. The joy of being on your own when you're twelve becomes boring at sixteen. And where to take your girl without the risk of getting caught is a problem as old as sex, I guess, but I had the place.

Helen hated the walk through the woods but loved the spot once we arrived. Here, we lost our virginity. I want to make it clear that I did not seduce Helen. That would be impossible. As usual, Helen read everything she could get her hands on regarding sexual intercourse and then lectured on the subject, making the actual act more of a scientific experiment than a major life-changing experience.

"You don't need a condom," Helen announced, after we set up housekeeping at the pond site. "I'm using the rhythm method."

If she was using rhythm you couldn't prove it by me. Helen had all the mobility of a Barbie doll and would only consent to what she called the missionary position. It sounded religious, so maybe she's saying her prayers while I'm bouncing up and down on this human trampoline. I can best describe sex with Helen by saying that I was the only guy in East Hampton High who had to think long and hard about making a date with Helen or with myself.

Helen brought two beach chairs to what became our

hideaway. One is now in tatters and the other went during a hurricane and is probably at the bottom of the lake, a place I now find repulsive.

After a few days of solitude, I relented and invited Helen to our old haunt. As promised, she made up a picnic basket, and I drove the old truck up Swamp Road, parking it on the edge of the woods. We walked the winding, familiar route to the pond. Still early spring, the air was cool but the sun warm enough to make the outing enjoyable. The water, when I stuck a toe in, was freezing. Helen remembered to bring wine and we indulged ourselves in food, drink, and carnal knowledge. The sex wasn't bad and I attributed this to the fact that we only exposed those parts of our bodies necessary to make contact. For me it's like doing it in the back of a classroom while the teacher is scribbling on the blackboard. A real turn-on. Another reason for my Academy Award performance was that I was thinking of Betty Zabriskie from beginning to end.

Yes, I admit it. Once you've tangled with Betty Zabriskie she'd hard to forget. She gets under a man's skin like the jock itch. Her fucking perfume has replaced the aroma of stale beer and Les's unwashed body parts in my home. Like a bloodhound I picked up her scent in every room of the house. This leads to raunchy thoughts and the need for instant relief.

I'm not the only one that's got Betty on the brain. Helen can't seem to get enough of her either and maybe that's why she's suddenly responding with more than just the usual slam, bam approach to lovemaking.

"Describe her hair again." "Was the blouse really silk or a synthetic?" "Pink nail polish?" "The perfume has got to be Joy."

"Joy?" I repeated.

"Joy by Jean Patou, about two hundred dollars an ounce."

I'm impressed. "So what does she want with Les?" I asked for the tenth time that day.

"The farm and what it can bring. She didn't deny it, Gay."

"No, but she didn't admit to anything, either. Why does a dame like that need more money?"

"Maybe she's running out of Joy."

Helen started putting the leftovers back in the basket while I began rolling up the blanket that was a usual part of the picnic provisions. The warmth of the sun was fading and the light breeze felt a bit more like winter than spring. "You've got to stop avoiding her, Gay. You've got to apologize for last Sunday's madness and start acting like a . . . like a . . ."

"Don't say it, Helen."

"Say what?"

"Start acting like a *son.*"

"I didn't say it, you did. But it's the only way we're ever going to find out where she came from and what she's up to."

"She came from the bar where Les met her. She's after the money Les is going to get for the farm, if Barrett ever gets off his ass and starts proceedings or whatever the hell it's called."

I tossed the blanket over my shoulder and Helen held the basket in the crook of her arm, and together—like Hansel and Gretel—we turned our backs on fairyland and marched off into the woods where the wicked witch was beckoning with long, pink fingernails and the aroma of Joy by Jean Patou.

"Gay . . ." Helen sighed in that way she has. "We've talked this out all week. Why would a woman like Betty allow Les to approach her? Even if she *is* a prostitute, of which you have no proof, Les is not the ideal john. Far from it. And if he did get close enough to brag about the Barrett deal for the farm, why would she believe him? Hookers don't work on speculation."

Before I could say anything she continued.

"She said she didn't hear about the farm from Les, and you believed her. So, who did she hear it from and how much does she know? Has it occurred to you that maybe she knows more than you?"

"What's that supposed to mean?"

"She's rich, you think. From Florida most likely. Maybe the Barretts go to Florida in the winter. That crowd usually does. Palm Beach is my guess, which is next door to Delray. Maybe she knows the Barretts. Or maybe she just knows Mark Barrett. Is it beginning to make sense?"

Like always, Helen was right. Jesus Christ, was she right.

"Play up to her, Gay. Find out what she knows."

"Don't tell me you can catch more flies with honey."

"That line sucks, Gay."

"That's why I didn't want you saying it."

"I didn't say it, Gay. You did."

Helen is an expert at verbal karate. She takes your words, twists them into a steel boot, and returns them with a good swift kick in the ass.

We got in the truck and as I pulled onto Swamp Road I asked, "So tell me, is Eddy getting into your pants too?"

She hit me with the picnic basket, drawing blood just over my right eyebrow.

Fourteen

Betty was sitting in Les's chair at the kitchen table, a lit cigarette in one hand and a drink in the other. It was early evening but the only light in the room, which wasn't much, came from the window behind her, so you weren't sure if the lady was sixteen or sixty.

"Well, well, well, the prodigal returns. Should I kill a fatted calf?"

"*The Prodigal?* It was a movie. A biblical epic."

"I'm impressed," she answered, pounding out her cigarette in an ashtray I had never seen in our home before Betty took over.

Score one for me, I thought, seeing how impressed she was with my answer to her smart-ass greeting. Maybe she thought I didn't know what a prodigal was. Well, now she knows better. I didn't get the part about killing a cow and didn't ask. Quit while you're ahead, I always say. "I know a lot about movies," I told her.

"Which accounts, I'm sure, for that big television set in your room."

"You've been in my room again?"

"No, Galen, I have not been in your room again."

Remembering I had to make nice to the lady, I said, "I don't mind if you were. I've got nothing to hide."

"Neither do I, Galen. Would you like a drink?"

"Some wine would be nice," I said, playing it cool, like her.

"Help yourself."

I poured some white into a wineglass, both of which were compliments of Betty Zabriskie because the Miller household didn't stock either. I turned to her and raised my glass. "Cheers."

She picked up her drink; it might've been a plain seltzer, straight vodka, or a combination of both. "Cheers to you."

I pulled out the chair opposite her and sat, stretching my legs across the floor like a movie cowboy. Betty was wearing a white turtleneck sweater. What it lacked in cleavage it made up for by her protruding breasts—distinctly separate, like a pair of cannons aimed right at my puss. They made it hard for me to focus on her face and she knew it. Betty is a fucking sex machine. The way she sucks on her cigarette and lifts her face to exhale in the direction of the ceiling. The way her finger rolls around and around the rim of her glass. The smile on her face that says she likes what I'm thinking. And the perfume. Always the perfume. Two hundred bucks an ounce and she bathes in it.

"So, what's a girl like you doing in a dump like this?"

"What's a boy like you doing with a nasty gash over his pretty blue eye?"

"My girlfriend hit me with a picnic basket."

"How quaint. What's her name?"

"Helen. Helen Weaver."

"You going to marry her?"

"Not if I can help it. You going to move in with your husband?"

"Not if I can help it."

And there the small talk ended. In the silence that followed, the sound of Les's snoring floated down the stairs and into the kitchen. She stared at the gash on my forehead and I stared at her tits. I couldn't help feeling that ours was not a typical mother-and-son fireside chat, but then nothing in the Miller house is typical of anything approaching the normal. She moved her now empty glass across the table and touched my hand with one long, cool finger. "Would you be so kind? Equal amounts of vodka and soda and there are ice cubes in the fridge."

Why the hell not? I went to the washstand bar and fixed her drink, using the cubes she brought with her. She must have learned earlier in the week that our fridge is reluctant to turn water into ice. While there I topped off my wine, which I did not need as I had consumed the lion's share of Helen's picnic Chianti. I served the drinks, and seeing as it had grown dark, I pulled the light cord that hangs over the table and ignited the single bulb inside its filthy globe. She winced and covered her face with one hand, shielding it from the sudden glare and my gaze. The harsh light left no doubt as to the lady's age and the day-old makeup didn't help her cause.

She lowered her hand and shrugged as if to say what the hell did it matter, anyway? And I felt sorry for her. Yeah, I did. She was far from home, wherever that might be, and alone with two strange men, never mind that one of them shared a marriage license with her. But there was a light in those dark eyes that told you the lady was alive and kicking. Whatever she was up to, I would put all my money on this dark horse.

I sat. "So, what's your story, Betty, not short for Elizabeth?"

"All of it?"

"Spare me the toilet training and pick up on the events leading to you and Les telling each other I do, I do."

"That goes back twenty . . ." She hesitated and again shrugged like she's letting it all hang out. "Twenty-five years."

"I got nothing but time."

She helped herself to another cigarette and offered me the pack. I accepted, struck a match and lit hers, then my own. She took a deep drag; I don't inhale.

"I was born in Jacksonville, as far north as you can get in the state of Florida. The town is not warm enough in the winter to attract attention and not cool enough in the summer to do likewise. Our economy, therefore, was perpetually flat. My father owned a gas station, two pumps in front of a shack we called home. Business was so bad we couldn't afford help, so I quit school at sixteen and took turns pumping along with Ma and Pa. I wore a pair of cut-off jeans and a halter that didn't quite cover all of me. Business picked up.

"I lost my virginity to a boy who looked very much like you. I did it for love. He reciprocated by joining the navy and forgetting I existed. I never did it for love again. One day a black car, somewhat larger than our house, pulled into the station. A distinguished gentleman was at the wheel. He took one look at me and said—"

"What's a girl like you doing in a dump like this?" I broke into her story.

Betty laughed, once again lighting up those dark eyes and looking real sassy, like an athlete who gets a second wind from the cheering crowd.

"Not quite that crude, but you get the idea. I asked him what choice I had and he told me to hop in and he would show me. Something told me that it was now or never and I decided on now. I filled his tank and hopped in, with the very few clothes on my back and not a backward glance at my point of origin. I won't tell you his name, to protect the innocent, but it was one that appeared on the front pages of the *Washington Post* and *New York Times* at least once a week. His wife's blood was a startling blue and her bank balance an almost vulgar green. He set me up in a cozy house in Delray, a suburb of Palm Beach, and I joined the demimonde. Do you know what a demimondaine is, Galen?"

"I'm just learning Italian."

"I see."

Betty downed another ounce or two of vodka and soda. A few more and we'd join Les in the master bedroom suite.

"A demimondaine is not quite a whore but definitely not a lady."

"His mistress?" I offered.

"Again, crude, Galen. We've got to smooth your edges if we're going to work together."

What the fuck did that mean?

"Posh resorts are filled with the demimonde, Galen. When my friend was with his family or rubbing elbows at the Chevy Chase Club, I had time on my hands and used it to get the education I was denied in Jacksonville. I discovered I had a flair for designing and learned to sew and make my own clothes. They were good enough to get me a few private customers, but not good enough to get noticed in New York or Paris. Always on the fringe, you see. Good, but never good enough. We dined in restaurants that catered to couples who like the lights dim and the waiters discreet. Good, but not good enough. We traveled in circles in which the right clothes were worn, drove the right cars, but didn't get invited to the right parties. Good, but not good enough.

"If this is beginning to sound like a soap opera, it's because soap operas imitate life."

She was well on her way to finishing her second vodka and soda. Or was it her third?

"I watched his family grow via photographs: marriages, divorces, grandchildren. I watched him go from sixty to eighty. He explained that he couldn't leave me anything in his will because he didn't have anything to leave. The money was all his wife's. I had the house and very little else. His last kind gesture was to set me up in business. A boutique in Delray, catering to ladies who did get invited to the right parties. The blue hair set, as they're called in Delray. Widows of rich men or wives of retired rich men. Mrs. MacAlister is typical of my clientele."

I almost jumped out of my chair, but Betty put out her hand in a restraining gesture. "All in time," she promised.

"Shortly thereafter my friend died. I learned about it from the eleven o'clock news," she went on.

" 'Betty Z' was my logo. Catchy, I thought. Business was good but like everything else in my life, not good enough. I began to notice how the husbands who accompanied their wives to my shop looked at me." She stubbed out her cigarette in the ashtray and immediately lit another, blowing smoke slowly into the air.

"They looked at me the way men have always looked at me, with sheepish smiles on their faces and impure thoughts in their minds. I created a small waiting area for these men who had time on their hands, money in their wallets, and were just beginning to realize that the parade had passed them by. I served wine and cheese. Not very original, but then neither is poverty."

I could see those poor husbands jiggling the change in their pockets, watching Betty Z pass around the Gorgonzola.

"While their wives were being fitted, I flirted, and before you could say Christian Dior, I had a sideline."

"Christ." I shook my head in disbelief. "You were hooking out of a boutique."

"Crude, crude, crude," she scolded. "You can do whatever you want in this life, Galen, as long as you call it something else. I accommodated. Doesn't that sound better?"

"And just how much did you charge to accommodate?"

"Two hundred dollars wasn't unheard of. But the older gentlemen, the ones who need a little something extra to make it all work, were often grateful enough to part with three of those bills."

I was amazed. I sat back and looked at this woman and thought she had to be the only dressmaker in the world whose clothes got in the way of her profession. "Les never had two hundred of anything in his life," I told her.

"He didn't need it, Galen. He came highly recommended."

I finished my wine and when I stood up to get another I was a little unsteady on my feet. Was it the wine or what I was sure would be the answer to my next question? "Who recommended him?"

"But you know the answer. Mrs. MacAlister."

Betty, I noticed, didn't ask me to freshen her drink.

Like all pros, she knew when to raise the ante and when to lay down her hand. I also noticed she didn't try to stop me from getting a buzz on. Some piece of work, this Betty Zabriskie.

"She came into the shop two weeks ago, on Saturday, the day before they were to leave for home, to pick up a skirt she had ordered. All excited, she told me about the man who drove their car north and south, who had just arrived and announced that this would be his last trip as he had come into money. A million or more via a land deal offer from a prominent attorney in East Hampton."

Damn Les, I thought. Can't keep his big mouth shut.

"In Delray we had heard about people in the Hamptons who'd gotten rich on second houses and land they purchased for peanuts years ago that were now worth fortunes. Why couldn't something like that happen to me? I thought, and then . . . and then I thought, but it *has* happened to me. Hearing about this man's good fortune, even secondhand, made me a part of it, didn't it? But what part? When Mrs. MacAlister said, with a blush to be sure, that dear Les was a widower and, it was rumored, had a weakness for pretty girls, I knew exactly where I fit in.

"You see, Galen, every year in Delray and elsewhere, there are more rich widows than rich wives. My cheese and wine fanciers were on the decline. The girl who pumped gas was almost pumped out. I had some work done. Under the eyes and the neck—they're the first to go. But it doesn't last forever. Nothing is forever. In a word, Galen, I was desperate, and for the second time in my life I hopped in without a backward glance. It was now-or-never time again and I picked now.

"I told Mrs. MacAlister the skirt wasn't ready. But she was leaving in the morning. Wasn't her driver taking her to the airport? In Fort Lauderdale? Well, when he headed north he could make a stop here and I'd have the skirt all ready to go. It would save me the trouble of mailing it. Never mind that the next day was Sunday. I'd make an exception and have the shop open just for the pickup. Old people are so gullible. By the time she left she thought I was doing her a favor."

"So, Les walks into the boutique, takes one look at you, and it's like shooting fish in a barrel."

"In fact," she answered, "the honeymoon was so delightful he proposed the next morning. I made a few calls, got my assistant to look after things, and followed Les in the Lincoln. The end."

"When did you find out he was a drunk?" I asked.

"One look and I suspected the worst. When he knocked back most of the wine in my waiting room, I was sure."

Then I sort of thought aloud. "But when Les was late getting here, Mrs. MacAlister didn't say anything about this."

"Why should she? A half-hour detour couldn't be the cause of the delay. But more likely, she forgot. Old people do, you know."

"Did they see you when Les took the car back?"

She shook her head. "Les delivered the Mercedes to their house and drove their rental to Hertz. I drove my car straight to Hertz and waited there for Les."

"You sure he didn't blab to the old couple?"

"Positive. I told him I would leave him if he did."

"And what Betty wants, Betty gets," I said.

"Something like that."

"Why are you telling me all this?"

She jerked her head back like she was shocked. "Why,

Galen, I thought you knew. We got off to such a bad start I want to clear the air between us. I want you to know what Betty Zabriskie is all about, so you can never say I was anything but honest with you. I want you to know where I came from and, more important, where I'm heading."

"You're not going to fuck me out of my share of the farm?"

She smiled like she was thinking something naughty. "If I'm going to fuck you, Galen, it's not going to be for a farm."

Check this lady! In the sweepstakes of stepmamas, I got all six numbers plus the fucking supplementary. "I don't have two hundred bucks, Betty."

"With what you've got, Galen, you don't need it."

Maybe it was the wine. Maybe it was because we were playing you show me yours and I'll show you mine. Or maybe it was because I leap before I look and shoot off my mouth before I think. "I got a little sideline too," I said.

"Really?" She raised an eyebrow in disbelief.

"A lot of fags come here in the summer."

"Galen, Galen," Betty said, rolling her eyes. "Men of alternate sexual persuasion. Or, if you must, gay men."

"I didn't mean to offend, Stepmother. I never conversed with a demimondaine before this delightful evening."

She dismissed this with a wave of her pink fingernails. "And what do you do for these men, Galen?"

"I 'accommodate' them. But I don't peddle my wares out of a fancy boutique like some people I know."

"Where do you peddle your wares, Galen?"

"The volleyball court on Two Mile Hollow Beach."

And just because I never know when to raise the ante or fold my hand, I go right on. "I wear a pair of white boxers that show everything, and for good measure I stuff my briefs with an athletic sock for the visually impaired. Ha ha. Helen told me that's what ballet dancers do. The men, I mean. They're my working togs. Of course the togs are not tax-deductible like a nurse's uniform, but this business is all cash off the books. Underground economy, right?"

Betty laughed. "Oh, Galen, you're the best thing that's come my way since that big black car pulled into Daddy's station. What do you charge to accommodate?"

"A hundred," I lied. I usually get fifty, but once I did get a hundred. The guy from Mulholland Drive, remember?

Betty extended her hand across the table and I shook it. "We're going to get along just fine, partner."

So where does that leave Les?

Betty got up and left the kitchen. Below the turtleneck she wore a pair of black slacks that showed off her tiny waist, flat belly, and a behind that looked as trim and firm as Helen's. The high-heeled shoes, black and pointed, were not intended for jogging. She returned wearing her coat. Not the fur this time, but something white and shiny, which on her looked like it was made of diamonds. "Do you have a decent pair of pants and a jacket?"

"Why?"

"Meet me at Gurney's tomorrow at noon. I'll buy you lunch."

Then she was gone, leaving me alone in the shadowy light with the sounds of Les snoring, the refrigerator grinding and the unmistakable aroma of Joy by Jean Patou.

Fifteen

The room could hold five hundred people, easy. But late March is still off-season on the East End of Long Island and Gurney's Inn must have been between conventions, because only a dozen or so tables were occupied. The hostess had managed to seat everyone along the restaurant's glass wall and because the Inn sits on a cliff hugging the shoreline, the view is all sky and ocean. It's like being on a luxury liner that rides the waves without making a ripple in your wineglass.

I saw Betty as soon as I entered the dining room. She was sitting at a corner table, a few empty tables away from the nearest diners, and even from a distance I could tell she was the classiest lady in the place. The hostess, a big blonde past her prime lugging a stack of oversized menus, looked me over and told me with her million-dollar smile that I looked more appetizing than the tomato surprise. I wore my navy blue blazer, which had set me back close to two hundred bucks, and a dress shirt, open at the collar; no tie. When I told her I was joining the lady sitting alone, the hostess turned her menus into a sail and her behind into a rudder and navigated our way across the parquet floor. Hey man, this is the fucking Hamptons.

"You look lovely," Betty said as I eased into a chair across from her.

"So do you."

The hostess was hovering, hoping our conversation would prove what I knew she suspected. A lovers' reunion between the married lady from New York and the boy who cut her lawn last summer, rehearsing for next season.

"Can I get you a beverage?" the hostess asked.

Betty's Bloody Mary looked tempting, so I answered, "I'll have whatever my mother is drinking," tossing a wet blanket on her dirty thoughts. She was so surprised she forgot to ID me, which saved her the trouble of pretending to scrutinize my phony driver's license.

Betty laughed as the woman fled. "You're a nasty little boy, but very perceptive."

"Not as nasty as the guy you married. Les wants to know where his bride is."

"What did you tell him?"

"That I didn't know, of course. I didn't think you'd care to have him join us for lunch."

"You *are* perceptive," she said again. I take it being a smart-ass is a trait she admires. "You sure he didn't follow you?"

"In what? I have the truck. Besides, the only reason Les goes out is in search of booze. Thanks to you, there's no reason for him to stumble any farther than the kitchen sink. *You're* very perceptive too. It must run in the family."

"He's happier than he's ever been in his life," she answered, as if that made it okay to keep Les zonked out on booze.

"And how long are you going to keep him happier

than he's ever been in his life? If you mean to kill him with whiskey and sex, let me tell you that his blood is a hundred proof and his dick stands up when it hears 'The Star-Spangled Banner.' You've met your match, Betty Z."

"I am not trying to kill him with whiskey and sex," Betty answered, just in time for the waitress delivering my Bloody Mary to overhear. The girl stared at Betty, then tripped over herself as she backed away.

"Now you've done it. If something did happen to your father she'd make a great prosecution witness." Annoyed, Betty lit a cigarette in defiance of the no-smoking rule.

"Prosecution? Hey, lady, leave me out of this. I'm just an abused kid who does volleyball, not drugs." I helped myself to my Bloody Mary. They were a little stingy on the gin.

"Nothing is going to happen to your father. He represents the farm."

"And what do you represent?" I asked.

"I represent him, because he's incapable, and I need you as an interested party." She sounded like a television lawyer.

"How interested am I?"

"Partners. A fifty-fifty split."

I know what I'm gonna say but I let her stew awhile. I had thought about nothing else all night. They were married, that was a fact. I knew that Les didn't have to give me a cent from the sale of the farm. But if he died without a will, before the sale, his widow gets half and I get half. So, she wasn't trying to kill Les, not just yet. And Les never made a will and I was here to make sure he never did. If she was offering me half when she didn't have to give me dick, I had no choice but to listen, agree to whatever she was up to, and kiss her backside for the privilege.

"So, what do you have in mind?"

"I thought you'd never ask."

First, she removed the roll from her bread plate and used the plate for an ashtray. Gauche. Then for the next hour I learned more about Long Island real estate, Mark Barrett, his wife and family, and their friends than I had picked up living in this town for nineteen years.

Barrett's motel-to-condo conversions, it seems, weren't exactly a huge success. Sales were never great and now, with maintenance costs soaring and demand for units on the decline, those that had been sold were for resale below cost and the empty units were competing with owners for summer rentals. Betty learned this by visiting some of them and playing the role of interested buyer.

"It was a case of too much too soon," Betty said. "The market's saturated where there was never much of a demand. Barrett is overextended."

The burger and fries I had been enjoying suddenly didn't taste so good. "You mean he's broke?"

"People like Mark Barrett are never broke, Galen, they're temporarily embarrassed, at most. His wife is a Boston Stiles. Millions, and she and her brother were sole heirs."

When Betty wasn't visiting condos, she was sitting in the library looking at back issues of the *Star,* where she read about Mark Barrett's business and social wheeling and dealing. "You know," she said, picking at her salad, "that Joseph Kirkpatrick lives in East Hampton—the media giant; radio, television. His daughter and husband are great friends of the Barretts. Reo is their name and the world is their playground, as they say. More millions. The old man had a heart attack New Year's Eve and is recuperating on Dunemere Lane. Do you know the house?"

I told Betty that Les & Son never had the pleasure of mowing the grass on Dunemere Lane and if we were ever invited for cocktails it escaped my notice.

Betty had also discovered that the maid assigned to her room was a local lady who had been changing sheets at Gurney's Inn for thirty years. Overtipping daily, Betty got the maid to talk and learned all the news the *Star* forgot to print about the Barretts of East Hampton.

"They have a son who will soon join the family law firm and a daughter who's persona non grata—that means she isn't welcome for Sunday dinner."

"I know what it means," I lied. "She was into drugs is what I heard, and they kicked her out of the house."

"And Barrett has a roving eye, or so says Ida, my domestic engineer."

"Did he come on to Ida?" I kidded, turning off the flow while I'm thinking of how Barrett always stops in Main Street Video to talk to Helen, and marveling at how much Betty has learned—fact *and* gossip—in less than two weeks in our town.

"No, Galen, but maids socialize with maids and a good friend of Ida's was once housekeeper to the Barretts. Mark Barrett used to keep an apartment in New York and there was talk of a divorce."

"So what are you doing?" I asked. "Writing a book?"

"No, gathering information."

"What has this got to do with selling the farm?"

"Everything."

"I didn't know we'd have to swap true confessions with the buyer. Wait till they hear *your* track record."

"Think, Galen, think. You shoot off your mouth before

you think." Christ, did she know Helen Weaver? "My gentleman friend, who was chin-deep in politics, told me that the way to wage war is to know everything about your enemy—his strengths and, more important, his weaknesses—and when you do, hit him where it hurts most. Barrett is hurting in the wallet, but thanks to family and friends, there's a neverending supply of capital he hopes to recoup. The marina is the best idea he's come up with and unless I'm mistaken he has old Kirkpatrick and the Reos interested. Something very posh and very exclusive. The Hamptons are hot and a Monaco or Positano on this side of the Atlantic is a strong possibility. We have movie stars—why not the international set with the Kirkpatrick clan leading the way?"

It was all bullshit to me but because I'm perceptive I asked, "You think we can put the squeeze on for more money?"

"That and more. Perhaps a percentage deal or one of the units as a lifetime gift. The place can't run itself. It'll need a manager or overseer, someone to see to its smooth operation from day-to-day maintenance to social functions. The possibilities are limitless."

And so was Betty's imagination. Christ, she was setting herself up as madam of the marina with Barrett as chief pimp. Smart? This lady was the best thing to come my way since lubricated condoms. I could see her rowing from yacht to yacht, picking up two hundred bucks a lay like a fucking doctor making house calls. "I don't want to mow any more lawns," I told her. "I just want my share of the money and I'm out of here."

She shrugged and signaled the hostess for the check. "Les tells me you want to go to Hollywood."

"I didn't know you and Les were on speaking terms."

"There's a lot you don't know, Galen, and that will be your downfall someday. Look, listen, and learn is my motherly advice. Do you have a contact in L.A.?"

I told her about the guy from Mulholland Drive. "And once another guy, this big Hollywood producer, told me I looked like a young James Dean. I told him the guy on the greenback he gave me looked like Grant when he should look like Ben Franklin. 'A hundred,' this punk says. 'A hundred. The surfers get a hundred. The volley-ball boys get fifty.' I didn't know I needed a prop, I told him. I didn't know this gig had a job description like the fucking steamfitters union." As always, I shot off my mouth to make an impression.

Betty was laughing. "Your greatest charm, Galen, is that you don't know you possess any. Forget the producer and stick to Mulholland Drive. If he remembers you."

"I'm hard to forget," I told her.

"Poor Helen Weaver," Betty sighed.

"Poor Mark Barrett," I sighed right back.

She patted my knee under the table. "We're going to get along just fine, Galen. Famously, in fact."

Her hand moved up my thigh, but the width of the table made it impossible for her to achieve her goal. Some business lunch this was turning out to be. "So, how do you persuade Barrett to see things our way?" I asked her. Grope him under the table, I thought, and maybe he's got a mousetrap inside his fly.

"If you're finished, I'll show you."

Betty signed the check and the hostess watched suspiciously as we headed for Betty's room. The units at Gurney's are stacked in tiers, giving everyone an ocean view. Betty had a suite and I made the mistake of gawking around like a kid in a toy store. "You've never been here before, have you?" she asked me, already knowing the answer.

"I'm a local and this is a tourist hangout."

She nodded. "It's that way in Palm Beach and, I suppose, in all resorts towns. The haves and the have-nots don't mix and mingle. But this should make you happy." It seemed she had also been to Town Hall, and opening a large brown envelope, she pulled out a surveyor's map and spread it across the writing desk. We bent over it like generals studying a war map. Pictured was a blowup of North West Harbor. To the north, Cedar Point Park; below, grids depicting lots. Our farm was outlined in red. "For the kind of operation Barrett is talking about you need room. Forty acres, at least. This crowd doesn't fancy living in the guy next door's pocket," Betty explained. "From this map you can see that the available plots are here." She pointed with her pink fingernail. "And our patch, thank God, is right smack in the middle. I mean, without our ten acres he falls short on either side. Also, ours is the shortest stretch to the harbor, which makes it key to the operation."

"You mean if we don't sell, he's shit out of luck."

"Crude, but you do get the point."

We looked at each other and grinned happily. A pair of con artists who had just spotted a mark. We were two of a kind all right. "You ever gonna move into the house?" I asked her.

"Tempt me."

In her high heels we were on eye level, our lips about two inches apart. I closed the gap. She put her arms around my neck, drawing me closer. My hard-on pressed into her thigh, my hand traced over the swell of her breasts. Her free hand found the target it was seeking under the table. We clung to each other, tongues entwined, fingers busy with buttons and zippers. She wasn't wearing a bra. I wasn't wearing shorts. I never do on a first date. I kissed her nipples, one, then the other. Going down on me, she returned the favor to the head of my shaft. A second later she had me moaning. She got my pants down without missing a stroke. When I couldn't take any more I withdrew and joined her on the floor; she stretched out and my hand went under her skirt. *She* wasn't wearing shorts either.

"I charge a hundred bucks," I told her.

"I charge two hundred."

"So," I said, getting into position, "when Barrett comes through, I'll owe you a hundred."

With Helen Weaver, I lost my virginity. With Betty Zabriskie, I lost my innocence.

Sixteen

The next day Betty moved in with her husband. Actually she moved into her husband's house, taking over the small bedroom between Les's and mine. Given the latest developments in this screwed-up family, I call her choice right on target. Helen told me that once upon a time there was this Russian empress who never went on an overnight trip without taking her bedroom furniture with her. Well, Empress Betty arrived with a new bed, bedding, a chest of drawers, and a wardrobe. She wasn't about to put her bare skin or fancy clothes in contact with anything in the Miller household except the bare skin of Les & Son. You go figure that one out.

Les went stomping around like a kid at Christmas as the men hauled in the furniture, offering them drinks and sandwiches and telling them to be careful not to bruise the walls. Holy shit. Did Les know that this was the first night his bride would spend under his roof since their wedding? I honestly don't know. Sometimes he talks sense and other times he talks crap or doesn't talk at all. But one thing's for sure—he can't get enough of Betty Z. He stares at her, grins at her, all but bows to her, an amazed expression on his beat-up face that says he can't believe this sexy broad is seeing to his care and feeding. Not to mention supplying his booze. I think he's afraid that one false step, one wrong word, and she'll disappear, taking the kitchen sink and the whiskey bottles with her. So Les sits and sips, stares and grins, and thinks he's got it made.

But to be fair, I've got to say that since moving in she's got the guy looking as presentable as is humanly possible. He doesn't come downstairs until he's washed and shaved and dressed in a decent pair of pants and clean shirt. She takes him out in the Lincoln and he sits in the passenger seat—sometimes he drives if he's up to it, proud as can be and dying to show off his wife and car, but Betty is very clever about sticking to the scenic routes and avoiding contact with anything that walks on two legs. "Low-profile" is how Empress Betty explains these outings.

She gave up her space at Gurney's but, as might be expected, took out membership in the hotel's spa, so she can take her daily hot shower and check out the sauna, masseuse, and beauty parlor.

Some family picture we made, Les & Son and Betty Z—all waiting on Santa Claus to fill our stockings with detached condos and yachts. Betty kept an eye on Les and I kept an eye on Betty. I don't know if Les was getting any, but every night my bedroom door was opened wide enough to admit the sound of Les's snoring and the aroma of Joy by Jean Patou. The perfume was all the lady wore as she hopped into my three-poster and slid her hand under the elastic band of my Jockey shorts in a successful search for the missing post.

"You're always ready," she whispered, those long fingers with the pink nails working me like she's had a lot of practice.

"So are you."

We explored each other's bodies with hands, lips, and tongues. I became as addicted to the taste of her perfume as I was to its aroma. Everything Helen would not allow seemed to be what Betty most desired, and she let her needs be known without ever playing the aggressor. She taught without leading and never achieved satisfaction without giving it.

"You're not as big as your father," she told me one night, stroking the thing that didn't measure up to my ol' man's.

"No one is," I answered, "except maybe King Kong. You doing it with Les too?"

"That's impertinent."

You believe this dame? She's whacking me off and I'm impertinent. Hand jobs seemed to be Betty's specialty. Maybe it came from working on all those old guys in Delray before the main event, if they ever made it that far. Betty Z had hands of gold.

"Helen is going to owe me a lot," she announced after one of our more successful unions. This, I think, is a gentle way of saying that our contact sports are nothing more than an amateur bout before the main event: waiting for Barrett to sign the contract. What she didn't know—we didn't know—was that our love boat was going to hit the sand long before Barrett got out his ballpoint.

You see, Betty never hits you with a brick. Not this lady. She gently pats your cheek with one hand, squeezes your dick with the other, and tells you to get lost all at the same time. You know you've been had, but how many women can give you a hard-on while giving you the brush-off?

It was Betty who suggested I tell the MacAlisters that Les & Son would no longer tend their lawn. "Maybe he should work," I said. "Some fresh air and talking to other people might get him looking and acting less like a zombie."

"He gets plenty of fresh air, and talking is something Les is apt to overdo. If it weren't for Les's big mouth you wouldn't have me to split with. Don't you ever learn?"

She got no sass from me on that score.

I went to the MacAlisters and told them Les had retired. "How nice," Mr. MacAlister said. "We've hired a local lawn maintenance company to see to our property." The MacAlisters did this not because they thought Les was coming into money—which I doubt they now believed—but because they didn't trust dear Les as far as they could throw him. Les had fucked up another meal ticket. Barrett had better come through, or Father would have to go back to mowing and Mommy and Sonny would have to go back to selling their tails for the price of leather jackets and Joy by Jean Patou.

I wondered if the denim skirt Mrs. MacAlister was wearing was designed by Betty Z. I wondered what she would think if she knew her dressmaker had married her ex–lawn person and was getting it off with his son. She wouldn't believe it because in her world shit doesn't happen. I don't know if I'm supposed to envy her or pity her.

In May the weather turned warm and I tried to drag Betty to the beach with me, talking up the joys of springtime in the Hamptons before the invasion of those who keep the money flowing and the traffic snarled.

"I don't think it's a good idea to be seen together," was her response.

"Why not? We're not criminals. And this is a small town—people are going to find out that Les has a wife."

Helen knew about Betty, but I could trust Helen to keep it quiet. I should say here that I was feeling a little guilty about Helen. Except for stopping in Main Street Video for a quick chat a few times, I had not really seen much of her since our picnic at the hideaway off Two Holes of Water Road. Well, it was Helen who told me to find out what Betty was up to, and that's just what I was doing, right?

I did miss my movie fix that Helen never failed to supply several times a week. When I told Betty how Helen and me (Helen and I?) were working on our college degrees by way of movie classics, she didn't seem interested. In fact, she never once asked to see a film on my giant TV screen. Betty had other fish to fry—only at the time I didn't know I was her prize shrimp.

"Galen," she sighed. "The less people know the better—how many times do I have to tell you that? If they see me, they're going to wonder why I married your father. I think I can say that and not be accused of arrogance. They'll speculate and if the MacAlisters talk, they'll know. Barrett must have confided in people locally. Bankers, town board members, his cronies at the Club. It won't take long for someone to fit the missing pieces together, and then what? Those who oppose such developments—and from what I've read, that's just about everyone in town—will have been forewarned and therefore forearmed. The people who own the surrounding parcels will jack up their price tags, making the deal unattractive if not impossible to finance. Other locations will try to lure Barrett and his associates by making better offers. In short, Galen, we'll be fucked. Get it?"

I got it.

"The best thing we can do is sit tight, wait on Barrett, and take the money and run. Unless we can interest him in the parcel and us as a package deal."

Us? Bullshit. She meant herself and I couldn't care less. I just wanted my half mil, and let Barrett deal with Betty Z. But as usual, what she said made sense, so I went along with it. And as usual, I never look before I leap and never think before I shoot off my mouth. Betty's passion for privacy and her "Get it?" attitude led to my boasting of my private beach. Then, of course, I had to show it to her. Like Helen, Betty complained of the walk from Swamp Road, but once we arrived she loved it. Tarzan had found another Jane. That same day, the big baboon noticed that the Lincoln had never left the front of the house and the pickup truck was missing, and even a zombie could figure out that Betty and Galen were occupying the same space at the same time.

Without pausing for breath, Betty told Les that I had dropped her off in town to shop and picked her up to drive her home. "I didn't take our car because I thought you might be wanting it and I hated to wake you to explain." The idea that she would actually leave the Lincoln for him so staggered Les that he all but knelt to kiss the hem of Betty's skirt. Is she cool, or what? Now, if Betty wanted to work on her tan, in private, my hole of water was the place to do it, but we had to keep Les from counting cars and noses while we were there. Betty, naturally, knew just how to do it, and so help me, her plan was fucking foolproof.

She had been to New York City a few times—taking

the bus—to shop and see how the other half lived, as she put it. Soon after our visit to the pond, she told Les that she would join the Wednesday matinee crowd and take advantage of the cut-rate round-trip fares the Jitney (as the bus is called) offered theatergoers. The following Wednesday, Les proudly drove her to the East Hampton bus stop and saw her off.

The bus makes its way west, stopping at the little towns along the way, until it arrives at Southampton, where it makes a final stop before the long trek to the city. In Southampton people get out for a smoke or to buy a container of coffee for the trip. Southampton is the Jitney's official depot, where a new driver takes over, relieving the guy who has just finished one round trip. This is a stop that generates a lot of coming and going, so when Betty gets out, lights a cigarette, and walks off to the parking lot where I'm waiting in the truck, no one notices or could care less if they did.

I drive Betty back to East Hampton, arriving at Swamp and Two Holes of Water Road without a fucking crease in her Wednesday matinee outfit under which is nothing but Betty, because when we sunbathe all we wear is a big smile.

Around six o'clock, I drive her back to the Southampton stop, where she boards the East Hampton–bound bus, arriving in time to be picked up by Les in the shiny Lincoln.

Foolproof? If this lady ran the CIA, we would own the fucking world.

So Betty and Galen are performing in Wednesday matinees the likes of which you'll never see on Broadway. Betty is not a swimmer but the sun is warm, the outdoor sex is cool, and Betty and I (Betty and me?) are

Bonnie and Clyde waiting for the bank to open. All thanks to clever Betty. Well, if this lady is so clever, how come she's dead under ten feet of water, where a zillion little fishes are eating her eyeballs and worms are crawling in her ears and out her mouth? Christ, how smart can you be?

Summer was fast approaching and not a word from Barrett. I was getting nervous but Betty made sure I didn't leap without looking. Besides, the Miller family—in its own perverted way—was enjoying life thanks to the generosity of Mama Bear, whose fat pocketbook was keeping us all afloat. "It's an investment. Do you know what that is? An investment is giving a little in order to get back a whole lot."

"In Las Vegas they call it gambling."

"Investments are calculated risks, Galen, but the wise investor always hedges his bets."

The following Wednesday I found out exactly what she meant.

We were late getting to the Southampton depot and the East Hampton–bound bus was just pulling out. The driver saw us, stopped, and waited for Betty. In her rush she forgot to take her carryall and the bus was well on its way before I noticed it on the seat next to me. It was a big leather pouch suspended from a shoulder strap, which held our lunch and a small bottle of wine besides Betty's personal items. Just the thing a woman would take to the city for a day and not arouse suspicion.

The bus driver, I was sure, would trust Betty for the fare, and as long as Les didn't notice she wasn't carrying the bag, there was no problem. If Les did notice, she could say she left it on the bus, fake a call to the Jitney, and pick it up the next day. Betty was never at a loss when it came to making up fairy tales.

The only reason I looked into the bag, and I admit it even though I'm not proud of the fact, was to get at the bottle of Joy and have a sniff. What I found was a white business envelope addressed to Mrs. Lester Miller with a Bridgehampton post office box as her address. Strange? The return address told me it was sent by a law firm in Southampton. Stranger?

I sat there at the bus stop, staring at the envelope on my lap, thinking about what I should do with this thing that was burning my fingers. Here's what I thought: I was having an affair with my stepmother and conspiring with her to take one half of the loot that legally belonged only to my father. So, why should I stop at opening an envelope not addressed to me?

". . . at your convenience, bring with you the deed and the affidavits, properly signed by you and Mr. Miller, and we will forward them to the County seat in Riverhead requesting a new deed to the property naming you and Mr. Miller as joint tenants."

I don't know how long I sat there staring at the letter, my vision going blurry with fury. I knew what this meant. Joint tenantship. The way Les had inherited from my mother, Betty would inherit from Les if he passed over, and if the letter on my lap was any indication, Les would be on the other side as soon as Betty's postal box yielded the new deed. Hedging her bet? The fix was in and Betty Z was going for the balls of Les & Son.

"Think, Galen. Think." That's what she always said when I shot off my mouth or jumped the gun. Well, I had the long ride home to do just that. The letter was dated three days ago, so she must have gotten it yesterday. She could talk Les into signing anything, but she also needed the deed and that was my trump card. It was hidden in my room. I found it in a desk drawer years ago and put it away for safekeeping. Les would have no idea where it was, so the search would be on. They could declare it lost and apply for another, but that would take time and that's just what I needed, time. Time to think some more.

When I got home I passed the bag to her with a sly wink. She blew me a silent kiss.

Blow this, baby, blow this.

In my room I jammed the back of a chair under the doorknob to keep out the aroma of Joy by Jean Patou and fell on the bed.

Think.

"Investments are calculated risks, Galen, but the wise investor always hedges his bets."

Seventeen

As I came through the kitchen on the way out, Betty was putting together a cold supper. I declined her invitation and pretended not to notice the look that passed between husband and wife. The hunt for the deed would get under way as soon as I left the house and only Christ knew what she had told Les to keep it all a secret from me. But I would lay odds that Les was going to get laid tonight. Happy hunting, I thought, as I stroked the deed I had hidden in the inside pocket of my leather jacket.

Helen wasn't in the shop at this late hour and that was okay with me. I didn't need her sharp tongue, nagging, and most of all, asking me why I wanted to see this particular film on a warm Wednesday night. The video store was busy and Mr. Weaver just had time for a quick hello as he checked me out on the computer.

When I got back to the house, Les and Betty were in Les's bedroom, and from the sounds coming from behind the closed door, they were tearing the place apart. As I came up the stairs I heard what must have been a drawer crashing to the floor. Betty screamed, so maybe it landed on her toes. I smiled for the first time since reading her lawyer's letter.

I barricaded my door once again, but it wasn't really necessary. They couldn't search my room with me in it. But I wasn't taking any chances. I didn't want either of them walking in on the middle of my movie. No, especially not the middle. Betty Z was many things but stupid was not one of them.

I set up the VCR, turned down the lights, and stretched out on the bed, my head propped up with two pillows. I aimed the remote, pressed the play button, and . . .

Paramount Pictures Presents

A PLACE IN THE SUN

BASED ON THE NOVEL AN AMERICAN TRAGEDY
by Theodore Dreiser

The first time I saw the opening scene—this guy George Eastman hitchhiking and being passed up by a beautiful girl in a flashy convertible—I knew this movie was all about me. George Eastman, ashamed of his parents, ashamed of his poverty, ashamed of the menial job his rich uncle gives him in the Eastman swimsuit factory, where he meets Alice and gets laid. The one lousy act that relieves, for a moment, his self-pity and boredom. The guy gets his rocks off and he has to pay for it with his fucking life. George gets noticed by his uncle, moves up in the factory, and meets all the big shots in this shit-ass town. He falls in love with the beautiful, rich girl who owns the convertible and she falls for him. The winning lottery ticket is in George's hand until

Alice turns up pregnant and all the sweet-smelling roses turn to shit.

George promises to marry Alice, but first he rents a flat-bottomed boat at a place called Loon Lake and takes his pregnant bride-to-be for a spin around the secluded pond.

I sat straight up when this scene came on the screen. They're in the boat, George and Alice, face-to-face, him rowing and her shooting off her mouth about how happy they're going to be.

"If I can only tell you how much I love you . . ."

"We can go to another town just like any other couple . . ."

"I'm not afraid of being poor . . ."

"What's the matter, George, you look sad . . ."

Alice gets up and starts to walk to him; the boat lists and they both fall into Loon Lake. Alice can't swim, a fact George knows, and George's troubles are over, except he's left a trail behind him with his name written all over it. George admits he was going to murder Alice but says he couldn't do it and what happened was an accident. The last we see of George Eastman he's on his way to the electric chair, movie style.

When we discussed it, Helen believed George. I mean, she saw the cottage with the white picket fence and the bicycle blocking the front door. I didn't buy it. If Alice hadn't tipped the boat, George would have tossed her out of it. When? When she says she's not afraid of being poor, that's when.

"If I were Alice," Helen said, "I would never tell George I was pregnant. I would go away, have the baby, who would be a boy, and when he's grown I'd send him to see George Eastman to beg for a job in the factory."

Christ!

"What would you do if *you* were George?" she asked.

"Get rid of Alice without getting caught."

"You don't have the nerve."

Don't I?

Eddy Evans

Eighteen

Thursday, June 26, will go down in East Hampton history as the day Lester Miller voluntarily walked into the police station on Pantigo Road, not handcuffed and more sober than drunk. We have often gone to see Les, but this is the first time the old sot has ever reciprocated. His purpose, we soon learned, was to report his wife missing.

So, the rumors that have been making the rounds of the local bars from Main Street to Montauk were true. Les had himself a new woman. This, granted, was not hot news. Les usually had a woman, although how he did it I can only attribute to an old Bonacker yarn. The story has it that Les and his cronies were drinking in a local pub one night some years back and when the subject turned from fishing to fornication, this city dude, uninvited, announced that he had the biggest dick in the room. One of the Bonackers pointed to Les and told the intruder that he, Les, held that distinction. The young man laid a ten-dollar bill on the bar and said, "Put up or shut up." Knowing a patsy when they saw one, all the old Bonackers anted up and the bragger covered every one of them. When the bets are all laid, this guy unzips and pulls out seven inches, limp. The old Bonacker looks at it, turns to Les, and says, "Just show him enough to win."

Like I said, it's an old Bonacker story, so consider the source. Look, I have nothing against Bonackers. We even have some on our police force, although our volunteer fire department is more their speed. Bonacker families have been in East Hampton as long as the landed gentry, who are the Osborne, Conklin, Baker, and Barrett families. The Bonacker founding fathers are the Bennett, King, Lester, and Miller families. They came here from Dorset, England, three hundred plus years ago and settled in Acabonack—the Algonquin name for this area adjoining Gardiners Bay. A good guess is that originally they were known as the Acabonackers, which was shortened to Bonackers. These two clans are not exactly the Hatfields and McCoys, although they often act like it; the gentry and the indigent comes closer to the truth. The Osbornes et al. owned the land; the Bennetts et al. worked the land. But over the past three hundred years more than one member of the gentry and one Bonacker was conceived on the wrong side of the blanket.

To this day the princes still reside on Main Street and, of course, in their oceanfront "cottages," while the paupers hug the bay side of town. The middle class is in the middle, where else? This infrastructure survives because in our kingdom by the sea, as in all kingdoms, the rich need workers and the workers need money. The gentry and the Bonackers still don't mix and mingle, but exist in a perpetual state of detente. Open hostility, from either camp, is redirected at the summer residents, whom the former ignore and the latter overcharge.

Me? I'm neither landed gentry nor native son, but one of a growing number of migrants from "Up-island," as

East Hamptonites call that stretch of Long Island from Westhampton Beach to New York City. Long Island, like Caesar's Gaul, is divided into three parts. From west to east, we have Queens, which is one of New York City's five boroughs; Nassau County; and finally, Suffolk County. Suffolk is divided down the center by the Peconic Bay, giving it a north and south fork. The south fork, bordering the Atlantic Ocean, is collectively known as the Hamptons; its most fashionable villages are Southampton, Bridgehampton, and, farthest east, East Hampton.

I was born in Queens and christened Edwin. Two strikes against me before I was big enough to lift a bat. My father's successful dental practice enabled us to rent a summer cottage in East Hampton from the time I started school. My parents had the good sense to buy it before the potato fields started sprouting the kinds of houses that get layouts in *Architectural Digest* and before summer bungalows, without basements and heat, became "quaint, charming, and picturesque" with price tags that were none of the above; when the movie house still had one screen; Main Street had a five-and-dime, and the drugstore soda fountain didn't feature a "scoop du jour."

I went to Southampton College, shunning the dormitories in favor of our second home. I never went back to Queens. Instead, I joined the East Hampton Town Police and rose, in stages, to my present rank of detective. My parents retired to Arizona, leaving me the house—which now has a basement, heat, *and* central air.

When I was a rookie, my first arrest was a drunk driving charge to none other than Les Miller—the same man who had just misplaced his wife.

I assume no photos were taken of the union between

Beauty and the Beast, as the locals are calling this supposed marriage, and Les's description of his spouse was as clear as those given by the few who had caught a glimpse of the bride. He wasn't sure of her height or weight, so I take it the couple never danced cheek to cheek, nor did Les carry his bride across the threshold. According to Les, we were to be on the lookout for a woman who was both "classy" and "beautiful." Ask for a show of hands answering to that description in East Hampton and we'd have a lineup spanning the length of the Long Island Expressway. Her age was also a mystery to the bridegroom. She sounded more like a blind date than a wife.

"Her eyes are real dark and her hair looks red in the sun."

A change of contact lenses and a hair rinse could transform her into a blue-eyed blonde.

One thing we know for sure. The lady owns an upscale car. Les drove it to the station house and even produced its registration, in the name of Betty Zabriskie, with an address in Delray Beach, Florida.

"Betty," Les informed us, "ain't short for Elizabeth."

Now there's a lead you could sink your teeth into.

It seems Betty took the Jitney into New York on Wednesday and hasn't been seen since. Seeing as it was now Thursday, we told him twenty-four hours is no big deal in the missing persons department. We promised to check with the New York police to see if a "classy" and "beautiful" woman had recently met with foul play in their jurisdiction.

Every officer and civilian in the station house had come out to the reception area to see Les and hear his story, including the Chief. Everyone on duty reluctantly returned to their desks to answer their phones when they rang, but came back as soon as they could to witness the phenomenon of Les Miller seeking help from the East Hampton Town Police.

When we finally hustled Les out of the station house with a promise that we'd be in touch, the Chief wiggled a finger at me and I followed him back into his office. Did I have a choice?

"She must have sobered up, taken one look at her bed partner, and caught the first flight back to Florida," I offered as I closed the door behind me.

The Chief sat and motioned for me to do the same. "And left him the car for services rendered? No man's dick is that big."

"The Lincoln in exchange for being free of Les Miller is a bargain."

The Chief wasn't buying that either. "It won't wash, Evans. I want you to follow up on this one."

"You're kidding. If we followed up on every domestic squabble complaint we get from those people, we wouldn't have time to write a traffic ticket." I bit my tongue as soon as the words were out of my mouth, but of course it was too late.

"I don't know who you mean by 'those people,' Evans, and I don't want to know. This is just the kind of pimple that can become a boil, and it's my ass on the chopping block. We police both sides of the highway, remember? Being accused of playing favorites, we don't need."

Seeing as the town police were currently involved in litigation, with lawsuits flying all over the place for just that reason, I didn't argue the point.

"We'll wait another day before we do anything. Check with Les tomorrow and if she's still missing try to get him to talk sense. See if he has a photo of the lady. If not, get as detailed a description of her as you can so we have something to give the New York boys if it comes to that. I want to know where those two met, if they're really married, and what Les Miller is doing with her car. The Lincoln, Evans, is the puzzler. Find out how Les Miller came into possession of that car and you'll solve the mystery of Betty Zabriskie." The Chief unnecessarily straightened the neat stacks of paper on his uncluttered desk.

"You think he did her in for the car?" I asked.

"I think, like you, the dame hightailed it out of here, but I want to know why she didn't make her exit in style and what else she might have left behind. The fact that she left Les, I understand. Sooner or later, they all do. Her speed worries me. And Evans, let's try to keep this out of the *Star?*"

"No way," I answered. "Les Miller's wife on the MIA list after three months of wedded bliss? This has got to be a bigger story than Sal Iacono getting his chicken farm splashed all over the *New York Times*."

"Let's not get this one splashed all over the *New York Times,* and try to keep it in the family." The Chief leaned back in his swivel chair and folded his hands over a belly that was beginning to put a great deal of stress on the buttons on his regulation blue shirt. "That's it, Evans."

"Why me, Chief?" I asked as I opened the door, letting in the sounds of ringing telephones and a chorus of disjointed conversations.

"Because you know Les's kid and his girlfriend."

I closed the door, not quietly, on the Chief's grinning face.

Les's kid is not a kid. He's a nineteen-year-old misdemeanor prepping for a felony. And Helen is not Galen's girlfriend. She's a sweet and caring person who unfortunately attached herself to Galen's coattails in grade school and is having a hard time breaking loose. I'm committed to performing the necessary surgery.

Galen is handsome, with a body to match. Me? I watch my diet, work out, sip a little wine, and get plenty of rest. The result is a hundred and sixty pounds on a six-foot frame, but I have to sweat to maintain this delicate balance. Galen lives on junk food and his most arduous exercise is lifting a beer can to his lips. The result of this is a body that keeps girls like Helen—who should know better—infatuated, and pretty Galen in business. Not mowing lawns, which is the business of Les & Son, but hustling the gay boys on Two Mile Hollow Beach. Galen thinks no one knows about his moonlighting. Well, I know because I shadow Galen like a cat stalking a fat mouse, just waiting for him to trip over his own cockiness.

And I know he doesn't confine his activity to the volleyball court on Two Mile Hollow. He also parades up and down Main Street on summer nights, strutting past Main Street Video where Helen's folks are making an honest living renting films. Brazen? Stupid? Or a whole lot of both?

Does he know what he can get from the men he's preying on? Does he know he can pass it on to Helen? I'm sure Gay and Helen are going at it, because I can't imagine two young, pretty, healthy people today who aren't.

I never discuss this with Helen because she would deny it, even if she knew it was true, and rush to Galen's defense as she's been doing since they met in the first grade.

Did I mention that Galen is ten years younger than me?

Am I jealous?

Yes.

Now I have to go looking for his stepmother.

Nineteen

"Did you find her?"

"We're looking for a person, Les, not a wallet. She's got two legs and knows how to use them. We think she took off for Florida." And if she did, I didn't add, she wasn't answering her phone. I got her number from information, using the address from the only factual information Les had given us—Betty's car registration.

"Why would she do that?"

Look in the mirror, I wanted to tell him, but I wasn't a marriage counselor. And remember, we had to tread easy these days. The fact is, Les didn't look all that bad. The lady must be responsible for that, but she was gone two days now and hubby hadn't shaved since she boarded the Jitney to God knows where. The kitchen, however, looked and smelled like a Bowery flophouse. Mrs. Miller was no Hannah Homemaker. And if she had set up the bar on the kitchen counter, her intent was to wish Les under the wagon rather than on it. The supply seemed to be running low, which accounted for Les's anxiety over her disappearance.

"You want a drink?" he asked, as if reading my mind.

"At ten a.m.?"

"You got a delicate stomach?"

I let that go too. I had come to get some facts, not to trade punches with a guy who was brain-dead. Les was sitting at the kitchen table. On the few other occasions I had been to the Miller house—in pursuit of Les—he sat in the same chair. Maybe he never sat anyplace else? Even slept there? Did Betty Zabriskie kiss him good night as soon as his head touched the table and then climb the stairs to her lonely bedroom? Not so lonely, come to think of it, with Galen snoozing in the next room. What the hell was going on here?

"Look at this." Les shoved a piece of paper across the table.

It was a marriage license. Les to Betty. So, fact number one: They were married. I got out my notebook and jotted down the vital statistics. The lady, I noticed, was forty-seven years old (if she was telling the truth). No spring chicken, but in great shape according to Les. And not poor if the car parked out front was any indication. So why does she hook up with a drunk who lives in a house that leaks like a sieve and smells like a barn? Her appearance, not her disappearance, was the real mystery.

I took the chair opposite Les and started asking questions from a list the Chief and I put together that morning. When I finished, all I had to show for the effort was more questions.

"A dress shop. And she owned it?"

"Real fancy." Les drained his can of Bud, sipped from a glass that looked like it contained water but I'm sure didn't, and had the nerve to ask me to get him another beer from the fridge. I was tempted to look under the table to see if he still had legs.

"Like they got here on Main Street, only with a waiting area where she served wine," he boasted, accepting the Bud as if accustomed to live-in help.

"So did you wander in thinking it was a bar, or were you looking to raise your hemline?" And damned if I didn't strike gold when he told me about the MacAlisters, the couple whose car he ferried north and south. I jotted down their East Hampton address, confident that they could tell me what I wanted to know about Betty Miller, née Zabriskie, and her dress shop in Delray Beach. Les was, as usual, shy on details, such as the shop's name and address, and he couldn't recall having been to his wife's house in Delray before he swept her off her feet. The fact that the lady served wine in her place of business was the only fact retained by Les Miller's soft brain.

"You want to have a look at her room?" Les asked.

The newlyweds, I gathered, were not roommates. "I don't have a search warrant."

"Go ahead. We got no secrets from the police." Les lit a cigarette. I bet his lungs and liver are in better shape than mine.

"Unless there's a picture of Mrs. Miller up there, I have no need to search the room at this point. What about correspondence?"

"You mean letters? Never seen her get any."

"You saw her off on the Jitney on Wednesday. What time, Les?"

"In the morning."

"Did she make a reservation for the bus?"

"Ask her."

"I can't, Les. We don't know where she is. Remember?"

"Yeah. That's right. So if she went back to Florida, how come she left all her clothes and the car?"

Les can't remember the details of his three-month-old marriage, but he comes up with the one question I don't want to hear. Why did she walk away with only the clothes on her back? How the hell do I know? Unless she met with an accident. The Chief was contacting the city boys, but all they would do is recite the statistics on how many people disappear in New York City every day. Strictly routine. No crime had been committed. The lady was free to take the bus to New York and points beyond if it pleased her. No law against it. But they could check the morgue and the hospitals to see if they had a woman's body no one was claiming. If she was comatose or DOA, any ID she was carrying, like a driver's license, would point to Delray.

I had to get to those MacAlisters to find out the location of the dress shop. If the shop was open, whoever was in charge might just know where the owner was or if they had heard from her in the last two days.

"She liked me," Les was babbling. It wouldn't be long before he went down for his morning nap. "And I never told her about the farm."

"What about the farm, Les?"

"How's it hanging, Eddy?" Galen, in person, came into the room like he was fired from a cannon.

"You've been here all the while?" I asked.

"Where else would I be, Eddy?"

"What about the volleyball court on Two Mile Hollow?"

"Haven't been there much this season."

"Doesn't the league miss you?"

"We don't have a league, Eddy. Just some guys tossing a ball across a net and letting it all hang out, if you know what I mean."

"I'm afraid I do, Galen. Helen hasn't seen much of you either."

"But I bet she's seeing a lot of you."

"We go out when it's convenient."

"Dinner dates, Eddy?"

"Who wants to know?"

"Touchy. Have you located my stepmother?"

"Where do you think she's gone?"

"Took off—back to Florida."

The little hooligan was in the hall all the time, listening. "Did you get along with her?" I asked.

He shrugged like he couldn't care less. "My room is my castle, Eddy, and the lady never tried to cross the moat, so we got along fine. She was good to Les, as you can see. You want a drink?"

"He's got a delicate stomach," Les answered for me. He seemed to come awake at intervals, resembling a mechanical toy triggered by a child with an itchy finger.

"What was Mrs. Miller wearing when she left here on Wednesday?" I didn't ask Les that question because I knew what the answer would be. His son proved to be just as helpful.

"Never saw her on Wednesday. I was still in my room when Les took her to the bus."

"What time was that?"

Galen walked to the refrigerator, opened it, removed a plate of what looked like fried chicken, and placed it on the table in front of his father. "Put something in your stomach," he cautioned the old man. Then, taking his own advice, he picked up a leg and began munching it. "Time? In the morning. Which narrows it to between midnight and noon, I guess."

"Answer my questions or don't," I told him, "but spare

me the wise guy answers. You haven't got the moxie for the role. You're still a punk."

"Hey man, I'm half an orphan for the second time in my life and you attack me? Where's your respect for the bereaved, Mr. Evans?"

Before I told him, Les woke up and said to no one in particular, "She had on her big pocketbook."

I turned from the son to the father. One of them knew more about the disappearance of Betty Zabriskie than he was saying. But which one? My money was on Galen.

"Her what?" I asked.

"He means a shoulder bag. A big-ass bag she carried when she went to the city. Brown. High-class Italian leather from someplace like Gucci or Pucci or Hoochy-Coochy. You know what I mean?"

It wasn't much, but it was something: a guess at her height and weight; hair that looked red in the sun, but the color could be changed in an hour; dark eyes; nice figure; carrying a designer shoulder bag. A composite that would resemble half the women on Long Island.

"Did you call Delray to see if she'd gone back?" I asked Galen.

"I wouldn't know where to call."

"Her address is on the Lincoln's registration."

"I never thought of it, and what would I say if I got her on the phone? Your husband misses you? Where should I send your clothes and car? If you're looking for alimony, file a claim with the New York State Department of Welfare?"

"Do you know if she had an address book or a diary or anything like that?"

"If she did, it would be in that bag. You want to have a look at her room?" Galen offered, knowing the answer.

"Not necessary."

He sucked on the chicken leg. "Suit yourself. I'd close the door so you could rummage through her nylon panties. I'd even give you a rubber to spare the lingerie, but in this house we don't stock size small."

Les banged his beer can on the table and cackled like an old crone. "That's a good one, Eddy, right?"

I had a .38 revolver, in a holster, under my jacket and suddenly, like an epiphany, I knew the meaning of "justifiable homicide."

Twenty

"That would be the nine-fifty from East Hampton. It gets into the city about twelve-thirty, give or take, depending on traffic, so they can grab a quick lunch before the curtain."

"If they're going to the theater," I interjected. "Not everyone on the Wednesday morning bus is going to a matinee."

"I didn't imply they were, Mr. Evans. The bus is timed for the matineegoers, is what I meant. I should think that was implicit in my statement."

Jan Solinsky, spokesperson for the Hampton Jitney in their Southampton office, was all business in a straight black skirt and white blouse. Her fair hair, pulled away from her face, contained not a ripple. The no-nonsense watch on her wrist and horn-rimmed eyeglasses completed the picture of a lady executive on the go. In the distance I could hear telephones ringing. It was the end of June and the bus company that linked town and country was in full throttle.

"I'm interested in last Wednesday. Do you have the passenger rosters for that day?"

"So you said on the phone. I have them right here, Mr. Evans."

"Eddy, please," I said.

"Of course, Eddy. I've never been questioned by a detective before."

I nodded, indulgently. "I'm looking for a Betty Miller or Zabriskie on the nine-fifty from East Hampton."

Jan shuffled through a pile of rosters, focused in on one and studied it. Finally, looking up, she shook her head. "Nothing even resembling those names," she informed me, looking pleased by the fact. "Anything else, Mr. Evans?"

"Eddy," I reminded her.

"Anything else, Eddy?"

"Do you get the names of every passenger on board?"

"Usually, yes. Or at least the name they give us. We don't verify who they say they are, Eddy."

"Must riders make a reservation?"

"This time of year, almost always. You might get lucky on weekdays, but weekends are booked solid well in advance."

"Do you check the roster as they board?"

"No. Going west, to the city, riders board at each pickup point and when the bus arrives here, in Southampton, our attendant boards with the passenger list. There are no more stops, so the attendant collects fares and ticks off the passengers against her roster."

"Suppose someone gets on without a reservation?"

"If we have room for them, we add their name to the roster and collect their fare."

"What if there's no room?"

"If we have more passengers than seats in Southampton, we take roll call and if you're not on our list we put you off the bus. Most people without reservations ask before boarding and the driver can usually tell them if there's space available."

"But not always," I added.

"No, not always. Boarding without a reservation, especially this time of year, is risky."

"What time would the matineegoers return?" I asked.

"There's a bus that leaves midtown at six, arriving in East Hampton at eight-thirty, give or take."

"Could you check the nine-fifty for the previous Wednesday, Ms. Solinsky?"

"Jan," she corrected.

Things were looking up.

She shuffled once again. "No Miller and no Zabriskie."

No sense checking the names that made the round trip. Betty obviously used an alias going and coming—if she returned last Wednesday.

"A favor, Jan. When you get a chance could you check the lists for the same Wednesday buses for the last two months?"

"I could."

"Today's Friday. Will Tuesday be too soon?"

"I don't think so."

Silence. Jan removed her glasses and looked at me as if she was seeing me for the first time. "So," she began, "*detective*. Not bad for a marine biologist. How long has it been? Five years?"

The charade was over and I silently applauded her performance, as I often did over three turbulent years as lover, housemate, and almost spouse of Jan Solinsky. If she was playing a part, which she often did, who was I to bring down the curtain before the star had completed her turn? When Jan and I met, at Southampton College, she was an aspiring actress whose role model was Katharine Hepburn. I couldn't decide between marine biology and computer science and went with computer science. When, after graduation, I followed my heart and joined the East Hampton Town Police Department, Jan threw in the towel—or rather, moved out of my house, taking all my towels with her.

"Competing with seaweed and software, I might tolerate," she explained, "but I draw the line on seven nights a week of *EHPD Blue*. Catch me on the silver screen, copper." Those were her parting words and I never heard from—or of—Jan again until today when, after leaving the Miller place, I called the Hampton Jitney. Explaining my purpose, I was connected to Jan. Thanks to Katharine Hepburn, I recognized the voice instantly.

"Jan? It's Eddy."

"Eddy who?" was what I got in return.

Her greeting, in person, was no more friendly.

"Six years," I corrected her, "and I went with computer science, remember?"

"Does that account for your rapid rise in the police department?"

"It helped. But I'm a good cop. You between shows?"

"Actually, I'm between husbands."

"Sorry."

"So am I." She reached into her desk drawer and took out a pack of cigarettes. "It's illegal, but what the hell." She lit up and blew smoke at the ceiling. "We were a team," she went on. "Lang and Solinsky. Not exactly Bogie and Bacall—we performed in a bistro on Columbus Avenue in the roles of waiter and waitress. He auditioned for an off-Broadway show. The producer was a rich lady, past her prime, looking for thrills—should I go on?"

"I get the picture."

"I'm sure you do."

"So how did you end up here?" I asked, with a nod at her tiny office in the Hampton Jitney facility.

Jan shrugged. "End up? I'm hoping it's a beginning." She opened another drawer and extracted an ashtray. "Native or transplant, no one ever really leaves the Hamptons, do they, Eddy? The very rich, the very poor, the potato fields, the windmills, the fishermen, the artists, the bad and the beautiful, and all within walking distance of the ocean."

"You sound like an ad in Dan's Papers for a half-share in a shack in Westhampton Beach."

Jan tossed her head back and laughed. A theatrical ploy I remembered well, accompanied by a chuckle, hearty and honest, that made you want to join in. "That's exactly where I got it from."

"That's why I made detective," I told her. "So, where are you staying?"

She drew on her cigarette. "Where else? A half-share in a tacky house in Sag Harbor. But I'm looking to up-grade. This gig"—accompanied by a wave of the hand—"is strictly for bread and butter, with compensations. A lot of show people ride the Jitney to and from the city and I get to talk to them."

"Still starstruck," I said.

"And why not?" she challenged, with yet another wave of her arm, depositing a pinch of cigarette ash on her desk.

"I hope you find what you want, Jan."

"And I hope you find Betty Miller, or Zabriskie. By the way, what is she running away from?"

"Her husband."

"Then I hope you don't find her."

"I'm not sanguine."

She smiled, her full lips, carefully painted, parted to reveal a perfect set of teeth that I knew to be genetic, not cosmetic. "I like your choice of adjective. You have class, Eddy."

Jan never minced words, a trait that often left me blushing or fuming and, it seems, still did. I prepared to leave. "Thanks for your help. I'll call you on Tuesday."

She stubbed out her cigarette and rose, too. "Nice seeing you, Eddy. Sorry if I was a little rude."

"You were a lot rude, but I'm all heart."

Just as I was about to open the door she called out, "Are you married?"

I turned. "Not yet."

"Engaged?"

"Nope."

"Seeing someone?"

"You might say that."

"She's married," Jan said, hopefully.

"Hardly. She's nineteen and I'm competing with a juvenile delinquent."

Jan put her hands on her slim hips. The skirt did her figure justice. "You're an anachronism, Evans."

"I can't be. I'm only twenty-nine."

"Going on forty. Crew-cut hair, blue suit, penny loafers, and the naïveté to admit you're panting after Lolita."

"Her name is Helen, I'm not panting, the hair is my

own, the shoes are comfortable, and the suit is paid for. So back off, Jan."

She ignored this as she ignored anything that got in her way, and scribbled something on a piece of paper. "Here, take this."

I retraced my steps, taking the paper from her outstretched hand. "What is it?"

"My home number. In case something comes up over the weekend."

"You've got a dirty mind, Jan."

"Me?"

I closed the door on her theatrical chuckle.

Twenty-One

I thought the old lady was going to drop dead at my feet.

"Betty and Les! Married!" she said, for about the tenth time. "Are you sure?"

"I saw the license, ma'am."

"But how could such a thing happen?" she asked, still dazed by my news and carrying on like it would take more than a marriage license to convince her of the fact.

"I was hoping you could tell me, Mrs. MacAlister."

"Me? I didn't even know they knew each other," she cried.

"Easy, Mother," old Mr. MacAlister advised, as concerned as I was with his wife's reaction to the union of Les Miller and Betty Zabriskie. "It's not really any of our business."

"I know, Mac," she snapped at her husband, "but that doesn't make it any more credible. That old man and Betty? Why, she's so young and pretty."

I guess when you're Mrs. MacAlister's age anyone under fifty is young. "According to Les, you sent him to see her. To pick up a skirt, I believe."

"I did, but I never dreamed it would lead to marriage, Mr. Evans. I may be old but I'm not daft. Not yet, anyway. How did they become intimate in a matter of minutes, and why? That's what I'd like to know."

"So would I, ma'am."

"Mr. Evans asked for one of Betty's business cards, Mother. Why don't you go upstairs and find one for him. It will give you time to digest the news and maybe you'll remember something that may be helpful to the police."

"There's nothing wrong with my memory," Mrs. MacAlister reminded her husband and not, I'm sure, for the first time. "But I bet you can't tell me what we had for lunch."

"If I can't, Emily, it's because we haven't had lunch today. It's nine-thirty in the morning and we just finished breakfast."

Mrs. MacAlister gave old Mac a look that said she would have the last word as soon as I was history, then left us with her chin high and not a white hair out of place.

The MacAlister house is on Egypt Lane, one of the more prestigious village lanes that run south from the highway to Further Lane. Just beyond Further Lane is Two Mile Hollow Beach, so when Galen finished mowing the MacAlisters' lawn he could slip on his volleyball uniform and moonlight down the road apiece. The homes on Egypt are old and large and important; lawns, backyards, and surrounding landscaping are as fastidiously tended as a Martha Stewart dream. The MacAlister patch is no exception, which verifies their statement that Les & Son are no longer their property's prime caretakers.

This interview took place in the kitchen, where policemen are usually received, a room slightly larger than so-called great rooms in modern dwellings. The appliances were old but dependable and the wide plank flooring stained dark and polished to a high gloss. An oak table stood before a row of windows looking out on a back lawn dotted with graceful willows, a copper beech older than its owners, and a flower garden I suspected was the pride, joy, and labor of Mrs. MacAlister. The rectangular table could accommodate ten but only two chairs were positioned, at either end. Maybe this was why I hadn't been invited to sit. I wondered if the MacAlisters took their breakfast here and shouted at each other over their cornflakes and bananas.

The old man began fidgeting as soon as his wife was out of the room, a sign I knew well. "You have something you want to tell me, Mr. MacAlister?"

"I do," he said, with a determined nod.

"About Les and Betty Zabriskie?"

"About Betty—Miss Z."

"And what's that, Mr. MacAlister?"

"Didn't want to say this in front of Emily, you know. She likes Betty and refuses to believe the rumors. Cuts people off if they mention any goings-on within her hearing, which is not too keen to begin with."

"What kind of goings-on, sir?"

"Talk down there is that Betty Zabriskie is available."

"Available? For what, Mr. MacAlister?"

"Sex, if that's what they still call it, young man—for a fee."

Was this guy for real? "You're saying Betty Zabriskie is a . . ."

"Businesswoman," he concluded. "Doesn't give it away, by God."

I kept a poker face, but my mind was racing like I was holding four of a kind. If the old man's story was true, Galen and his stepmother were two of a kind. Was I about to expose a unisex brothel, operating between East Hampton and Delray Beach, Florida? Did the old man know what he was talking about?

"Is this pure gossip, Mr. MacAlister, or do you know someone who made a purchase in Betty's shop that wasn't wearable?"

"It's a fact," he said, examining his feet.

"Look, Mr. MacAlister, I don't want to get personal, and professionally speaking, I don't care one way or another, but are you speaking from experience?"

"That's all I'm saying." He folded his arms across his skinny chest and continued to admire his shoes.

This was getting more fantastic by the minute. The guy had to be pushing eighty-five, and if I was reading him right, he was still dipping his wick. I was spared a response by the return of Mrs. MacAlister, who came floating into the kitchen waving a small white piece of pasteboard that I presumed was Betty Z's business card. "Sorry I took so long, but it wasn't where we keep merchants' cards and it wasn't in our address book or phone directory."

"Where was it?" her husband asked. Better him than me.

"In my sewing box."

"Why?" The old man eyed her suspiciously.

"Because she's my seamstress, that's why. And it seemed like a good idea at the time," she added, before Mac could question this logic.

I took the card. "Thank you, Mrs. MacAlister." I now had Betty Z's business address and phone number. We had faxed the Delray police but Florida would freeze over before we heard from them, and if the New York boys came up with her body, it was their turf and their problem.

So why did I refuse to let go? Why was I on Egypt Lane on Saturday morning, interviewing a couple old enough to be my grandparents? Because after speaking with Les & Son and Jan Solinsky yesterday, I had all last night to ponder over what little I had learned. And I'll admit I also conferred with Helen, hoping she could add some insight based on her tight relationship with Galen. If she knew anything, she wasn't admitting it, but she couldn't hide her enthusiasm for attempting to solve the riddle of Betty Zabriskie's final trip on the Jitney.

The facts, as I knew them, were the following: Galen Miller had not made one appearance on the volleyball court of Two Mile Hollow Beach all spring; Galen Miller had hardly seen or been in touch with Helen Weaver for the same period; Les & Son were out of business and living high on the hog, if a well-stocked drinking bar and fried chicken are any indication—all this since Les's mysterious marriage to a mysterious lady who mysteriously disappears.

Les wants his wife back but little Galen doesn't seem a bit worried. If the lady is their bankroll and if I know little Galen, and I do, he not only knows where Betty Z is, but is in touch with her. So what's their game? Now, if that isn't enough to turn me into a shamus, tell me what it.

"Did you tell him?" Mrs. MacAlister asked her husband.

"Tell him what?" The red lines in Mac's parched skin glowed.

"About Les's million. Or did you forget?" She could hardly contain her glee.

"Million what?" I asked.

"Dollars," the old lady answered. "Les was coming into a million dollars."

"I didn't tell him, Mother, because I never believed it." Turning to me, Mac said, "I think Les Miller has lost his mind."

"Please, one at a time. You say Les was coming into a million dollars. How?"

"From the sale of his farm," Mrs. MacAlister announced triumphantly.

And I was back to zero. These people were living on Egypt Lane in body only. From the neck up, they were in la-la land. Could I believe anything I learned from them? "Have you ever seen the Miller spread, Mrs. MacAlister?"

"No. I've not."

"Les couldn't pay me enough to take it off his hands. It's miles from the ocean and the areas that have skyrocketed in value in the past decade," I explained to her.

"But that's what he told us. Said it was his last trip ferrying the Mercedes, and just a short time ago the boy came here and informed us they were no longer in the lawn care business. Not that I minded. Les gave us a real scare when it took him over a week to drive here from Delray, and now that I know the reason for the delay I'm sorry we ever got involved with Les Miller. He drinks, you know. And Betty Z? I just don't understand any of it, Mr. Evans."

Neither did I.

"I never believed his story," Mac repeated.

Then I got a brainstorm. "Mrs. MacAlister, did you tell Betty Zabriskie Les's news?"

The poor lady pursed her lips and was silent for a long

time as her husband and I stared at her. "I don't remember," she finally conceded.

"It was a long time ago, Mr. Evans. How do you expect anyone to recall a casual conversation in a dress shop." This from her gallant husband.

I liked the way the guy backed her up, and from the way she was beaming at Mac, so did she. Married sixty years, minimum, and beneath the nitpicking they were still on their honeymoon. "Mrs. MacAlister, when you went to Betty's shop—I don't mean that last time, but usually—did you gossip with her, and I use that word in its broadest context?"

"Well, yes, I did. I enjoyed Betty's company, Mr. Evans."

And you were not alone, if your husband is telling the truth. I didn't doubt for a minute that the old lady told Betty Zabriskie Les's cock-and-bull story. Then Les pays a call on Betty. So who's conning who? And where does Galen fit in? Right in the middle, is my guess.

"Married," Mrs. MacAlister said. "I don't understand it. That Les is so . . . so ungainly."

No one with a million bucks is ungainly, I was thinking.

"You say she took the Jitney to the city and never returned?" Mrs. MacAlister asked for the fifth, or was it the sixth time?

"Yes, ma'am. Last Wednesday."

"Perhaps she's come to her senses and is back in her shop in Delray, Mr. Evans."

"Perhaps she is, ma'am."

Twenty-Two

The town parking lot was filled with parked cars and hopeful drivers cruising the narrow lanes, ignoring the directional arrows, looking for spaces, dropping off shoppers, and idling to pick up passengers. All of it par for the weekend before the Fourth of July. I pulled into the one space reserved for official parking, conveniently located directly in front of the new public rest rooms. I flipped down my visor, displaying my official permit in hopes of not being ticketed by the boys and girls in pretty chinos and starched white shirts. These are our auxiliary police persons, employed every summer to keep traffic and pedestrians moving and to enforce the two-hour town parking law. Everyone thinks the auxiliary force is cute, and so do they.

I picked up a container of coffee in Dreesen's and walked down to the intersection of Newtown Lane and Main Street, the hub of East Hampton. Both streets were crowded with second-home owners and summer renters shopping, and the DFDs (Down for the Days), window-shopping or shoplifting. The latter was a new phenomenon, but when you take on the mantle of Rodeo Drive

East, you hire the private security guards that go with the territory.

I crossed Main and started for the video shop. Passing the movie house, I spotted Galen coming out of Main Street Video and getting into the Lincoln that was parked directly in front of the shop. The kid was born under a lucky star. Seeing him in the Lincoln riled me as much as the fact that he had run straight to Helen after my visit to the farm. He was listening behind the kitchen door yesterday, not missing a word of my interview with his father and cutting in before I learned from Les what Galen didn't want me to know. The million-dollar offer. Fact or fiction?

I waited under the marquee, sipping my coffee, until the Lincoln pulled away from the curb and joined the traffic. He handled the car like it was his. I saw a couple of young girls staring at his blond head as he drove by in the fancy car.

"My room is my castle, Eddy, and the lady never tried to cross the moat, so we got along fine."

Maybe Betty Zabriskie didn't have to storm the moat. Maybe her stepson lowered the drawbridge and waved the Lincoln in.

The shop was crowded and there was a line at the counter waiting to check out videos. Helen was on duty, being her efficient self and looking great, just as she did the first time I entered Main Street Video almost a year ago. For me it was love at first sight, just like in the movies that Helen dispenses to her customers. Today her hair was in a ponytail, a style I liked and one that suited her. She was wearing a white T-shirt that boldly proclaimed, "THE CHRISTIAN RIGHT IS NEITHER." Helen is very opinionated.

Seeing Helen, I thought of Jan Solinsky and was ashamed of the association. The piece of paper with Jan's number on it was burning a hole in my pocket. I considered trashing it, but in the course of an investigation one collects facts, discarding none until the case is solved. And if that isn't a commandment in the detective's bible, it should be. I didn't need or want Jan Solinsky back in my life at this juncture and I would have to fight the temptation like a dieter in an ice-cream parlor. Was Helen thinking the same thing about Galen's sudden appearance? Strange, come to think of it. Betty Zabriskie disappears and Galen Miller surfaces. Or, going back a bit, Betty Zabriskie appears and Galen Miller disappears. Betty disappears and Galen appears. They were like a couple of jack-in-the-boxes working at counterpoint. Up pops one and down goes the other. But who was working the trick?

The line moved slowly because everyone knows Helen and enjoys chatting her up or asking her movie recommendations. Helen is a walking encyclopedia of film lore, and Galen shares her enthusiasm. Me, I know what I like but Helen says what I like isn't art. You want art, you go to a museum. You want to be entertained, you go to the movies. I did vow to watch *Gone With the Wind* on the anniversaries of David O. Selznick's birth and death, but failed to win Helen with this generous offer.

When she was finally free I moved to the counter and foolishly greeted her with, "What is Galen up to?"

"Hello to you too, Eddy," Helen answered, not overjoyed at seeing me. "Galen wants to know what *you're* up to, so why don't the two of you exchange game plans and eliminate the middleman, namely me?"

"I'm on a case, Helen. You could be more coopera-
tive."

"Case? You mean you're looking for Les's wife?"

"Her husband reported her missing. It's my job. I think
she took a powder, like all of Les's women. What I want
to know is why she married Les."

"Ask Les."

"I did, but he's a bit vague on the subject and I think
Galen knows more than he's saying. What has he told you
about this?"

"Excuse me, Eddy, but there are cash customers behind you. Do you mind?"

I stepped aside and waited as people gave Helen the
little tags that hang below the display-video covers, indicating their selections. Helen had to run into the back and
get the actual cassette. Then the renters flashed their
membership cards as Helen keyed data into a computer,
aimed a gun at bar codes that activated a printer, pulled
receipts and dupes out of the electronic typewriter, and finally collected money in exchange for the printed tran-
scripts. The shop would need extra help now that the
season was starting, but Mr. Weaver would wait for the
weekend of the Fourth and not a moment sooner before
parting with a minimum-wage paycheck.

I was back as soon as she was free, but there were still
a few people browsing the racks. "What did you tell
Galen?"

"I told Galen that you went to the Hampton Jitney office yesterday and learned that his stepmother used an
alias every Wednesday."

I refrained from pounding the counter with my fist. "I
wish you wouldn't report everything I tell you to Galen."

"Then don't ask me to report everything Galen tells

me to you." Her ponytail bounced up and down as she punctuated each word with a nod of her head.

"Okay, I won't. If you'll just answer one question."

She sighed and raised a finger. "One."

"What do you know about a million dollars?"

She squared her shoulders, elevating "THE CHRISTIAN RIGHT" to new heights before letting me have it. "Very little, I'm sorry to say. But I do know that when the lease on this store expires next year, the landlord wants to double the rent. He's under the impression that Main Street is now an extension of Fifth Avenue. I know we can't afford the increase and will have to close the shop. My father doesn't know what he'll do if this happens, and my mother is sick with worry. I know I might be living on the street this time next year. In short, Eddy, I know very little about a million dollars."

She was shaking with rage and the tears that refused to fall gave her brown eyes the glassy, unseeing stare of a child's doll. Being on public display only added to her tension. I felt like a heel and that, I imagine, was her purpose. Helen was not the hysterical type, far from it, so I couldn't help wondering if the Millers' financial prospects (fact or fiction) had more to do with her outburst than the Weavers' financial prospects. She had been protecting Galen Miller since both were children, a task that grew more arduous with the passing years. Was she coming to terms with the fact that her childhood sweetheart was beyond redemption? If so, she had to make her own peace. As much as I wanted to, I couldn't help her, and attacking Galen would defeat the objective. Instead, I proposed.

"Marry me and you won't have to live on the street."

She stared at me, her mouth wide open but nothing

coming out. I think I was looking at her the same way. Did I really say it? I must have. Why else were we staring at each other with our sound systems short-circuited?

Someone touched my shoulder and I jumped. "How much longer will you be?" the woman behind me asked.

I moved away, still looking at Helen. There was the slightest smile on her lips now and a blush on her cheeks. I thought of a bride, walking down the aisle to be united with the guy in the tux and bow tie.

The customer left and I inched back to the counter. "I meant it, Helen."

"Eddy, please. It's so busy." She started stacking a pile of computer checkout receipts. "Sorry about the lecture."

"I don't mind. Everyone is having a hard time with our new prosperity." This got a laugh. "Helen, don't see Galen anymore." I had resolved not to say it ever, but the mouth is quicker than the best of intentions.

"Don't ask me that, Eddy."

"It's not because I'm jealous, which you know I am. It's because something funny is going on at the Millers'. It worries me, Helen, and all I'm asking is that you take care not to get involved."

"You mean Les's wife running off? Galen has nothing to do with that, Eddy. I've known Gay all my life and he'd never do anything that would harm me."

Harm? Her choice of word, not mine, and who was she trying to convince, herself or me? "That million dollars I mentioned. I learned that the old man is boasting someone offered him a million for the farm."

She hesitated a moment and then shrugged off this startling piece of information. "So? I've heard a lot of folks have made a lot of money in real estate in East Hampton. Why not Les and Galen? Are they any different because they're locals? Their roots go back as far as the Barretts', so isn't it about time they got a piece of the pie?"

"When you climb down from your soapbox, I'll explain."

Two more people lined up behind me. "Tonight?" I asked.

"Tonight."

I was relieved. She hadn't made a date with Galen.

"Eddy," she called when I was almost to the door.

"Yeah?"

"I'll think about what you said."

Saturday night.

Helen opened the car door but didn't get in. Instead she asked, "If I promise not to talk about films, will you promise not to talk about your case?"

"I promise."

She settled in beside me.

"Where to?" I asked.

"The movies. Where else?"

I can't win, but then maybe I don't want to.

Twenty-Three

Monday. I called the shop in Delray Beach and made contact with Yolanda Gomez. She sounded young. Did she moonlight along with Betty Zabriskie?

"I'm looking for Betty Zabriskie," I began.

"So am I," Yolanda answered.

"Who are you?" I asked.

"Who are *you?*" Yolanda answered.

"Eddy Evans. I'm a police officer."

"You were here yesterday."

"I'm not the Delray police. We alerted them. I'm calling from East Hampton."

"That's where they said Betty was living. They said she got married. I think they're nuts."

"It's true, Ms. . . ."

"Gomez. Yolanda Gomez."

"Betty Zabriskie married a man from here. Lester Miller. She left him and he's trying to locate her."

"I can't believe this. Betty didn't say anything about getting married when she left here."

"I take it you work for Betty Zabriskie. Or Betty Miller."

There was a pause before Yolanda asked, "How do I know you're a police officer?"

Yolanda Gomez is no fool, I thought, and was encouraged by this fact. "Call the Delray police and give them my name. Ask them for the telephone number of the East Hampton Town Police in New York and call me at that number. I'll be here, waiting."

There was another pause. "I don't mean to be rude, Mr. Evans, but I'm very worried about Betty."

"So am I, Ms. Gomez. I hope you can help."

"I'll try," she responded.

"Do you work for Betty?" I asked.

"I help out in the boutique and sew a little. Alterations. Betty left in March."

"Why, Ms. Gomez? Why did Betty leave?"

"She told me it was an emergency. Business hasn't been too good around here and she was worried. I thought she went someplace for help. Financial help."

She did. And if you saw Lester Miller you would know how desperate poor Betty was. At Betty's age I imagine her sideline was falling off as well.

"I don't ask questions because the pay is good," Yolanda continued. "She put me in charge. She calls every Monday. I did what I could. She sends checks to pay the bills, but we haven't got any new stock since she took off. We haven't got many customers either. I keep an eye on her house too. The only thing higher than the grass on her front lawn is the pile of mail I stack on her kitchen table. Mostly bills too. She told me to sit tight. She'd be back as soon as she took care of some pressing business. Things were taking longer than she expected."

"When was the last time you heard from her, Ms. Gomez?"

"Last Monday. I thought you might be her calling. I told the police I would call them as soon as I heard from Betty. They said she was reported missing and they left. I don't get it, Mr. Evans."

"It's a domestic case, more or less. The police don't like to get involved unless a crime has been committed. So far, there's no evidence of any crime."

"Thank God. Betty is a good woman, Mr. Evans. She had a gentleman friend but he died. He was very good to Betty. I never believed the rumors."

If the gentleman friend was dead, knowing who he was wouldn't help find Betty, and I knew what those rumors must be so didn't follow up that lead.

"Why is she missing? Did this guy beat her?" Yolanda asked.

"This guy is usually too drunk to stand up."

"Why did she marry a drunk? Where did she meet him? How come she didn't tell me she was getting married? It's all very strange, Mr. Evans."

Yolanda Gomez had more questions than answers, just like me. "It's a long story, Ms. Gomez, and I'm calling long-distance." The Chief wanted to spend as little time and money resolving Les Miller's love life as political correctness permitted. I was on a short leash. "Do you have a picture of Betty?"

"There's one in her house. In a frame."

"Do me a favor, please. Take it out of the frame and send it to me overnight." I didn't tell her to take it to the Delray police and have it wired to the station because I doubted they would make it their top priority.

"How much will it cost?"

"Do you keep a petty cash drawer?"

"Petty is the right word, Mr. Evans."

"Take the money from there. Call Federal Express, I'd like to have that picture tomorrow, Ms. Gomez."

I gave her our address and phone number. "If you hear from Betty, call this number anytime—day or night—and I'll get the message."

"You don't think I'll hear from her today, like usual?"

"I doubt it."

"What should I do, Mr. Evans, if Betty doesn't call?"

"Does she have a lawyer? An accountant?"

"An accountant. He comes once a month. I know him."

"Call him and tell him what's happening."

"Maybe she's on the way home, Mr. Evans."

"If she flew or took a train, she would have been there days ago."

"Maybe she drove and made stops."

"She didn't take her car, Ms. Gomez. It's here."

"What! Now I know you're all crazy!" Yolanda Gomez cried. In her excitement she seemed to lose command of her almost perfect English. "Betty loved that car, Mr. Evans. She say she couldn't really afford it but she had to make a good show for business purposes. You know what I mean? She take very good care of that car. If her car is in East Hampton, so is Betty. Believe me."

Twenty-Four

"I had a busy weekend, Jan."

"Really? I didn't."

It was not going well, but with Jan one always had to prime the pump. Anticipating her resentment at not hearing from me since Friday, I waited until Betty's photo arrived and then called the Jitney office, inviting her to a late lunch. After telling me the research I requested had yielded very little toward solving the mystery of Betty Zabriskie, she agreed to give me forty-five minutes of her precious time. Before I could tell her to meet me at the diner on Route 27, she told me she would be waiting for me to pick her up at the depot. This would cut considerably into my allotted forty-five minutes but that was Jan's way of getting even.

The diner I refer to is in Southampton, a short distance from the depot. It is a real, honest diner as opposed to the diner in East Hampton, refurbished and taken over by celebrity restaurateurs who have created, of all things, a designer diner, but not, alas, any haute cuisine. One of its most puzzling aspects is its hours: one never knows when it will or will not be open for business. I've heard it said that this diner's hours are worked around the social schedule of its owners and staff, which is as good an explanation as any, since there aren't any others.

I chose the Southampton Diner because it was a favorite haunt of Jan's and mine in our college days; while we sometimes did eat breakfast or lunch there, my fondest memories of it are as the final stop, usually with friends, for a cup of coffee after a party or night on the town. When a few awkward tries at "Remember when . . ." and "Whatever happened to what's his name . . ." failed to resurrect the past, I gave up, feeling like a guy trying to impress his date and failing miserably.

I wore jeans, a polo shirt, and sneakers. Jan declined to comment on this show of modernity. Today, her hair was a mass of curls. "A perm?" I asked.

"A wig, silly."

Knowing the fluttering eyelashes were an extension of her own, I ventured, "So what have you got on that's real?"

"Why, Eddy, I thought you would have remembered."

I had a tuna salad on a seeded roll. Jan ordered the low-cal special that looked like a mountain of Jell-O.

"I was busy on the case all weekend," I told her. "Don't marry a cop, Jan."

"Have no fear, Eddy."

"Did you turn up anything?"

"Very little." Now all business, she opened her purse and removed a small notepad. Lifting the cover, she read aloud, "A Betty Miller made a reservation for the nine-fifty on Wednesday, May the twenty-first. She was a no-show."

"Meaning?"

"Just that. When the fares were collected and the passenger list checked off, there was no Betty Miller on the bus. She never boarded."

"This was after the bus left the Southampton depot, correct?"

"Like I told you on Friday."

"She could have boarded and then got off any stop between East Hampton and Southampton."

Jan gave this some thought as she poured a packet of sugar into her coffee and stirred vigorously. "We do take passengers on short hops between the villages but one wouldn't make a reservation to New York for that. Besides, I think the driver would notice if a passenger left the bus before Southampton if they hadn't already stated their destination. You see, they would have to pay the driver directly for the short hop."

"Could I speak to that driver?"

"Sorry, Eddy," she said sincerely. "He's no longer with us."

"Could I speak to any of the drivers who make that Wednesday morning run?"

She sipped her coffee. When she returned cup to saucer she answered, "I'll see what I can do but I'm not sanguine, as you would have it." She explained: "The drivers' schedules vary and they often accommodate each other by swapping schedules when they need time off. And, not surprisingly, we have a big turnover among our driving crew. But I'll see what I can do."

"It's appreciated. I understand you ask the passengers for a contact number when they make a reservation."

She nodded, and answered before I asked the obvious. "She gave us a number, Eddy, and I confess I dialed it. Couldn't resist."

"And?"

"The operator answered. There is no such number listed in East Hampton. She made it up. Your Betty Miller began burning her bridges way back in May."

Jan handed me her notebook and I glanced at the number Betty had given the Jitney. The first three digits were the East Hampton code numbers and I thought I recognized the remaining four numbers as those for Betty's shop in Delray. Any doubt that this was my Betty Miller was instantly forgotten.

Indicating the manila envelope I had carried into the diner, I asked Jan if she wanted to see a picture of Betty.

"Why not? But I seldom see our passengers, Eddy."

I removed the eight-by-ten and gave it to her.

"Nice-looking woman," was her comment.

Betty Zabriskie, in fact, was a beauty. Auburn hair and dark eyes. Fair complexion. The photo, a head shot, was very professionally done, giving Betty the appearance of a movie star or model.

"She's older now," I said.

"Aren't we all," Jan lamented. She returned the photo and I slipped it back into the envelope. "Did you see Helen this weekend?"

"The subject of age wouldn't have anything to do with your question, I hope."

"You hope wrong."

"We went out Saturday night. Dinner and a film."

"Sweet. Did you hold hands in the theater?"

"That's none of your business."

She was enjoying this and let me know it with a dazzling smile. I wondered why Jan never modeled for a toothpaste manufacturer.

"And the next day you abstained?"

"She was working."

"On Sunday?"

I explained Helen's job in her father's video shop and regretted it when I was once again treated to a display of dental perfection. Jan would visit Main Street Video the first chance she got.

The depot, when we returned, was as animated as an anthill. A Hampton Jitney, headed for the city, had just pulled in. The driver got out, followed by passengers grabbing a smoke before the two-hour ride to New York. Those waiting to board began lining up. Cars were constantly moving in and out of the semicircular driveway; people arriving and departing, scurried in and out of the vehicles. I pulled into an empty spot, and as Jan opened the car door she spotted the bus driver, talking to another man also in a T-shirt bearing the Hampton Jitney logo. "There are two of our drivers." She pointed. "I'll introduce you before I go in and you can show them Betty's picture."

I thanked her and promised to stay in touch.

"I'm not sanguine." Jan got in the last word.

"I had that run a few times," one of the drivers said, looking at Betty's picture. "But I don't recognize her. Pretty lady. It's a busy time and I see a lot of faces, so I'm not saying I never picked her up in East Hampton."

The other man took the photo and studied it a long time. I waited. He removed his baseball cap and scratched his balding head. "I wouldn't swear . . ."

"I'm not asking you to swear to anything. Tell me what you think even if you're not sure."

"I think I picked her up here a few times."

"Here? In Southampton? On the run to New York?"

"No. On the return trip. Her, or an older version of this one," he said, indicating the photo.

"That's very possible. I think this picture is at least ten years old. You picked her up here and took her east?"

"Yeah. To East Hampton. She's a regular at the health club." He meant the facility that shares space with the Jitney offices and several small shops in this minimart on Route 27.

"That's what she said," he explained. "Carries her workout clothes in a big leather bag. Told me her husband drivers her to the club but she has to take the bus back to East Hampton."

"Do you remember the dates and time?"

"The dates? Never. Time? Five, six in the evening, something like that."

"Can I have your name and address?"

"Look, I wouldn't swear to this in court."

"I don't think that will be necessary, but I might want to speak to you again."

Reluctantly he gave me the information, and I scribbled it on the manila envelope.

I ran into the health club and spoke to a young man behind the reception desk after showing him my ID. I asked him to check the club's member list for a Betty Miller or Zabriskie. He consulted a computer and shook his head. "Sorry. No Miller or Zabriskie."

I once again displayed Betty's picture, reminding him that she was now older. He shook his head. "Never saw her. She's not a member."

"You know all the members by sight?"

"Pretty much so. We're not that big."

"Can people buy a day pass to the club?"

"Sure. Oh, you mean maybe she used the club a few

times when I wasn't on duty. It's possible. Is she a crook?"

"No. She's a missing person."

"Is there a reward?"

Betty Zabriskie never went to New York every Wednesday. She lied to Les. Not surprising. He swore he saw her get on the bus each time and picked her up when she returned to East Hampton about six in the evening. Jan told me the matineegoers were just boarding the bus in New York at that time. She didn't go to the theater, and I'm sure she didn't go to New York at all. She either made a reservation, using a phony name and a nonexistent phone number, or as I now strongly suspected, didn't make one at all, except for once in May. And if the driver was right, her Wednesday ride on the Jitney was a round trip from East Hampton to Southampton. Judging from the scene I had witnessed there today, it would be very easy for a person to get lost in that mix.

A *modus operandi* was beginning to emerge, but like Yolanda Gomez, I had more questions than answers.

"If her car is in East Hampton, so is Betty," Yolanda had said. "Believe me."

I was beginning to believe.

Michael Anthony Reo

Twenty-Five

This morning Vicky asked me if I was lunching with Milly at the Club, adding "as usual" by way of accentuating the negative. I told her I was not, as Milly had better things to do today. Score one for me.

I asked Vicky if she was spending the day in Mark's office, the "as usual" implied rather than stated. She informed me that she was not, as Mark had better things to do today. Score one for Vicky.

Our first skirmish of the day ending in a draw, we could now go on a reconnaissance mission to ascertain the strengths and weaknesses of our respective positions for future reference. Maddy, coffee urn in hand, circled the breakfast table, listening intently, like a mole in drag. Their inheritance secure, John and Maddy now observed our sparring from front-row seats, and no doubt were putting their money on Mark Barrett to succeed the master, in more ways than one. I assume Annie and her spouse reported daily from their end. Well, the domestics were in for a big surprise. It's the *frog* that turns into a prince, kids, not a fucking WASP.

When Vicky and I were courting, we used to meet at a popular coffee emporium on Lexington Avenue whose motto, emblazoned on paper place mats and napkins, advised:

> *As you wander on through life, brother,*
> *Whatever be your goal,*
> *Keep your eye upon the doughnut*
> *And not upon the hole.*

I didn't heed it and now, twenty years after the fact, was paying the consequences. Waiting for the hole to disappear, it never occurred to me that if and when it did, so would the doughnut. Well, I wasn't about to make the same mistake twice. And, I should add, it was easier than ever to keep my eye upon Vicky, who had metamorphosed into a butterfly since coming into her own.

Upon her father's death, Vicky had become the chief administrator of what was the ninth—or was it the eighth?—largest trust foundation in America. My wife was now a woman with a purpose. Rushing to keep appointments with her lawyer and winning the competition with her father for visibility (whoever dies first loses), Vicky no longer faced her vanity mirror with the intensity of an artist contemplating a bare canvas. The result was remarkable. A natural tan was now all that came between the world and her lovely complexion, with only a stroke or two of lip gloss to complete the age-old ritual.

Her green eyes, unadorned, resembled the color and tone of antique jade, and not using a rinse to highlight her blond hair, recently cut and shaped to follow the line of her jaw, had allowed her usual brassy appearance to give way to a softer, warmer—and definitely sexier—Vicky. Even the affectations had succumbed to a more reflective, if somewhat distant, persona.

And, she had obviously been raiding the boutiques on Main Street. Not buying "labels," but rather good-quality clothes that suited her. This morning she wore a printed summer shift reminiscent of the heyday of Lilly Pulitzer, which showed off her figure and shapely legs. The legs were the reason Vicky seldom wore slacks. A wise decision promoted over the years by yours truly. That I had not been consulted regarding her makeover prior to the fact was a reminder of her newly found independence. Vicky, it appeared, was erasing all traces of her old self. What other aspects of that old self was my wife planning to dispose of?

"So what's Mark up to?" I asked, not taking my eyes off the *New York Times* that I was scanning rather than reading.

"MJ has finally wrapped up his life in Boston—apartment, furniture, and girlfriends, I assume—and arrives home today. Mark's driving to La Guardia to meet him."

I knew MJ was expected today, of course. Milly had talked of little else for the past week. So, I wasn't seeing Milly for the same reason Vicky wasn't seeing Mark. Finally we had something in common again. Well, it was a start.

What I didn't know was that Mark had volunteered to play chauffeur. The current head of Barrett and Barrett wasn't always on the best of terms with the incipient partner of the family firm.

"Why not MacArthur?" I asked, referring to a commercial airport more convenient to the Hamptons than La Guardia, which is on the opposite end of Long Island.

"The Delta shuttle out of La Guardia is more convenient," Vicky, who had returned to smoking with a vengeance, lit a filter-tipped Marlboro 100. "And Mark has business in the city," Vicky continued. "He's going to leave the car at the airport, then taxi into town and back in time for MJ's arrival."

She certainly knew the details of Mark Barrett's day-to-day existence. I wondered if the trip into New York included a visit to the MET Tower building. Instead I asked, "Is Mark going to prep MJ for the bar exam?"

Vicky shrugged. "Why do you ask?"

"Just curious. Mark told me to cool it with MJ this summer."

Vicky looked genuinely surprised. "He thinks I'm a distraction and wants MJ to concentrate on passing the bar on his first try."

"Well, the boy does follow you around like a puppy and you don't discourage it."

"Why should I?"

"Because you're old enough to be his father."

"Maybe that's the attraction," I answered. "Barrett's about as warm as an orphanage warden with his son." I waited for Vicky to respond and when she didn't I continued. "What with the Kirkpatrick windfall, I gather Barrett is anxious for MJ to qualify so the boy can handle whatever incidental business might come over the transom." I was goading her, but I was subtle.

We were into August, more than a month since Kirk's death, and not once had we discussed his will and our future. Vicky had put a barrier between us the length of the Dunemere Lane house. A bruised pride had reduced me to licking my wounds and complaining to Milly rather than simply asking my wife why she had left my bed. And damned if I would sniff around the money pouch like the servants groveling after their share of the spoils. Need I add that—the Incident—as I euphemistically dubbed it—off Two Holes of Water Road continued to haunt me, awake and asleep, although I had resolved to "let it go," as they advise in twelve-step programs. As far as I knew, a support group for recovering murder witnesses did not exist. Where was Dr. Kevorkian when you needed him?

Kirk had been such a force in Vicky's life and our marriage that his sudden absence had her acting like a schoolgirl when the teacher leaves the room. Boundless freedom is a very heady proposition, especially when it comes with an unlimited supply of money, so it wasn't surprising that Vicky had turned for guidance to a representative of a profession rooted in reality, rather than to a husband her beloved father had deemed a fop. But this fop knew that the fastest way to lose his wife was to tell her the guy she was leaning on had legs of clay and a bank balance in need of a transfusion.

Was Vicky's silence concerning things that mattered on advice of counsel? I knew how easily she could be manipulated, thanks to Daddy. But her makeover was her own doing and that show of independence sparked my hope.

Labor Day was fast approaching. We would be heading back to the city and plans would be under way for that promised memorial ceremony for Joseph Kirkpatrick. There would be a press release regarding the posthumous testimonial, and at that time Vicky would have to announce her plans as head of the foundation, and also what she would do—aside from the foundation—to perpetuate her father's name in the entertainment industry. When Kirk was forced into retirement, I suggested forming a production company under the Kirkpatrick logo. The mogul, who couldn't resist a moneymaking scheme, especially with his logo riding the crest, like the idea but not the messenger. The fact that my interest in and knowledge of the industry made me a likely choice to head up the company only strengthened his resolve not to act on the suggestion.

Was the idea still on the table? I shuddered to think what the result would be with Mark Barrett horning in on the project. If he knew as much about film production as he did about real estate, Kirkpatrick Productions Presents Bankruptcy would be our star-studded disaster epic.

I had to save my marriage and I needed a chance to prove my worth. Which was more important? Perhaps they were intrinsically linked; one without the other would be a compromise and I was too old, too tired, and too tough to settle for either/or. I wanted it all and if I was falling in love with my own wife, I doubt I was the first man to do so. The new Vicky needed a new Michael, a role I had been coveting for twenty years.

It wasn't all an uphill battle. We still sat down to dinner together every night, served by John and Maddy. We traded gossip, complained about the heat, the traffic, the summer residents, and the fact that Main Street had more boutiques per square foot than Madison Avenue. Like a suburban couple in reverse, what we did not discuss was her day at the office and my day at home. Without Kirk (and by the way, Vicky sat opposite me as usual, leaving Kirk's captain's chair empty), we gushed a plethora of chatter with a paucity of perception. If Kirk's death ended our twenty-year honeymoon, the period of adjustment did not have the luxury of that time frame. Something had to give. And soon.

"Mark is not our only lawyer, as you very well know," Vicky was saying. "We have an entire floor of them in the

Met Tower building. It's a huge estate I've come into, and besides the personal business, Mark has been translating a mountain of paperwork from legalese into English."

"And what does Michael Anthony Reo translate into?"

She stubbed out her cigarette. "What do you mean?"

"Just what I said. Does Mark find it strange that I'm not involved in your day-to-day business affairs, or was it his recommendation that keeps me from being enlightened?"

Vicky poured herself another cup of coffee and looked at her cigarettes wistfully, but made no move to pick up the pack. "I know you're upset about Father's will, Michael, but—"

"We're not talking about Kirk's will. We're talking about Mark Barrett. I know Kirk left a large estate. I know that you have a battery of lawyers in New York. I know there's a mountain of paperwork involved in all this, legalese and otherwise. But none of it justifies the amount of time you spend in Barrett's company or your silence on what the two of you are up to. A rich, pretty woman and an ambitious lawyer, not yet past his prime, are the stuff of trashy novels."

She shook her head vigorously, her new coiffure swaying in perfect cadence to the sudden movement of her head, offering a visual testimony to the cleverness of her hairdresser. "I moved out of our bedroom the night Father died because I needed to be alone to think about our future." And Vicky went on the defensive. Finally.

"'Our'? I'm honored to be included. But don't you think I should also be consulted?"

"You know what happens the minute we get into bed." This drove her to picking up the Marlboros and clutching the pack as if the act would allow her to absorb the nicotine by osmosis.

"I do. And there are a zillion couples who envy us that problem."

"That's just my point, Michael. The most we ever had in common was our bed and a taste for the good life. Now, especially, we have to face that fact. Father's death has saddled me with a responsibility I was never taught to cope with. The rehearsal is over and opening night has arrived."

I was amazed. The new Vicky was more than just a pretty face. "I want to shoulder that responsibility with you. That's what husbands are for."

"You've never shown any interest in responsibility, Michael."

"Neither have you."

"I was never given the chance."

"Nor was I," I reminded her. "Did Barrett advise you to withhold my conjugal rights?"

"No," she said adamantly.

"But he encouraged it."

No comment. But there was no need for one. "He called you on Kirk's private line the night you moved into Kirk's room."

"You were listening?"

"Only long enough to hear the phone ring. I was about to knock and see if you needed anything."

"I would have welcomed your company."

"I was angry."

"I suppose you had a right to be."

"The funeral arrangements. Private. The memorial service in the fall. Were they Barrett's ideas?"

"No. Mine. I told you, I needed time to think. I didn't

want a crowd of insincere mourners invading East Hampton, crying on cue, sucking up to the press, and drinking my good whiskey."

"Bravo! But I wish you had shared that with me instead of your lawyer."

"Mark has been helpful," she reminded me.

"And Kirk told you to listen to Mark Barrett."

She didn't answer and refused to meet my gaze. I saw an opening and plunged right in. "Are you having an affair with Barrett?"

She tossed the pack of Marlboros on the table, upsetting a dish of now cold toast. "Have you been faithful to me throughout our marriage?" she challenged.

It was my turn to examine the tablecloth. "I'm sorry," I apologized. "It's the future, not the past that matters."

She bowed her head, covering her face with her hand. "I'm so confused, Michael. And frightened."

At this poignant moment Ms. Johnson's gray head came peeking through the swinging door from the butler's pantry. Yes, the nurse-cum-secretary was still with us, but only on a part-time basis; three days a week, I think. Ms. Johnson has become so skilled with the fax machine and computer I fear she will never return to the world of bedpans and rectal thermometers. Medicine's loss is Silicon Valley's gain.

"Mrs. Reo. Mr. Reo. Good morning. I'm here."

And that was as keen an observation as you were ever going to get out of our Ms. Johnson.

Vicky regained her composure and answered with a weary smile: "Good morning, Ms. Johnson." If the woman had a first name I didn't know it and probably neither did Vicky, who now rose, and—out of politeness—so did I.

"Still at it?" I asked.

"We're down to the acknowledgments, which must be handwritten. My hand, I'm afraid."

"We'll talk later," I said to Vicky.

She nodded and as she walked past me I touched her shoulder. She paused and looked up at me. I kissed her cheek and saw her blush under her tan.

I retreated to my room with a cup of coffee, feeling like a man who had finally mustered up the nerve to invite the woman of his dreams to dinner and didn't get turned down. Not yet, anyway.

Then the telephone rang.

"Michael? Something has happened. I must see you. Can you come here? Now?"

"Milly?" She sounded distraught and very unlike the poised lady of the manor I had come to rely on since my once ordered life turned into a shambles of fear and uncertainty. "What's wrong? What happened?"

"I don't want to discuss it on the phone. There are so damn many extensions in this house. The help. You never know."

No, you never do. Good grief, what now?

Twenty-Six

I rode my bike to Barrett House because crossing Route 27 in a car in August would defeat Moses. Pedaling past the perfectly manicured lawns of Dunemere Lane, I recalled the coffee klatch social set, Maddy and Annie, who conferred daily at Dreesen's market. Was phone tapping also on their agenda? After delivering her distress message, Milly had rung off with a ta-ta. In sync with this drama, I listened for heavy breathing and the clandestine click of a disconnect on my end before hanging up. What the hell was happening to us?

My first thought had been that Milly's call had something to do with the Incident, and Pretty Boy's face popped into my mind's eye with a chilly clarity.

Next, I speculated that perhaps Milly had caught Mark with his pants down. That Milly would care if she had was as irrational as connecting her with the Incident. However, this wasn't the first time that the lady under the lake had immediately brought to mind the man under the influence of my wife's money. A quick fix for a pressing problem. The association was unsettling, to say the least. But it was summer in East Hampton, when and where a young man's fancy lightly turns to thoughts of sex, sand, and blood.

I dismounted at the end of Dunemere Lane. To my right was Guild Hall, which houses the John Drew Theater. To my left the old cemetery hugged the bank of our town pond, its long, narrow roller-coaster terrain resembling a gigantic snake toting a load of tombstones. I walked the bike first across James Lane (which flows into 27 just past the John Drew) and then onto 27, already wall-to-wall with autos moving east and west. In less than five minutes a car with two bicycles mounted on its roof took pity and paused on its way to Amagansett or Montauk. Nodding my gratitude, I advanced, cautiously, to the double dividing line, where a woman driving a station wagon, incensed at my presence on her turf, blew her horn at me; a monstrous dog, riding shotgun on the bed of a pickup truck, barked at me; a young man in a convertible winked at me; and finally, a farmer driving a plow at fifteen miles an hour happily waved me by.

Once again on the bike, I rode past the library, the newspaper office, the 1770 House Restaurant, the Osborne-Jackson House, now home to the East Hampton Historical Society, and finally up the Barretts' gently curving driveway. Several men tended the lawn, shrubs, and trees, now all at the height of fruition. Here, the sound of traffic was strangely muted, as if the idyllic setting refused to allow anything unnatural to infringe upon its domain.

One of Milly's young girls answered the door. I assured her I knew my way, and found Milly in the great room looking as pale as the white Norma Kamali print dress she wore. On the table beside her was a cup of tea and a bottle of rye whiskey. Catching my gaze, she quickly explained, "It's medicinal, Michael. I fainted at the Elvis."

Not knowing whether to laugh or console, I repeated, "At the Elvis?"

The Elvis, for those not familiar with East Hampton, is the Ladies' Village Improvement Society—LVIS when appearing in print, or simply the Elvis, colloquially. This society of formidable East Hampton dowagers is practically solely responsible for making and keeping East Hampton Village the pastoral gem of the Hamptons, or perhaps even all of America. The Brown House, their headquarters on Main Street, is a few opulent doors from Barrett House.

"Would you like a cup of tea?" Milly asked.

"Not laced with booze before noon," I answered.

"You might, after you hear what I have to say."

"Milly, what is it?"

"Sit down, Michael."

"I prefer to stand, thank you."

"If you enjoy falling from great heights, be my guest."

This chatter did nothing but accentuate Milly's agony. She was on the verge of tears, and if the dam overflowed it would not—judging from the sorry state of her eyes— be the first time today.

"You fainted in the Elvis," I prompted.

Milly sipped her tea. "If I had a cigarette, I would light it this very moment."

"You don't, and neither do I. You fainted at the Elvis, remember?"

"I was looking for a book," she stated. The Elvis thrift shop is noted for its fine and abundant used-book section. "Mark's gone to meet MJ at the airport."

"I know. Vicky recited the itinerary to me at breakfast."

She waved this aside, a gesture stating that my problem was insignificant compared to hers. "I don't expect them until dinnertime, so I went to the Elvis to find something to read. I was browsing when another woman came into the room. A young woman. And lovely, Michael. Oh, so lovely I had to restrain myself from staring. She was as poised and smartly dressed as a model in a magazine. A movie star, I thought. The town is suddenly filled with them." Milly drank more tea. I hoped it was moderately spiked.

"I kept glancing at her. Rude, but one does, you know. I was trying to place her from films or television. After a few minutes I noticed that she was staring at *me*." Milly had obviously replayed the scene in her mind again and again.

"Then, quite suddenly, she was approaching me, smiling, and a moment before I recognized her, Michael—a moment before—she said, 'Hello, Mother.'"

I sat. "But I thought—"

"Those old rumors," Milly interrupted, "that Mark paid her to stay away. We settled a monthly stipend on her when she said she wanted to remain in California, but she didn't sign a contract, for pity's sake. She was a high-spirited girl, Michael, with a father who didn't or wouldn't understand, and the victim of malicious gossip, most of it unfounded."

So, lovely Sarah had decided to give up her stipend for a summer in the Hamptons. Why all the fuss? Her father might not like it, but as Milly just said, the girl didn't sign a contract.

"I didn't know what to do," Milly continued, her eyes

brimming over. "'Is it you? Is it really you?' I said. Oh, Michael, how foolish I must have sounded."

This was all anticlimactic, to say the least. "Where's she staying?" I asked.

Milly named an acclaimed financial wizard whose home on Georgica Pond had become a tourist attraction and a bonanza for a guy who rented canoes to those who like to snoop on the rich and famous. Well, Sarah Barrett wasn't roughing it in a B&B with a blond surfer.

"'I've come home, Mother,'" Milly quoted verbatim, or so it sounded. "'We're renovating the old Beaumont house. I'm Mrs. Stephen Fletcher now.'"

Twenty-Seven

"I was stunned," Milly said, shaking her head. She spoke as if begging my indulgence. "Maybe paralyzed would be a more apt word. I didn't know what she was talking about. The name meant nothing, and then, quite suddenly, I remembered that I had heard it before. Here, at dinner, you told us who had bought the Beaumont house and that he was— Oh, Michael," she cried, "I didn't know what to say."

"Congratulations would have been nice," I blurted.

"That's unfair. *Unfair!*" Milly shouted, bringing a frustrated fist down upon her knee. "I was shocked at seeing Sarah, so confused, so overwhelmed. How can you think . . ." She burst into tears, burying her face in her hands, sobbing, abandoning all control.

I went to her and knelt. Placing my hand under her chin, I gently urged her to raise her head. Forced into making eye contact with me, she tried to break away, but I refused to yield and she surrendered, her blue eyes wide, her cheeks wet and shiny. "Forgive me, Milly. Please forgive me. Just shooting off my big mouth. You reacted the way anyone would, given the circumstances."

She leaned toward me and I felt her relax in the embrace of my arms. "I was shocked, Michael, shocked," she kept repeating. I patted her back reassuringly and rocked her, like a babe in arms. I felt her tremble, and thinking she was going to lapse once again into a crying jag, I squeezed her shoulder to steady her. But Milly wasn't crying. She was laughing. Like a child whose tears are forgotten by the promise of a new toy, she announced, "And then I fainted."

"At the Elvis," I said, relieved that her sense of humor had not gone the way of her composure. A moment before my comforting embrace gave way to embarrassment, I released my hold on her and retreated to my chair. "Did you hit the floor, Milly?" I asked along the way.

She shook her head. "No, thank God. My knees sort of buckled and Sarah put a firm grip to my elbow. You know, there isn't a chair in that damn place, Michael, except the ones on sale, and if you alight on one of those you own it."

"I hope the result of your folly wasn't the purchase of a bogus wing-back upholstered in hideous crewel."

"Worse," she moaned. "I commandeered Sis Parker's seat at the register."

"Sis Parker? I thought she was banished from the checkout. She once rang up fifteen hundred dollars for an ancient copy of *The Sun Also Rises*. I told her it was tagged two-fifty and she said the rest must be tax because the Democrats are in power, don't you know."

Milly laughed, blotting at her eyes with the back of her hand.

"How did it end, Milly? I mean, how did you get from the Brown House to here?"

"The way I got *there*. I walked. Sarah insisted I drive

with her, but I refused. She was in a little red sports car. Very expensive, I would imagine."

"Why, Milly? Why didn't you accept the ride? The truth."

"I'm not ashamed of my daughter, if that's what you're thinking. I fear for her."

"Mark?"

"Yes, Mark." Our moment of frivolity ended as abruptly as it had begun. "He was always a bit awkward with Sarah when she was little, and when MJ came along he practically ignored her. She grew up rebelling and refused to conform. East Hampton is a small town, as you very well know, and the Barretts are landed gentry. She did everything to embarrass her father and now . . ."

"The ultimate slap in the puss," I concluded. "Marriage to a black man. But a very rich one."

"Oh, Michael, what does the money matter? Mark will kill her. He will. He will kill her."

"Easy, Milly. Easy. Mark won't kill her." The sentiment wasn't as insipid as it sounded. Sarah's marriage was a fact. A *fait accompli*. Mark had nothing to gain by such an act except putting into headlines the very thing he wanted to suppress. If Mark retaliated it would be with a vengeance his daughter could appreciate in the here and now. He couldn't cut her off financially and he couldn't snub her socially. Stephen Fletcher was a frequent visitor at the White House and it was rumored he had gotten a certain duchess out of trouble, financially and otherwise, on more than one occasion. Even Buckingham Palace owed Stephen Fletcher.

"Once MJ was settled, I had planned to go to California to reconcile with Sarah," Milly said.

And there it was again. The blunt reminder that she intended to leave Mark in the very near future. Well, how nice for all concerned. Milly would have her children, her money, and her villa in Italy. Sarah would have her red sports car and her black husband. MJ would inherit Barrett House and all that went with it. The Reos and Mark Barrett were still unaccounted for in this wave of fortune's bounty.

I had paid my dues, lived up to my side of Joseph Kirkpatrick's stringent bargain, and for this I get a nomention in a will that devoted two pages to the care and feeding of the servants. Life was to begin when Kirk died. However, we had failed to notice that life was passing us by while we waited. Was it too late for Vicky and me? No. And now that a dialogue had opened between us, my optimism was based on more than just hope.

Was Milly still planning on retreating to Italy? I had never accepted or declined her invitation. In fact, the subject had never risen again since the night I announced that Fletcher had bought the Beaumont house. And hadn't that bit of news come full cycle? In the bright light of the next day, was Milly sorry she had made the offer, even if it was just a kind gesture to a guy feeling sorry for himself? I doubt Milly would risk endangering our special relationship by suggesting it was anything more than platonic.

Whatever, it would have to be addressed. Not to do so would be rude. But not now. There was too much uncertainty in both our lives to make plans beyond lunch tomorrow, and with both MJ's and Sarah's return, even tomorrow was open to speculation. Would any of this be happening if Kirk were still alive?

Thoughts must indeed have wings, because Milly suddenly lamented: "New Year's Eve, when Kirk fell over his dinner plate, was a harbinger, Michael. Like a curtain coming down on act two of our lives. One gets the feeling that nothing will ever be the same for any of us."

"It would make the old bastard happy to know he was still pulling the strings, posthumously."

We were silent for a while, perhaps out of respect for these weighty pronouncements. Milly broke the spell. "When the curtain goes up on act three," she said, "what will be revealed?"

I shrugged. "The script is still being written, or hadn't you noticed?"

"Ominous," Milly said. "Or, like a mystery writer's clue, meant to beguile?"

"When are you going to clue Mark in on the arrival of his daughter and son-in-law?"

She actually shivered. "I'm not."

"You're kidding?"

"Not tonight. MJ's first night home. I wanted everything to be perfect and it is going to be just that." Poor Milly. There was little conviction in that statement.

"You should have invited Sarah and made it a real family reunion. And don't be foolish, Milly, you have to tell Mark. The sooner the better. Sis Parker might not be able to add, but the only thing sharper than her eyes is her tongue. I bet she spotted Sarah before you did and was on the phone before the two of you were out the front door."

Milly nodded hypnotically, as if seeing in startling detail her confrontation with Mark. "Of course, I must tell him and MJ. I wish you could be with me when I do," she added.

So do I, I thought. Just for the pleasure of seeing Barrett's smug face get its comeuppance. The three banes of East Hampton society are Canadians, gays, and show folk. For the pure of heart, "Canadian" is the code word for Jew. It makes chatting in public places so much easier: "The town is filled with Canadians, my dear." Blacks are so far down the social scale they pose no threat, so can be treated with politically polite tolerance. But tolerance, especially when it's self-serving, has its limits and Sarah had exceeded that limit by megamiles.

It occurred to me that if I wanted to trip Barrett on his mad sprint for my wife, I couldn't have contrived a more potent diversion.

"If we hadn't met as we did, Sarah said, she was going to call this evening," Milly told me. "Imagine if she did, just as we were sitting down to dinner." The initial shock had passed and the chatter was now retrospective rather than narrative. "I told her we were expecting MJ this evening and that he was coming home to stay and prepare for the bar. We didn't discuss her father except for civilities—what a dreadful word when talking about family. She knows that Mark will be difficult. He always was, wasn't he? She never mentioned my embarrassing reaction except to make sure I was all right."

"And how did you leave it?" I asked.

"She gave me a phone number where I can reach her. I said I would call tomorrow. She's so poised, Michael. So sure of herself," Milly babbled, sounding like the proud parent of a precocious two-year-old. "I felt like a child and I suppose I acted like one. And beautiful. Did I tell you how beautiful my daughter is?"

"So is her mother."

"You won't get an argument from me."

"Did I hear the siren announcing high noon a while back?"

"You did."

"I'll have that drink now, Milly."

"Martini?"

"Bloody Mary."

Twenty-Eight

The Barretts' driveway is graded toward Main Street, so I was able to coast from the front door to the street. A bit unsteady, thanks to Milly's drink recipe that was more vodka than bloody, I approached Mark Barrett's office just as the front door of the converted carriage house flew open and a blond head thrust itself from the doorway. The scowl on the face below the golden mane expressed dissatisfaction with the services of Barrett and Barrett. The young man bounded onto the driveway without bothering to look right or left; I applied the hand brakes, but not in time to prevent my front wheel from hitting his leg.

"God damn!" he exclaimed.

Looking directly into Pretty Boy's face, I could do little more than gape in stunned silence.

"You all right?" he asked, thinking, I'm sure, that our collision had brought on a stroke in an old fart who shouldn't be on a bike in the first place.

I nodded. While I could think lucidly, I was finding it difficult to speak. Perhaps I *was* in the throes of a stroke.

He was about to continue down the drive when he turned and, placing his hand on the offensive front wheel of my bike, asked, "You been at the house?"

"Yes." I didn't recognize my voice, but then I so seldom hear it in competition with the beat of my heart. I was also conscious of the pulse in my forehead. Specifically, the left side. Definitely a stroke.

"Is Mr. Barrett home?"

"No." Why was he questioning me about what was clearly not his business? "I believe he's gone to the city." And why was I answering? I couldn't have been more at his mercy if he held a gun to my head.

He eyed me with a menacing squint—to see if I was dying or lying? Nodding toward the office, he stated, "That's what she said," and appeared satisfied with the corroboration.

He turned once again and this time walked smartly down the driveway, head high, shoulders squared, and tight-assed.

I watched until he walked off the property and disappeared up Main Street. I pulled a handkerchief from my back pocket and wiped my forehead. My shirt was so damp it clung to my back. When I got off the bike I didn't think my legs would support me, but determination overcame trepidation. I engaged the kickstand and went into the offices of Barrett and Barrett, the door left ajar by their last visitor.

"Hello, Mr. Reo." Susan looked up from the keyboard of her computer to greet me. She was a pleasant-looking girl, not more than nineteen or twenty I would say, with brown hair, eyes to match, and a figure that had not been a hindrance in getting her the plum job of private secretary to Mark Barrett.

"Mr. Barrett's not here today," she informed me before I asked. "Neither is your wife," remained unspoken.

"I know, I've been visiting with Mrs. Barrett." Might

as well tell the truth—thanks to Milly's copious staff, in and out, Barrett House was as private as a fishbowl. "I almost ran over a young man as I came down the drive. Who is he? If it's none of my business, just say so."

She blushed, misinterpreting my curiosity as I'd intended, to throw her off the scent. How easily one can slip into a spying mode when one's peace of mind—if not life—is at stake.

"Galen didn't come to see me, Mr. Reo."

Galen! Not an easy name to forget, and I was certain I had heard it before.

"He's been pestering Mr. Barrett for the past few weeks. First on the phone and now in person. he's a nuisance, but harmless." Her fingers tugged the tiny gold cross suspended from a delicate chain that hung between the modest cleavage her blouse exposed. A rather cute nuisance, if body language did indeed mirror our thoughts.

"Is he a client?"

She laughed at what appeared to be my naïveté regarding the caliber of Mark Barrett's clientele. "Hardly. I think he wants to enlist Mr. Barrett's help on behalf of his father."

"Isn't his father able to speak for himself?"

Again the patronizing smile. "His father is . . ." She hesitated before asking, "What's the polite term for town drunk?"

"Try town drunk," I advised.

She leaned across her desk conspiratorially, anxious to tell all she knew and screw semantics. "Les Miller, Galen's father, is always in trouble. Mostly DWIs and disorderly conduct in public places, like bars and liquor stores that refuse him credit. When Galen began calling I thought it was because Les needed a lawyer for the usual reason. Most of the lawyers in town who handle that sort of thing have given up on Les because he can't afford their fees. Mr. Barrett, of course, would never consider representing Les Miller. We don't do that sort of thing."

Of course, I silently agreed, helping poor people in need must not interfere with helping rich people in need. The poor will always be with us, while a Victoria Kirkpatrick comes along once in a lifetime.

"But when I read about Galen's stepmother, I knew that's why he wanted to see Mr. Barrett, although I don't know why he thinks Mr. Barrett can help."

Stepmother? "You say Galen has a stepmother?"

Susan couldn't have been more delighted with the question, and plunged right in. The only thing lacking in her performance was a microphone. It seems this Galen's father had gone to Florida last spring and come back with a wife. Words like young, pretty, smart dresser flowed from Susan's lips. "And a fur coat. Real mink, according to Ida."

I racked my brain but could not place Ida in the world of haute couture. Seeing my dismay, Susan explained that Ida was a domestic at Gurney's Inn, where the bride resided, sans bridegroom, while waiting for her furniture to arrive from Florida. Ida's daughter cleaned for Susan's mother, hence the real mink coat connection.

"Why would this woman want to marry the town drunk?" I asked, hoping to inject reality into what was beginning to sound more like hearsay than fact.

The question prompted Susan to tug on her gold cross until I thought she would succeed in tearing it from its chain. "Well," she said coyly, a delivery that must have driven the little boys of East Hampton High wild, "they say Les Miller always had a way with women, if you know what I mean."

I didn't, but I figured the better part of valor was to admit it. "You said you read about Galen's stepmother. Do you mean a wedding announcement?"

"Oh no!" Susan cried. "Didn't you read about it in the *Star* about a month ago?"

The only thing I read in the *Star* is the weekly column titled "The Way It Was (in East Hampton) . . . 100 Years Ago, 75 Years Ago, 50 Years Ago, and 25 Years Ago." A bit of nostalgia that reassures the reader that (in East Hampton) that's the way it still is. "I must have missed it," I said. A wave of anxiety, like a nudge from a part of my brain that was beginning to add two and two, swept over me.

"She's gone missing," Susan cried. "She went to a Wednesday matinee in the city and never returned."

"Wednesday?" I felt my bowels loosen. Was this really happening? "Do you mind if I sit, Susan?"

"Of course. Please. Are you all right, Mr. Reo?"

That was the second time in five minutes I had been asked that question. I wanted to shout, "NO, I'M NOT ALL RIGHT. I think I know where that wretched boy's stepmother can be found and I am on speaking terms with her murderer."

"I'm fine, Susan. Fine. Just want to sit a moment. Must be the heat."

"The air conditioner is on high, Mr. Reo."

I sank into a Windsor chair of great value as I coped with my second stroke of the day. "You did say Wednesday?"

Susan was so enthralled with imparting the mystery of Galen's missing stepmother that she never noticed my reaction to the story. As she spoke of Wednesday matinees, a luxury car, closets full of expensive clothing, I saw the lovers once again through my binoculars: the boy called Galen and his stepmother. There she was, leaning back in the ancient boat, one finger trailing in the cool water, the brown nipples of her breasts shiny in the bright sun. And there he was, her naked gondolier standing to guide the craft to the center of the lake, his blond pubic hair invisible in the glare of sunlight on still water, resembling a lewd drawing of a prepubescent boy endowed with a man's genitals. I heard her scream as the boat capsized. Did she scream? Or had I added a sound track to a silent film?

"Do you think she left him?" Susan asked in conclusion. "Just like that?"

I stood. "I think I'd better get home or my wife will wonder if I left *her.*" I had to escape before I exploded. "MJ will be home tonight," I added as I made for the door.

Again a blush and a tug at the gold cross. So, sweet Sue had pretensions. I must remember to tell MJ. This could be the answer to his problem, if the problem still existed. With the very young, one never knew. She wasn't of the blood, but between his Barrett father and Stiles mother, MJ had blood to spare and then some.

"He'll be working with us," Susan proudly announced.

"Can you handle both of 'em?" I asked, my tone rife with innuendo. With a wave of my hand I was out the door before the poor girl strangled herself with Christ's burden.

I walked my bike back to Dunemere Lane, fearing I would wind up on my ass—or worse—if I tried to pedal, navigate, and think at the same time. The traffic on Main

Street had not abated and I could see people strolling and window-shopping along the business district east of Barrett House.

Galen Miller. Calmer, and away from Susan's gaze, I concentrated on recalling where I had heard the name, and came up with the answer before reaching home. At the Barretts', the same night Milly had first heard the name Stephen Fletcher. Who would have thought that the evening's innocuous banter was a prelude to today's momentous bombshells?

Galen Miller. Having been preoccupied with the wanton condition of Mark Barrett's fly (oh, I haven't forgotten), I have no idea why the boy was being discussed by my hosts, but there was now no doubt that he was known to Mark and Milly. According to Susan, Galen was in hot pursuit of Mark Barrett. Why? Not on his father's behalf, as Susan believed. Did the boy want to confess and elicit Mark's help? Mark wasn't a criminal lawyer, or would that fact be lost on Galen Miller? He didn't appear retarded. On the contrary, he had street smarts written all over that pretty face. There must be some other connection between him and Mark Barrett, judging from the boy's relentless pursuit.

Why confess? Except for me, he was home free, and I was now sure that Galen Miller had no idea that I was witness to his crime. If he did, he was the coolest murderer to come down the pike since Cain. Also, I now knew why the two caroused on Wednesdays and the identity of the lady under the lake.

All the pieces of the puzzle were in place except for one glaring gap in the center: Why did Galen Miller kill his stepmother? Perhaps the cause, not the crime, was the reason Galen wanted to see a lawyer. Specifically Mark

Barrett, Esq. As I pushed my bike up our circular driveway, I thought it might be prudent to learn the answer.
For this, only Galen Miller could help me, and I had a
strong suspicion our paths would cross again. In fact, the
kid kept popping up with the regularity of a bill collector
and was just as welcome.

So, we could add miscegenation, incest, and matricide
to our list of things to do in the Hamptons. I wondered if
they were faring any better in Newport.

Twenty-Nine

That evening I had recovered sufficiently to take Vicky to Gordon's for dinner. It was our first night out in public since her father's death, and because Gordon's was the only restaurant Kirk patronized—outside of the Club of course—I thought it fitting for the occasion. Located in Amagansett, Gordon's is East Hampton's premier bistro, a fact happily known only to those whose names appear in print when they're born, when they marry, and when they die. George, the owner/chef, is uncompromisingly professional when wearing either hat. We were seated in the corner banquette, adjacent to the small bar, where one enjoys a commanding view of the entire room and comparative privacy at the same time. At Gordon's, nothing is left to chance.

The dinner date, while welcome, should not be construed as indicative of an end to the war of the Reos, but rather as a sign that a truce had been called due to the extraordinary developments in the camp of Vicky's ally and my adversary. Our breakfast chat had opened a dialogue, as they say, and we both now knew where we were coming from, if not where we were going. I hoped dinner, outside the Dunemere Lane house and its memories, would point us in the right direction.

Vicky couldn't get enough of the news of Sarah's return as Mrs. Stephen Fletcher. I suggested we dine out, away from the ears of John and Maddy, if we wanted to gossip. Vicky agreed that the corner banquette at Gordon's was the last of the "unwired spots" in East Hampton; hence the evening found us indulging in George's superb mussels along with a very fine pinot grigio and the promise of the veal chops to come, while lamenting Mark and Milly's dilemma. I'll spare you the "one man's meat" line.

"Do you think she married him to embarrass her father?" Vicky, wearing a white skirt and a very tailored navy blue blazer questioned Sarah Barrett's choice of mate.

"That's what everyone will think, unfortunately, and no one, me excepted, will hope she married for love."

"You sound like Father," Vicky exclaimed.

Was that a compliment or a death blow? Then I recalled that not only had Joseph Kirkpatrick supported the civil rights movement both editorially and financially, but at his insistence, WMET was the first network to run a black sitcom and the first to feature blacks and women as staples of the six o'clock news. "Kirk was color-blind, I'll say that for him."

Vicky waited until our waiter withdrew after refilling our wineglasses before she answered: "I wonder how color-blind he would have been had I married a black man."

"So you married me. Half wop, half mick, and he wasn't happy about that."

"Your mixed blood didn't bother Father. Your good looks and vanity did."

"I am not vain."

"Michael, you are the most narcissistic man I know."

"But that's only because I have every right to be."

She laughed. A sound I had not heard since the start of the new year. "You've got an Irish tongue," Vicky said.

"And an Italian stomach," I reminded her as the bus-person removed our mountain of black mussel shells to make room for the veal chops.

"Will Milly have them to dinner?" Vicky wondered aloud, prompted perhaps by the meal now spread before us. Was she enjoying Milly Barrett's plight? Or do we all, no exceptions, take a sadistic pleasure in another's troubles? Why else were disaster films so popular? We seem to love watching others suffer from a safe distance while munching on buttered popcorn in a plush velour seat.

As stated, there has never been any love lost between my wife and my ladyfriend. Milly, a true thoroughbred, had little time for pretense, and Vicky, especially in her youth, was as guilty of that as I was of vanity. What a pair. And, Vicky was always a little jealous of my friendship with Milly. Was retaliation a factor in her attraction for Mark Barrett?

"She told me this afternoon she intends to give a reception for the newlyweds."

Vicky, fork poised between plate and mouth, appeared either startled or impressed. "At Barrett House?"

"Where else?"

"The Club," came her expected answer.

"You're kidding. Milly wants to give a party, not start a revolution." Catching Billy's eye as he sauntered past our table toting a tray full of drinks, I drew his attention to our now empty wine bottle. Billy is George's brother and works the room in whatever capacity the moment demands, from bartender to maître d' and all stops between. The brothers are from Greece, and in the old days Vicky and I referred to them as "the Boys from Syracuse" before plunging into any one of the memorable Rodgers and Hart songs from that show. Oh, we used to have fun, and hopefully the best is yet to come. Hopefully.

"Besides," I went on, "at the Club there would be more gawkers than guests. I think it's going to be a very small affair. Strictly the crème de la crème."

"That lets us out."

"Speak for yourself, lady."

Pressed for time, and because it was our second bottle, Billy spared us the ritual of my tasting the wine before our glasses were replenished. "It's good to see you again, and our condolences to you and Mrs. Reo," Billy offered.

"Thank you, Billy," Vicky answered for me. "It's a pleasure to be back."

When Billy retreated, Vicky prophesied, "The *Star* will report the reception with relish and the world will know."

I put down my knife and fork and picked up my wineglass. "Vicky, wake up. When the *Star* comes out on Thursday, everyone will know. They didn't report the sale of the Beaumont house to Fletcher, either because they didn't know about it or didn't care if they did. But when they find out he's married to a Barrett, especially *that* Barrett, they'll headline the sale and the nuptials."

"But does anyone know besides Milly?"

"By now, Mark and MJ know." I wondered how poor Milly was faring. "And Sis Parker must have guessed who Sarah was and wondered at Milly's reaction to her daughter's homecoming."

"She fainted at the Elvis," Vicky said, as if I didn't know. "No one has ever fainted at the Elvis. It's an all-time first."

"There's a rumor that a hundred years back someone discovered a headless corpse in the Brown House. Whoever found it might have fainted. And don't forget who Sarah is staying with. That guy in Georgica who has more money than you. He's got a big mouth and loves to see his name in the newspapers. He's not going to let house-guests like Stephen Fletcher and wife go unnoticed."

Vicky put a finger to her lips before pointing. "He's sitting right there."

"With the blonde?"

"That's him."

"Is she his wife?"

"I hope so."

With our coffee, Billy offered dessert and a complimentary Remy. We declined the *dolce* but it would have been rude not to accept the brandy. "I enjoyed this very much," I said in lieu of a toast.

"So did I. It was a good choice. Father always liked it here."

A moment of silence seemed to be called for at this juncture and I respected it. Thankfully, Vicky wasn't teary. In fact, she appeared more content than I'd seen her in weeks. The effects of a satisfying meal and the vintage beverages or the company? This morning she had confessed to feeling confused and frightened. A bold admission for my wife. It was my job and intention to enlighten and protect her. Therefore, it would never do to admit to a similar state of mind. We had enough to sort out without making the Incident a part of our marital woes. Having been in the spotlight since birth, Vicky would understand, I think, why I didn't go directly to the police. I also hoped she would fear for my safety. What I didn't need was for her to suggest I speak to a lawyer, even though it was her lawyer, paradoxically, who could tell me what I wanted to know.

Taking advantage of our reflective mood and the familiar ambiance, I thought it might be the right moment to find out what Vicky remembered about the name Galen Miller without arousing suspicion.

"Do you recall the last time we dined with Mark and Milly?" I asked. "Shortly after Kirk's funeral."

Did I see the faintest flush to her cheeks, or was it the light in the crowded room? She nodded. "Yes. It was the night you told us Stephen Fletcher bought the old Beaumont place."

"Am I imagining it or did the name Galen Miller also pop up that evening?"

Vicky gave this some thought and then answered, "Yes, it did. That lovely name. Hard to forget."

"Do you remember why he was discussed?"

Again, the pensive look. Vicky shook her head. "He wanted to see Mark, I think. He'd been pestering Susan for an appointment, or something like that. Why the sudden interest in Galen Miller?"

"I ran into him this afternoon, after leaving Milly. He came storming out of Mark's office. It seems he's still trying to get that appointment."

"How did you know who he was?"

Gross error. "I didn't. I literally ran into him—I was on my bike—and he assumed an attitude. I went into the office and asked Susan if she knew him."

"Did she say why he wanted to see Mark?"

I shrugged and signaled the waiter for our check. I had already said too much, and the longer we stayed on the subject the harder it would be to conceal my interest. "Something about his father and his stepmother who has flown the coop."

"Yes," Vicky said. "Now I remember. His father is a dipsomaniac and his mother—his natural mother, that is—used to work for Milly. A local family. What's the boy like?"

"Too handsome for his own good, I'm afraid. The kind of good looks that make one soar or get stuck in the mire." Bad choice of metaphor, I lamented, signing the check with a flourish.

Thirty

It was raining when we left the restaurant, reminiscent of the night of Kirk's funeral. Leaving Amagansett, I drove past The Stephen Talkhouse, the Amagansett club that showcases a potpourri of musical talent, ablaze with its facade of Christmas lights spilling over the crowd of young people queuing up for the late show. Gordon's and the Talkhouse are the bookends that flank the shops lining Amagansett's two-block stretch of commercial real estate.

Arriving on Dunemere Lane, I parked the Rolls at the front door, leaving it for John to deal with in the morning. Like me, he enjoyed driving the Rolls. The house was lit but depressingly quiet. I took off my jacket and Vicky removed her high heels before volunteering to make us coffee. I went into the den and opened the doors leading to the patio. The gentle rain was fast turning into a summer thunderstorm, again reminiscent of the night of the funeral. As I stepped outdoors I glimpsed a streak of lightning illuminate the sky over the Atlantic.

Protected by the patio's canvas awning, I sank into a deck chair. The rain had brought the long-awaited relief from the blistering heat of this August day, and when the wind kicked up I was anointed with a welcoming spray of cool rainwater. Content, and slightly soused, I closed my eyes and played the "if only" game.

If only I had never heard of Two Holes of Water Road.

If only I had minded my own business and not gone into Mark's office to pump Susan.

If only Vicky had turned to me when Kirk died.

If only Mark Barrett would disappear.

If—

"Only milk. No sugar," Vicky announced, carrying two cups with saucers onto the patio. "Not too cold out here?"

"Not cold enough," I said, taking both cups from her and placing them on one of the white cubes that serve as end tables for the patio furniture. Vicky stretched out in the chair on the other side of the cube. Stockingless, she wiggled her toes as they caught a spray of rain. I noticed that her toenails were not painted. Vicky had shed all her veneer. Shed? If only I hadn't made that astute observation.

"Reminds me of Cortina," I said, "remember? It was supposed to snow and it rained for three days."

"What were we doing in Cortina?" Vicky wondered aloud.

"The Burtons were giving a party. How lovely she was. I was fascinated by his pockmarks."

"I thought they made him look sexy."

"So did his wife, I guess."

"Why were we invited?" Vicky asked.

"Kirk, I'm sure. They were looking for backers for yet another of their forgettable epics."

"Father—always Father. Do you think we would have

been invited anyplace if I wasn't Joseph Kirkpatrick's daughter?"

"Certainly not, and why should we?"

"We were half of an attractive couple." She spoke in a tone usually reserved for more joyous reflection. "Cutiē and Croesus. Wasn't that our epithet?"

I wasn't looking at her but I could imagine her smile as she spoke. The label, whispered behind our backs and more than once blind-itemed in some lurid tabloid, always made us laugh. For the first time I wondered if Vicky's laughter was meant to hide her tears. How odd. So many "first times" for a couple married twenty years. If we were ever to make love again, would that too be like the first time? If so, it was something to look forward to. I felt a stirring in my groin and wondered what Vicky was thinking. Like old times, I thought wistfully.

"In case you haven't noticed, you've taken on both titles, even if I wasn't consulted regarding the new look," I said.

"I'm glad you approve and—on that subject—I doubt if I'll ever again need to consult with you or anyone regarding such momentous decisions."

I wasn't aware that we were on any particular subject and I refrained from asking if Mark Barrett was included in that sweeping statement. "Kirk's passing has unleashed a fury. Why am I reminded of any number of Bette Davis films?"

This got a laugh, as intended. "You and your movies." Then, after a short pause: "Passing. What a strange word for dying. We know where we pass from but not where we pass to. And don't kid yourself, Michael. Father will always be with us."

On that profound note we sipped our coffee and

watched nature's fire-and-water display. I could sense Vicky fidgeting next to me, and fearing she would flee before anything was settled between us, however tentative, I sighed contentedly and said, "A cigarette would turn mere bliss into ecstasy."

"Strange, I was thinking the same thing."

She produced her Marlboros and handed me her lighter. I could feel the tension subside as she drew on the flame I offered before lighting my own. I imagined the glow of our cigarette tips would resemble a pair of fireflies on a seesaw if seen from the south windows of John and Maddy's accommodations over the garage. Looking up, I noted that their lights were still on. "Waiting up for us, do you suppose?"

"Or watching themselves on the telly," Vicky replied.

"What?"

Vicky, puffing contentedly, expounded, "Promise you won't repeat this, but they taped the WMET news broadcast the night of Father's funeral. We're all in it, I guess."

So is someone else. Damn Galen. Out of sight did not mean out of mind with that boy. "Did Maddy tell you this?"

"No, Mark did. Annie, the Barretts' cook, said she had seen the funeral on the late news that night and when Mark said he had missed it, she told him John had made a copy."

"Everyone is entitled to their fifteen minutes of fame," I philosophized.

"Some of us were overblessed."

Did I detect a slight whine in her voice? The poor put-upon Victoria syndrome? Not all traces of the old Vicky had passed along with Kirk, but then I never expected they would. Thirty-nine years are not totally obliterated in thirty-nine days.

"Oh, come on now, it wasn't all that bad," I told my wife. "The Golden Princess was the envy of many a little girl. Still is, I'm sure."

"Envy is the seed of malice, as in gossip. Everything I did was scrutinized under a microscope and came up bigger and nastier than the true picture."

"I never believed—"

"Yes, you did." An octave higher and it would have been a shout. Was I destined to have a lifetime of suppressed resentment thrown in my face every time I touched the wrong nerve? "So did Father," she added. "I had my share of affairs, but not any more than other so-called debs at that time. Thanks to the Kirkpatrick name, a goodnight kiss became an orgy over the morning coffee."

While venting was good for the soul, carried to extremes it could prove dangerous, like a third-world nation suddenly in possession of an arsenal of atom bombs and hell-bent on revenge for past grievances, real or imagined. As the thunder subsided to a less threatening rumble, Vicky's lament seemed to take up the slack. "Father didn't agree to our marriage as a means of salvaging my reputation. The bottom line was that he didn't give a damn what others thought. If you were the answer to a maiden's prayer, you were also the answer to my father's quest. Oh, he wanted to see me married, but to a son-in-law he could manipulate. Your looks, your passion for show business made Daddy certain you would not make any waves and threaten your place next to the throne. To put it more dramatically, Daddy worked the spotlight we paraded under. One false step and the light would go out.

"Following the ceremony, he took the bride and groom from the top of the wedding cake and put them in a cage where, for the next twenty years, we obediently sang for our supper. I hoped, one day, you would be the breadwinner. I was wrong."

"I didn't make any waves because I didn't want to estrange you and your father." The gift of the goddamned Magi. The stuff of romance novels. "I thought you loved your father, Vicky."

"I do. I did. But I wanted him to reciprocate in kind, not with pride of ownership. His creation. His Golden Princess." She stubbed her cigarette into the ashtray with a series of quick, forceful jabs. I reached for her hand. It was cold and unresponsive. The rain had stopped and so too the breeze that had accompanied it. The moist air would soon turn to steam.

"I proposed to you, not to your father. Why did you accept?"

"Because I loved you. Because I wanted you desperately. And since I was used to getting what I wanted, I didn't care that you were using me."

"I had my dreams . . ."

"And you believed my father could make those dreams come true."

"I admit I thought Kirk would help me pursue a career. When he made it clear he wouldn't and read me his terms, I accepted them because I didn't want to put you in the position of having to choose between your father and me and a future that was uncertain, to say the least."

"Would you have married me if Father had read you his terms, as you put it, before we were married?"

"You're asking me to turn the clock back twenty years and see into the past. That view can be as foggy as gazing into a crystal ball. I was young, impetuous, and in love. Yes, I was. I would probably have told him to go screw himself, and for that bit of bravado I would have lost you."

She removed her hand from my grip and lit another cigarette. Mine was burned down to the filter. I flicked it onto the lawn, where a mist now rose from the wet grass. In the distance the dull roll of the surf came to us, carried on the still, night air.

"You're right," she replied, softly. So softly she could have been talking to herself. "I wouldn't have married you if Father hadn't given his consent." I knew the emotional toll the admission had extracted and admired her courage. I reached for her hand again, but it was busy transporting the adult pacifier to her lips.

Instead, I offered a bit of solace. "He knew that. So he read me the riot act after the fact to be sure you got what you wanted."

She was crying, brushing the tears with the back of her hand. "What I wanted or what I deserved?"

That did it. I sat up in the recliner, placing my two feet firmly on the ground, and faced Vicky across the white cube. "If you got what you deserved, then you deserved the best, because that's what I gave you. The best I had to offer, and I never disappointed."

"You strayed," she accused.

"Not so anyone ever noticed." If this was the moment of truth, I wasn't going to play the prude.

"Milly." She spoke the name as if addressing the person.

"Milly and I are friends. Nothing more. And you know that."

She smoked in silence, staring into the night. The

storm had passed and as the black clouds withdrew the tall oaks and maples that graced our backyard became visible, their leaves shiny with moisture.

"Did you ever wonder why we never had children?"

"Often," I answered.

"And blamed Father, somehow, for my barrenness."

"It crossed my mind."

She shook her head. "I never did anything to prevent a pregnancy and Father never mentioned the subject. We didn't have children because we were children."

"Are you saying we weren't blessed because we were naughty?"

"I think we *were* blessed. Imagine the mess we'd be in now if we had children to consider."

"We have ourselves to consider and that's all that matters."

Another half-smoked cigarette got pounded into the ashtray. "We should have had this conversation twenty years ago."

"We're having it now, Vicky."

"Now is too late."

"It is not," I pleaded. "Kirk is gone. The cage door is open. Let's fly off together and become the people we might have been if you weren't Joseph Kirkpatrick's daughter."

"But I am his daughter and always will be."

"Then let's use that legacy to strengthen our marriage, not destroy it. Together we can put the Kirkpatrick name back where it belongs: in lights."

"Father was considered redundant, remember."

"We're not your father, Vicky. We're us and we can do it. Do you remember my suggesting a production company under the Kirkpatrick logo?"

"Of course. I've discussed the possibility with Mark."

I wanted to pull her out of that deck chair and shake some sense into that blond head. Instead I asked, "And what does he think?"

"He likes the idea and so did Father."

"Kirk never told me he liked it."

"Daddy thought you were . . ." She searched for the right word and found it. "Frivolous."

"It was the role he assigned me and the one I played to keep the spotlight from going out. Remember? And it was my idea, for Christ's sake. I have forgotten more about the entertainment industry than Barrett ever knew. It's me you should be consulting, not your lawyer."

"Mark has asked me to marry him."

The words struck like a knife between my shoulder blades. The confession wasn't totally unexpected, but that didn't ease the pain. "Jesus Christ, the guy is married and so are you."

"He and Milly never had a real marriage."

"Because he couldn't keep it in his pants, that's why. What's he putting up as his share of the production company? His dick?"

"You're incorrigible, Michael."

"And you're blind, Victoria. Kirk bowed out of the business without a fight because he knew the ground rules were changing and he was too old to learn a new game. He could have kept the Japanese at arm's length, for a while, but chose not to because it was time to fold his tent and bail out with a platinum parachute. The worlds of communication and entertainment are in a state of flux—satellites, saucers, web sites, ROMs, digital equipment. The future belongs to the young and the bold.

The Joseph Kirkpatricks of the next century. Mark Barrett is not among them."

"And you are?"

"Yes, damn it, I am. Let me prove it, Vicky."

I rose and went to her, extending my hand. She took it and I gently helped her out of the lounge chair. We looked at each other for a good half minute before I took her in my arms. She didn't protest. I kissed her with passion, my arousal unmistakably in evidence. Her arms clasped my neck and her lips parted to my probing tongue. I withdrew long enough to whisper her name, "Vicky."

Her hand caressed my swollen flesh. "Is this how you intend to prove yourself?"

I covered her hand with mine. "With this, I already have. The rest will take time."

"I'm short on time," she said, the pressure of her hand making her meaning implicitly clear.

"Should I sweep you off your feet and carry you up to the bedroom or ravish you here?"

She answered by unzipping the fly of my trousers.

I lifted her skirt and pushed aside the crotch of her panties. She was moist, ready. I dropped to my knees, bringing the white nylon undergarment with me. I kissed her again.

"Michael!" she screamed. "Oh, Michael."

Thirty-One

MJ Barrett had begun his campaign to seduce me when he was twelve and twelve years later was still at it. For ten of those dozen years, Vicky and I were often abroad, making fools of ourselves in watering holes from Ascot to Zanzibar and thereby seriously curtailing MJ's campaign. The boy's attraction was no doubt prompted by the fact that he knew, as children know, that he and I were aliens in a society that frowned on strangers. Kindred souls, as it were.

Not being a pederast, thank heavens, I found the handsome little minx easy to resist. When he became legal, I was far too fond of him (and his mother) to allow any such thing to spoil my relationship with either of them. Still, MJ never missed a chance to put me in a compromising situation—hence his refusal to shower at the Club after our tennis date and insistence on driving us to his convenient oceanfront apartment to perform our ablutions. The apartment, need I add, was in one of his father's motel-to-condo conversions in Amagansett.

When MJ's father flaunted his pedigree, MJ's sexual persuasion became my ace in the hole. A card I could play when Barrett senior announced, presumably without malicious intent, "I told that wop mechanic that a Jaguar—I'm sorry, Mike. No offense, I hope. Just a figure of speech."

"Not at all, Mark. By the by, did you know MJ was a cocksucker? No offense, I hope. Just a figure of speech."

I could, but I never did. However, knowing I could was my invisible shield. My stiletto poised at Mark Barrett's heart. The fact that MJ was gay would not mortify Mark, but the fact that it was common knowledge would. The Club had its share of gentlemen who dabbled in what used to be called "forbidden fruit," and it was tolerated as long as it remained something one did in the dark.

But today, MJ had announced that he was going to "come out" to his parents and, presumably, to the world, and the devil take the hindmost. The love that dares not speak its name was entering the new millennium with its tongue wagging, and I for one heartily approved. However, this left my ace in the hole looking more like a deuce and my stiletto as lethal as a long-stemmed lily. Add to this—Lord forbid I should forget it—there was that woman rotting under a hole of water and her murderer on the prowl to be dealt with.

I was consoled by the fact that in my ongoing match with Mark Barrett I had won every round, proving the better man with his wife, his son, and the precious members of his precious Club. I enjoyed the game when it didn't bore me because Mark Barrett and his ilk are as innocuous as an ant at a picnic. But now this pest had overstepped his bounds and was threatening to walk away with the entire feast—my wife and her fortune. Vicky and I were only just recently reconciled and one night of passion does not a marriage make. Mark Barrett still had to be stopped.

We literally raced east on Further Lane in MJ's silver Mercedes convertible under a cloudless sky, the sun fast sinking behind us and an ocean breeze confronting us. In our tennis whites, we were the quintessential East Hamptonites, having fun. And please note our polo shirts, distinctive for their lack of circus animals stitched over the left breast. As the Good Book says: To those who have it shall be added and to those who have not, crocodiles and polo ponies will not help.

MJ had the Barretts' straight black hair and his mother's blue eyes. We could have passed for brothers, I like to think, but father and son was more likely. MJ was shorter than his father, not quite six feet, but handsomely proportioned and blessed with a smile that was beguiling and a manner that was a paradigm of manly grace. (Poor Susan. Poor all the Susans of this world.)

Home less than a week, MJ was already up-to-date on all the latest East Hampton gossip and eager to pass it on. As we turned onto Bluff Road in Amagansett, MJ divulged the story of a renowned singer/actress who had turned down an honest offer from her handsome actor/lover because the gent refused to have his au naturel appendage circumcised to please her. This, of course, did not excuse the lady from seeking consolation in the arms and bed of Seventh Avenue's wunderkind who was, of all things, a "designing woman."

"I don't believe a word of it," I said.

"But it's the rumor-of-the-week," MJ insisted, turning into the parking lot that fronted the ex-motel, "which in this town is like religion. You don't have to believe to participate." He removed the key from the ignition and placed it, and his hand, on my bare knee. "Do you know them?"

"Who?"

"The rumor-of-the-week couple."

"Of course not."

"I thought you and Vicky knew everyone."

"We know everyone that counts, MJ. There's a difference. And if you move your hand an inch higher, I'll scream."

"You sound like a virgin on her first date."

"You act like one."

"Ouch!"

I stood under the gleaming chrome showerhead, turning my face upward into the liquid needles in an attempt to cool my fevered brain. It didn't work. To compensate, I was generous with MJ's expensive soap, turning the stall into a perfume factory. The bathroom window of the corner suite afforded a clear view of the ocean beyond a stretch of white sand that was the condo's beach. Indeed, all the windows of the desirable units faced the ocean, with a deck or terrace running the length of the apartment. After rinsing off, I wrapped a towel around my middle and stepped into MJ's bedroom.

Having showered first, MJ was stretched out on his bed, air-drying as he called it, wearing a smile and little else. As I entered, he sat up, planting his feet firmly on the carpeted floor, and instead of reaching for his shorts, he rose and asked, "Would you like some juice?"

"With a dash of vodka, thank you. I'm not a health nut."

"It shows."

"Fuck you."

"Finally, a proposal."

"The juice, MJ. Now."

I helped myself to a cigarette from a pack he kept on

his dresser. These were not for himself, but for the occasional guest who might desire something more bracing than sea air.

"Those will kill you," he said, returning with two glasses of juice. Grapefruit was my educated guess.

"Not as readily as your disclosure to Daddy dearest." MJ knew there was no love lost between his father and me. But did he know Mark was ready to leave the nest for greener pastures? If not, he wouldn't hear it from me because I hoped to prevent it from ever happening. How? I hadn't a clue. "Are you going to issue your coming-out proclamation at dinner, or post a notice on the bulletin board at the Club?"

"Neither, but I went to the airport party last Saturday night with a date and I imagine that was last week's rumor-of-the-week."

I took my street clothes from the tote bag I had carried with me and stuffed it with my Jockeys, tennis shorts, polo shirt, and socks. I removed the towel and stepped into my clean shorts. "If an airport party is the jet set's version of an old-fashioned bon voyage, it might have been prudent to jump aboard—with your date."

MJ was back on the bed, stacking the pillows for a headrest. He balanced his cold juice glass on his naked belly, threatening to deluge a masculine extremity that would surely please the aforementioned actress. "The airport party," he lectured, "has become the social event of Gayhampton. It's held in a hangar at the East Hampton Airport as a fund-raiser for an AIDS support group here on the island. It draws a lot of big names, gay women of course, and a thousand gay men."

"A thousand gay men in one hangar? I hope you kept your back to the wall." I put on my shirt. "If it's a benefit, you could pretend to be there as a supporter of the group and not a member of the Club."

"You mean play the game? Get married to our Susan? I'd die of saccharine poisoning. Move into an overpriced cottage on Lily Pond Lane, father two-point-five children, spend a lot of time in New York on business, and take a special interest in intramural sports at the high school."

Picking up my jeans, I answered, "You wouldn't be the first."

"Sorry, Mike, but I can't play both sides of the fence."

"Then you're missing half of nature's bounty." I put on the jeans.

"Half is the operative word." Hell having no fury like a gay man with a cause, MJ spoke like a zealot. "The trouble with bisexuals is that they know a little bit about a lot of things and a whole lot about nothing."

"Strange, I remember when sex between consenting adults was less pedantic but a hell of a lot more fun."

Ignoring this, MJ continued to impart his plans for the future. "Next year I'm thinking of offering Barrett House for the Pride party."

I sipped my juice, which was well laced with firewater. One thing about the Barrett clan, they knew how to make a drink. "I'll bite. What's a Pride party?"

"The Empire Pride Agenda. It's a gay and lesbian New York State political group. They hold a gathering out here every year, usually at one of the designer showcase mansions." MJ named some of the past venues and they were very impressive indeed. "It draws a big crowd for big bucks, and a prestigious location is vital." He sipped from his juice glass and replaced it on his belly. One couldn't help but stare.

"It's not your house, MJ. At least not yet. And don't you think your parents have had enough disclosures for one season?" I said "parents" as a matter of form. Personally, I was concerned with Milly while secretly thrilled at the idea of Mark Barrett acquiring a black son-in-law and a gay son all in one week. But it wasn't enough. Nothing was enough for that prick.

"Sarah?" He smiled as he spoke his sister's name. "Mother—and I'm sure you and Vicky—thought Daddy would go ballistic over Sarah's latest caper. Instead, he's opening the doors of Barrett House for a reception in their honor. So, why shouldn't I be accorded equal time?"

It was true, and I wouldn't have believed him if I hadn't heard it from his mother. Milly told me Mark took the news of his daughter's return and marriage with calm resignation. "Quiet," was how she described her husband after learning the facts. "Pensive," I think, was also incorporated into the conversation. When Milly timidly suggested a reception at Barrett House to introduce the bride and groom, Mark readily acquiesced. True, he never said he approved, nor did he call his daughter in a welcoming gesture. On the other hand, he didn't go ballistic, as MJ would have it, which I think is what we used to call going ape-shit. But even lacking that more picturesque idiom, I smelled something rotten in East Hampton. Mark Barrett was a snob and a bigot, and beware of both when they come bearing gifts.

"Has Mark seen Sarah?" I asked.

"She's been to the house. He was cordial but not overjoyed. Civil, I guess you'd call the encounter. Of course Mother is out with Sarah just about every day. The two couldn't be happier."

I knew most of this via Milly herself, but pretended ignorance. "Has your father met Fletcher?"

"Not yet. But I've visited their digs on Georgica Pond and you know who their host is. Christ, the guy has more security than the White House and all armed to the teeth."

"Any sightings of the canoe brigade?"

MJ laughed, seriously imperiling the family jewels. I wished he would drink the damn juice and put on a pair of pants. "They're kayaks, actually," he told me. "You slip into them like waders, so all one sees is the paddler's torso. They're all over the pond like June bugs, and Sarah, in a bikini, waves. Her audience must think she's a goddess, she's so beautiful."

"And you told her your news?"

Finally, he picked up the glass, downed the grapefruit juice, and placed the empty glass on a nearby nightstand. "She was delighted," he said, proudly.

"I would expect nothing less. California and all that jazz." I sat to don my sneakers, then went into the bathroom to flush my cigarette, knowing MJ would frown at a nonhuman butt cluttering his clean ashtray.

"And she asked for you," he was saying when I returned.

"She remembers me?"

"Very well. She also knew I was hot for you."

"Observant little cuss, ain't she?"

"Nothing escapes our Sarah."

"What's he like?" I asked. "Fletcher, that is."

MJ thought this over as he tugged on his right earlobe. I prayed he wasn't thinking of having it pierced. "Distinguished," came the reply. "Regal, even. Proud without a trace of arrogance. Even a touch of gray at the temples."

"I assume he's also human."

MJ finally rose and once again planted his feet on the floor, examining his toes. "He is. And very much in love with Sarah, if I'm any judge. They took me to the Beaumont mansion. They're restoring it, you know. Workmen all over the place along with their New York architect. What a place, Mike. On a clear day you can see the south shore of Connecticut across the bay. Did you know the house has twenty bedrooms and as many baths?"

"And on a clear day you can hear the plumbing moaning."

"True, it's old, but before Fletcher is done every one of those baths will resemble a spa. The guy is rich, Mike. Rich, rich, rich."

Finally, and posed as an afterthought, I asked the question that was the sole purpose of my tennis date with MJ Barrett. "By the way, do you know a Galen Miller?"

MJ looked up, startled, and laughed. "Why, you dirty old man."

Just as startled, I looked at him questioningly. Seeing my dismay, he went on, "He works the volleyball court at Two Mile Hollow Beach. At least he did last year."

"He's a professional volleyball player?" I foolishly asked.

This drew a raucous laugh. "No, Mike, he hustles the men at the gay beach."

What with all that had happened in my life these past few months, I thought I was impervious to future shock. I wasn't. And while this new piece of information sent my mind spinning like a wheel of fortune sailing past the jackpot slot, I murmured out of politeness, "I didn't know the fraternity had its own beach."

"The boys and girls more or less took over Two Mile Hollow Beach years ago and retain it by squatters' rights. Galen was last year's star attraction. You had to wait in line, but I heard the kid was partial to producers and directors. I guess our Galen wants to be in pictures. If you've ever wondered how those pretty boys get started in porn videos, keep your eyes on the bouncing basket of Galen Miller. He and his father operate a lawn-mowing . . ."

MJ rattled on, filling me in on data already familiar as I mentally ran down my list of facts.

Galen Miller has an affair with his stepmother.

Galen Miller drowns his stepmother.

Galen Miller makes a pest of himself trying to get an interview with Mark Barrett.

And last, but certainly not least, Galen Miller is a hustler.

What was Mark Barrett doing in the middle of this plot? And would knowing help me get the guy out of my hair and my wife's pocketbook—and other places I didn't want to think about?

A link? But how, why, and so what?

MJ finally pulled a clean pair of undershorts out of his dresser drawer. "Big cocktail party tonight," he was saying, having allotted Galen Miller as much time as a Barrett deemed proper.

"Where?"

MJ recited the name emblazoned on the elastic band of the briefs he was pulling over his slim hips.

"For a lawyer, MJ, you talk just like a hairdresser."

Galen Miller

Thirty-Two

I watched the Jaguar approach from my bedroom window. When I first spotted it, I didn't know it was the Jaguar. Mark Barrett's Jaguar. From a distance it looked like a giant black bug kicking up dust on the winding dirt road that leads to our farm. When I thought it could be the Jaguar, or when I began praying it was the Jaguar, I could feel my heart pounding in my chest like it did the day Les told me about Barrett's offer. Like it did the day I found the letter from Betty's lawyer. Like it did the day I shoved Betty out of the boat. Don't think about Betty. Don't ever think about Betty. Makes me crazy.

I've been waiting for the Jaguar since Christmas—over six months ago. It could have been six years for all the shit that's gone down the tube since that freezing day. Today was boiling hot, so maybe the big bug was a mirage like they get in the desert when the sweltering air begins to act like a movie screen. If it was a mirage, no one was pulling the plug on the projector, because the bug kept coming closer and closer, and my heart kept pumping and pumping so that I was finding it hard to breathe. Something else was getting hard too. It does that when I get excited over something—I mean something that has nothing to do with sex. Why? I don't know. Maybe Helen knows. Maybe Helen knows too much.

It was the Jaguar. Barrett's Jaguar. Big and black. Like his new son-in-law. That's what I heard. His daughter, the one he kicked out years ago, is back in town and married to a nigger. Yeah, a Barrett married to a nigger. Maybe Barrett will take his son-in-law to his club for a few holes of golf. The fucking grass will turn brown under every step they take. Rich spade is what they're saying. Big television producer. I got this from my clients at Two Mile Hollow. I'm back at it. What the fuck else could I do? Betty's money ran out weeks ago. Don't think about Betty. Business ain't so good. Isn't. Business isn't so good. Fucking gay liberation. They don't want to pay for it anymore. And they're scared shit of AIDS. They want me to put on a rubber. Christ! Why don't they just chew on latex and forget the stuffing?

But I won't do it for fifty bucks. Ten dollars an inch, I tell them. It turns them on. Think it's gonna set them back a hundred and twenty bucks. Queers got rich imaginations.

The bug stopped in front of the house. I mean the Jaguar. Was this what it was like when the pot of gold you've been dreaming about came driving up to your front door? Heart pounding. Dick hard. Bowels loose. What do you do for loose bowels? Shove a screwdriver up your ass and tighten them. Ha ha.

Eddy ain't been around in weeks. More than a month since Betty disappeared. That's right. Disappeared. That's all I know. She disappeared. Try Nevada, Eddy. I hear prostitution is legal in Nevada, so Betty's gone legit. I haven't been near Helen. Given Eddy plenty of space to move in. Maybe if he's busy with Helen he'll forget about

Betty. But if he gets too close to Helen, maybe she'll tell him about our secret place. Maybe she'll ask him to take her there. Maybe something floated to the surface. Does it? Can it?

I'm clean.

But I'd be cleaner if Helen didn't know about Two Holes of Water. What am I thinking? Whatever it is, it's crazy, just when I have to think straight.

The money got out of the bug. The money walked up to the front door. The money arrived. The money I needed to get away clean. The money was carrying a brown paper bag. Long and slim. Stoli for Les? A celebration? I felt better. I was thinking straight. Straight as an arrow. Straight as a million arrows.

I opened my bedroom door so I could hear them talking. Barrett's voice. Smooth like silk. Then Les, cackling like a fucking hen. At least he was awake. He must have smelled the Stoli. I heard their voices but I couldn't hear what they were saying. I gave them a chance to toast the sale before I made my entrance.

In the bathroom I splashed cold water on my face. The mirror reflected a handsome son of a bitch. The excitement had put a glow to my tanned cheeks. Good skin. Never had a zit in my fucking life. Cute as hell is Galen. Man, I was so turned on I could have jacked off just looking at me. I winked. The guy in the mirror winked back. Nice trick, eh?

Mr. Barrett was wearing shorts. Bermuda shorts, they're called, and a dress shirt with the sleeves rolled up, the top two buttons open and no T-shirt. Very informal. But then the Millers have never been big on formal dress. Good-looking guy, Barrett. Real ladies' man. Why not? Nice tan. A little gray in the hair. Flat belly. He looked like my clients. He's got a son. Mark junior. I heard something about him on the beach. What? Who knows? Who cares? Today the money changes hands and that's all that matters.

Les was seated in his usual place. Mr. Barrett was standing opposite him. Both held glasses containing a clear liquid. Stoli. Why not champagne? Because we're Millers, that's why. The two were laughing like little boys telling dirty jokes.

"Here's Galen," Les shouted. "Tell him. Tell Gay, Mr. Barrett."

"Hello, Mr. Barrett," I said.

"Hello, Galen. You see, you didn't have to storm my office. The mountain has come to Mohammed."

What kind of Muslim talk was that? Maybe his son-in-law converted him. "Didn't mean to intrude, Mr. Barrett. Just wanted to . . . well, check up on things."

That passed with a wave of his hand. The hand that wasn't holding the Stoli. "Sorry about your stepmother," came next.

Not as sorry as she is. "Yeah. Well, it happens."

"The police are on top of it, I understand."

"Yes, Mr. Barrett. They are. I think she got amnesia. I saw a film once . . ."

"Amnesia." Les was bouncing around in his chair. A bad sign. Hyper, from not cutting the vodka with beer chasers. "That's what I said. Amnesia. That's how come she forgot the car and her clothes. She'll be back. When she comes around, she'll be back. Now tell Gay, Mr. Barrett. Tell Gay what you told me."

"It was between us, Les. I don't want to embarrass the boy." It was Mr. Barrett who looked embarrassed.

"I'm not a boy, Mr. Barrett." To prove the point I

helped myself to a cold beer. I didn't want to be empty-handed when it came time to toast the sale.

"Tell him," Les insisted.

"Well . . ." Mr. Barrett began reluctantly. "I was telling your father about this cocky guy who needed to be put in his place. His wife came to see me on business and later we were to meet him and go on to dinner. I got this idea when we left my office. I opened my fly, like I forgot to zip up after a quickie, and when we met her husband I made sure he saw it, like I was taking his picture. Snap. Snap. He never said a word. But he suspected. I know he suspected."

Stupid story, but I laughed. Les, of course, sent up a howl. If Mr. Barrett farted, Les would think he smelled Joy by Jean Patou. Forget that. But it was the kind of story Les liked and Mr. Barrett knew it. Why was he buttering up Les? Where was the contract? Where was the down payment? Fucking bloodhounds sniffing at my tail and he's telling raunchy stories. Give me a fucking break.

"That's just between us, Galen," Mr. Barrett said above Les's cackling.

"It won't go past this room," I told him, being certain that he never told the stupid story outside this room.

"We're all family," Les shouted. "All family telling stories around the kitchen table, like we used to. No one goes tattling outside the family. Right, Mr. Barrett?"

"That's right, Les. Like it used to be before the invasion." Mr. Barrett sounded like he was talking about a war East Hampton lost. "One of us got trouble, we all got trouble. Like this business with your stepmother, Galen. Do you want me to talk to the police? See what I can do?"

"Thanks, Mr. Barrett, but they're doing all they can."

"Who's your liaison in the department? I mean, who keeps you posted on their progress?"

I fucking know what it means. "Eddy Evans," I told him.

Mr. Barrett nodded. "I've seen him around. Good man."

"She'll turn up," Les said. "Soon as she comes around, she'll turn up. Got a closet full of clothes up there. And a mink coat. How much you think it's worth? A mink coat."

"Shut up," I yelled, and was immediately sorry. Straight. I had to think straight.

Mr. Barrett acted like he didn't hear nothing. Anything. Like he didn't hear anything. "You know, Galen," he said, "we go back a long way in this town. Our ancestors. Our roots."

Our blood. Our sweat. You telling me something I don't know?

"And we've seen a lot of changes in East Hampton." Mr. Barrett sounded like he was the graduation day speaker at East Hampton High. "The artists. The tourists. People moving in on our turf. Trying to shape us to suit themselves. I think we have to resist those changes. Keep things the way they were. The way they should be."

"Damn right," Les agreed, forgetting the mink, I hoped.

Keep things the way they were? Keep the farm the way it was? The way it is? I didn't like this. "Not all change is bad, Mr. Barrett, and the city people bring in the dollars."

"Don't sass Mr. Barrett. . . . The boy don't know what he's saying." Like always, just when you think Les is on another planet he lets you know he hasn't even left the room.

"The boy is right," Mr. Barrett said. "Not all change is bad and I didn't mean to imply it was." He put his glass on the table. He hadn't taken a sip since I came in the room. Not to worry. In this house it wouldn't go to waste.

"I wonder, Galen, if you would excuse us for a while. I'd like to have a private word with your father."

Did I say the wrong thing? My heart started up again. I wondered if Mr. Barrett could hear it. "No secrets in this house, Mr. Barrett."

"Humor an old man, son." Mr. Barrett wasn't smiling.

I put down my can of beer, also untouched, and picked up the keys to the Lincoln. "I have some errands."

"Good boy, Galen. And remember, if I can help . . ."

"Thanks, Mr. Barrett. Thanks a lot."

Is this how real estate deals are made? In private? I don't think so. I don't fucking think so.

Now what?

Eddy Evans

Thirty-Three

August. Over a month since Betty Zabriskie Miller boarded a Hampton Jitney to oblivion, and we're no nearer a solution to her disappearance than we were the day Les reported his wife missing.

On the evidence I've managed to turn up, the Chief agrees that Betty never got past the depot in Southampton on her Wednesday outings. We also agree that Betty married Les because of his boasting about a million-dollar offer for the farm. We differ on events following the honeymoon. The Chief thinks Betty is the victim of an alcoholic blackout. Because she married Les, he assumes Betty is also addicted to booze.

Alcoholic blackouts are a medical fact. They can last hours, days, months, and maybe years. The victim, while functioning normally in the blackout state, has no recollection when he recovers of where he was or what he did. It's a totally blacked out period in his life. Alcoholics have been known to "wake up" in another state, far from home. Some find themselves with a new spouse, having never divorced the old one. There is the case of a well-known actor who married, lived with his wife for ten months, divorced her, and later had no recollection of this except for what friends told him. He says that the marriage license, divorce papers, and dent in his bank account are the only reason he believes his friends are telling the truth.

The Chief's theory is not a bad stretch, except that we have no evidence that Betty Zabriskie was alcoholic, and it doesn't explain her weekly trips to Southampton.

I think the lady's stepson can set us straight on both those issues. Why? Because every time I question Galen he insists that he and Betty were barely on speaking terms; he doesn't know why she married his father and he never heard of any offer for the farm. Thanks to Helen, I now know this is a bold-faced lie. So is everything Galen tells me, which isn't much. Here is a pretty, sexy lady, with a fancy car and lots of money she's not timid about spreading around—sleeping in the next room. Could little Galen resist? No way. And could Betty Zabriskie resist the charms of Galen Miller? Hard to admit, but I doubt it.

If the pair were getting it on every Wednesday in a Southampton motel, what did they talk about when they weren't going at it? A million dollars? Then what? Did Betty Zabriskie Miller get greedy?

"A lot of smoke," the Chief says, "and no fire."

What he means is, we don't have a body and can't prove a damn thing.

The last week of July and the first weeks of August are typically the height of the summer season. The town was overflowing with vacationers, all of whom appeared to be four-car families. Every man on the force was pulling double shifts a few times a week. Just when I was certain the Chief was getting ready to pull me off the Zabriskie case, I got a reprieve from a higher authority. The FBI.

A serial killer was being hunted in South Beach, Florida. His latest victim was a fashion designer of such renown that the crime drew headlines around the world. It was determined that the suspect, a good-looking stud whose victims were gay males, spent last season in East Hampton, entertained by the rich and famous gay men who keep summer homes here. If he managed to escape the dragnet in Miami, would he return to East Hampton where he knew his way around? The FBI wanted us to keep our eyes open and alert the gay community. What better excuse for me to pay a daily visit to Two Mile Hollow Beach and follow the career of Galen Miller, who was once again showing his face, among other things, to the crowd the FBI was using as live bait to snare their suspect? The Chief had no choice but to agree.

Yes, Galen was plying his old trade. Amazing how everything was back to business as usual in the Miller household since Betty departed for points unknown. Except for the fact that they were no longer in the lawn care business and forgetting her car and clothes, one would never know Betty Zabriskie had ever been a part of their lives.

I didn't tell Helen where Galen could be found almost daily. However, I strongly suspected that Helen no longer cared. She has finally outgrown her high school crush on Galen Miller. I attribute this to my persistence, if not my masculine charms. Others disagree. Others such as Jan Solinsky. I knew Jan could not resist paying a visit to Main Street Video. Still, when Helen told me an old flame had called on her, I was furious.

"Just because you're back in East Hampton," I told Jan, "doesn't mean you're back in my life. Please keep away from Helen."

"Don't be silly, darling." Jan was doing her star turn—a role I knew too well. "I'm doing you a favor."

"Favors like this, I don't need."

"Oh, Eddy, shut up and listen. You've been competing with this juvenile delinquent, as you call him, for ages and where has it got you?"

"I don't need this, Jan. Not from you."

"But you do need it and especially from me. I know about these things."

"So how come you lost your husband?"

"That hurt, Eddy."

"You just made my day."

"I made your day when I showed Helen there was a glamorous, rather sexy, and mysterious woman in your life."

"You have a high opinion of yourself, Jan."

"In my profession, it's necessary."

"Expediter for a bus company?"

"I'll pretend I didn't hear that."

"You pretend too much, Jan."

"And you, not enough. You're cute, Eddy, but dull. I added a new dimension to your life and gave Helen something to think about. In other words, darling, she's going to have to put out or get out."

"You're vulgar, Jan."

"I'm real, Eddy. Get a life."

"I have one and it doesn't include you."

"Trust me, Eddy."

Did I have a choice?

And what difference did it make? Helen has become more receptive to my cause and that's all that matters. I even help out in Main Street Video when I'm off duty, schmoozing up to her father. I don't know if Mr. Weaver approves of me as a son-in-law or as a source of free labor. In spite of her reluctance early on, Helen is now intrigued with the "mystery of Betty Z," as she calls it. In fact, she's become my chief accomplice, offering theories I know were based on movie plots that could be found in the mystery section of Main Street Video.

She refuses to implicate Galen, in fact or theory, and I won't intrude upon her loyalty. It's enough to know I'm the only man in her life: to hold her hand when we stroll along Main Street, indulge in hot dogs and a beer on the few occasions we can get to the beach, feel her reluctance to break away from my goodnight kiss when I take her home after a date.

She even went so far as to tell me what she knew about the million-dollar offer for the Miller farm. Mark Barrett, a local lawyer who is known as a heavy investor in East Hampton real estate—mostly motels—is the interested party. I wanted to question Barrett about the offer but knew the Chief would never allow it. The Barrett family is among our landed gentry and right now Mark Barrett had more on his mind than purchasing a derelict farm site. His daughter recently arrived back in town from wherever she'd been, married to Stephen Fletcher, the richest black man in America—if not the world. The talk is that Fletcher bought the old Beaumont mansion on Gardiners Bay and will settle here.

There's to be a reception at the Barrett House for the newlyweds. I know this because Mr. Barrett asked the Chief if he could spare a few men to help with traffic and party crashers the night of the party. I was one of the men the Chief volunteered.

If Helen's free evenings coincided with mine, we usually went to dinner and a film. This particular night she invited me to her house for dinner. Her parents were holding down the fort in Main Street Video. I made hamburgers on the outdoor grill and tossed a salad with my own special dressing. Helen tended to the french fries, which came frozen in a box. Like most people with hearty appetites, Helen is a lousy cook.

After dinner, comfortable on the living room couch, I brought up the subject of Barrett's offer for the farm.

"Galen must have been upset when Les showed up with a bride. I mean, it was just him and Les and suddenly it was a three-way split or maybe Galen was completely out of the picture."

"Sure he was upset, but what could he do about it?"

The startled expression on her pretty face told me she had thought of an answer before I supplied it. Was this the first time she saw the possibility of Galen's involvement in Betty's sudden disappearance? I wanted to take her by the shoulders and shake some reality into that analytical mind that had come up with a dozen logical reasons for Galen lying to me about the offer for the farm. Distrust of authority was the leading contender. If the police represented authority to Galen Miller, it was the first I was hearing about it.

Her gray eyes clouded over and I wished I could crawl behind them and learn what had passed between her and Galen on the subject of Betty Zabriskie. Surely that's what she was recalling as she looked at everything in the room but me.

"What did he say at the time, Helen?"

"Galen? What didn't he say? You know him. He shoots off his mouth before he thinks. He wondered how Betty knew about Barrett's offer. He and Les had agreed to keep it between them. I told him there might be a connection between Betty and Mark Barrett because the Barretts have been known to winter in Palm Beach. I think it's near Delray."

"But now we know that's not true. Mrs. MacAlister was Betty's source. And why didn't he just ask Betty what he wanted to know?"

"Because he refused to acknowledge her existence, that's why. It was me who told him he could learn more from her by being a friend than an enemy."

"And did he take your advice?"

"I don't know. The season was just starting and business was picking up for both of us. I didn't see much of him after that."

I didn't remind her that Les & Son were out of business, so what was Galen busy with?

Not liking the direction our sleuthing had taken us in, Helen cut it off by suggesting iced tea. I preferred beer but accepted the offer because I guessed she wanted some time alone to think over what I knew she now suspected. Patience had gotten me into her heart. More of the same would take me into her confidence.

When she returned with our drinks I lightened the conversation by reminding her of the psychic she used to consult. "You know, the New York police sometimes use a psychic to help them find things, like missing loot and bodies. Do you think she can find Betty?"

"You'd have to consult a psychic to find her. She left East Hampton months ago."

"Before the season? Why?"

"Maybe she saw more rain than sun in East Hampton's future."

Helen drank her tea and I played with mine, stirring

the ice in the tall glass with a finger. "Do you mind if I get myself a beer? Iced tea is not my after-dinner favorite."

"Help yourself."

I did. When I was once again settled next to her on the couch I asked her why she went to the psychic.

"Curious," was her answer.

"I know you, Helen. You had a reason. Let's hear it."

"No. It seems so foolish now."

"We all do foolish things. I used to sit outside at dusk, every evening, so I could wish on the first star."

"What did you wish, Eddy?"

"That you would tell me why you went to the psychic."

"You won't laugh?"

"Cross my heart."

"I wanted to see if she could contact James Dean."

"Helen, he died before you were even born."

"I know, Eddy. That's why I needed a psychic to contact him."

"What did you want to ask him?"

"He looked a lot like Galen," she answered, and that seemed to explain everything. I put my arm around her and drew her close enough to prevent even a memory from coming between us.

Jan didn't confine putting her nose into my love life to just one visit to Main Street Video. Not Jan. She became a regular customer of that shop and impressed Helen with her knowledge of cinematic lore. This was their common ground, besides the fascination Helen had for Jan's theatrical career, such as it was. Also of interest to an impressionable girl like Helen was Jan's marriage and divorce. Helen told me that Jan had volunteered her services as an usher at Bay Street Theatre, our celebrity-owned-and-operated playhouse in Sag Harbor. This, I take it, was in preparation for Jan's theatrical debut on the other side of the curtain.

Jan invited us to her half-share in the Sag Harbor house and it was a fun evening, with Jan playing the grand actress and flirting shamelessly with me. I especially enjoyed the way Helen kept a possessive hand on my arm throughout our stay.

Helen never asked me if Jan and I were once lovers, but then I never sought the same information from her regarding Galen.

Everything was going great, and then suddenly, it all changed.

Thirty-Four

Mr. Weaver was behind the register, totaling up the daily take, which I'm sure was generous as it had rained most of the day. Main Street Video and its neighbor, the movie house, had both done record business. We had had a run of perfect beach days for the past two weeks, which is not good for shop owners in general and video rentals in particular. In our community, the farmers and the merchants pray for rain while the second-home owners and renters pray for sun. So far this year, God had turned a deaf ear on the sowers and retailers. Today, He gave them a break.

It was late. Near midnight. The store had been closed for an hour. I was straightening display jackets and checking the titles on the tags below them to make sure they corresponded. Helen was in the back room filing returns, which she didn't have a chance to do all day. The girl Mr. Weaver had hired for the summer, Doreen, had called in sick.

I was trying to figure out a good excuse for me to drive Helen home, letting her father go on alone, when Mr. Weaver's voice broke my concentration.

His chatter ended—I think—with the words, ". . . buying diamonds."

"Who's buying diamonds?" I asked, hoping it was the correct response.

"According to our landlord, everyone is buying diamonds. He told me a jeweler is interested in renting this space and has made him an offer that sounds like a telephone number. Laundering money, that's what's going on. What are the police doing about it, Eddy? Nothing. That's what. We even have a restaurant called The Laundry. The only thing we don't have is a place to wash your dirty underwear. But why wash 'em? Throw 'em away. Buy new. Cover your behind with diamonds."

Mr. Weaver had to be forgiven. He was a good man who was being nailed to a cross and it hurt.

"We can move to a new location." This from Helen, reassuring her father from the back room. "A better location." It wasn't a new line, but I imagine Helen was too tired to think of anything more original.

"Before we do," Mr. Weaver called back, "tell Galen to return that damn tape and charge him what's due."

I turned to the counter, where Mr. Weaver was fiddling with the computer. I saw Helen come out of the back room, looking the worse for wear. It had been a long day.

"Galen hasn't rented anything all summer. You must be looking at ancient history." She had come up behind him, peering over his shoulder.

"Last June, Helen, is not ancient history, even to someone of your tender years. It's right here, Wednesday the eighteenth. I remember the night he came in. I guess you weren't here. See, *A Place in the Sun*. We have two copies and I want the other one back plus the past-due money he owes us."

Wednesday the eighteenth. A week before Betty disappeared. Les reported her missing on the twenty-sixth. I knew those dates like I knew my own birthday. I arrived at the counter just as Helen's gaze went from the computer screen to my face. She looked ill. "What's this about Galen?" I asked.

"Nothing. He rented a movie. That's why we're in business." Her tone was so defensive even Mr. Weaver looked at her askance.

"Why don't you go home, Eddy. We're almost through here," Helen said.

"I thought I'd drop you off."

"That's silly. I'll go with my father." She pushed her hair back with her left hand, leaving a dark smudge on her cheek. I never saw her so out of control.

"What's wrong, Helen?"

"Nothing, Eddy. I'm tired. Just go, please." She turned and all but ran into the storage room.

"I don't get it, Mr. Weaver. Why all the fuss over a film?"

"It's not the film, Eddy. Doreen didn't show up and poor Helen's been here since ten this morning—a double shift on the busiest day of the summer. She's a little stressed out. If you're planning on marrying her, get used to it."

I didn't believe him.

Michael Anthony Reo

Thirty-Five

For Mr. and Mrs. Stephen Fletcher's debut, Vicky had selected a pale blue sheath that cleaved to her figure with the slightest motion of her body.

"New?" I asked.

She nodded at my reflection in the vanity mirror.

We were in Kirk's room (I refused to think of it as Vicky's room), where Vicky was applying the finishing touches to her makeup. Standing behind her image, I saw myself in a dark blue summer suit and rep tie. The dress code this evening was semiformal.

"Everyone will be ogling the bride and groom," Vicky predicted.

"Brides and grooms are supposed to be ogled, but this crowd will do it with great discretion."

Vicky turned from the mirror. "Gloves?"

"No. Less is always better and this is August in the Hamptons. Pomposity will be frowned upon, believe me. Are you ready?"

"Ready."

I offered my arm and she took it.

"We'll be the most attractive couple there," I said, opening the bedroom door.

"You are the vainest man I know."

"Not without cause—and I did include you."

"Oh, Michael."

After the night we sat out back, watching it rain and performing a verbal autopsy on our marriage, we faced each other the next morning like newlyweds who had spent their wedding night in separate bedrooms: uncertain, but willing to try again. Vicky had not moved back into our room but we were once again acting more like man and wife than boarders in a residential hotel. In retrospect, I now saw all the things I had done wrong since they carried off Kirk in an ambulance that chilly January morning. Major among them was underestimating Vicky's potential. I took it as fact that she would always need someone to guide her and that I would always be that someone. Poor pompous Michael.

While I was riding my bicycle up and down Two Holes of Water Road, Barrett had been conferring with Kirk and commiserating with Vicky. In hindsight, the Incident had me more concerned with guarding my back than seeing what was going on before my eyes. But I knew, or thought I knew, that when Kirk went, Vicky would turn to me for guidance. She didn't, and who could blame her? Pouting over Kirk's will, I withdrew my shoulder when she needed it most, while Mark Barrett was laughing all the way to the bank.

When I asked Vicky how she responded to Barrett's proposal, she told me she laughed. That did not discourage her Lothario, I'm sure. In fact it must have been what he expected. But the seed was planted and he was watering it with my sweat. The fact that Vicky had not laughed when she told me about Mark's offer proves the point. Mark Barrett would not be easily discouraged. However, if I underestimated my wife, Mark Barrett underestimated my relationship with her. For twenty years Vicky and I were friends and lovers, a claim few married couples, including the Barretts, could make. Her father's death and my preoccupation with another death put a strain on the union, but in spite of Barrett's efforts, these events had not broken the bond.

I knew Vicky was as happy to have me back in her confidence as I was to be there. When I talked about what I hoped would be our future together, she listened, joined in, and began to see the possibilities not only for a resurgence of the Kirkpatrick legacy, but for Mr. and Mrs. Michael Anthony Reo as well.

"But is this what Father would want?" was her mantra.

"No," I stated honestly. "Not with me at the helm. But that no longer matters. You're in command and what you want is all that matters."

Tonight I would show Mark Barrett, and his world, that what my wife wanted was me. I was going on the offensive and the competition was awesome: Sarah Barrett's reintroduction to East Hampton society as Mrs. Stephen Fletcher; MJ Barrett peeking out from behind the closet door; Milly packing her bags for an extended stay in Italy; Mark, undoubtedly furious at both of his offspring and at his wife, in pursuit of Vicky; and a boy named Galen Miller in pursuit of Mark.

The mother of the bride wore beige, a color I long suspected was invented for mothers of brides. On Milly it looked original. The hug with which she greeted Vicky and me was far from perfunctory and, I thought, more a gesture of farewell than welcome. It was not without a twinge of foreboding that I said, "If this is the third act, Milly, you have put together a spectacular finish."

Long-stemmed white roses, a delicate reminder of the gathering's purpose, dominated the decor in the great room. Milly's "girls," present and alumnae, moved among the guests with pride of position, offering an array of delicacies flawlessly arranged on their silver trays. A bar had been set up at one end of the room, attended by two young black men who exuded the charm and air of Harvard undergraduates moonlighting. Bravo, Milly.

Another bar was visible in the library, off the great room, that looked out to a flagstone patio, offering a safe haven to smokers. The guests—perhaps fifty—moved about to the background music of a cocktail pianist playing Gershwin, Porter, and Rodgers on the polished Steinway grand. Here were the elite of East Hampton society, which means there wasn't a celebrity in the crowd except for the lovely Dina Merrill, whose charm and talent transcend both worlds. Most were here to see what they had been discussing for weeks: the goings-on at Barrett House. Reactions were impossible to gauge by either their manner or conversation, proving there is much to be said for a proper upbringing.

"Third act?" Vicky questioned. "What does that mean?"

"It means," Milly said, "*la guerre est fini.*" With a smile and a nod she moved off to greet the next arrivals.

"How do you spell *guerre*?" Vicky asked.

"M-A-R-R-I-A-G-E."

"Mr. and Mrs. Reo, how nice." Sarah Fletcher, with her husband at her side, moved toward us as she spoke.

Milly and MJ had described Sarah as a beauty. Their praise was modest. Sarah Barrett Fletcher was exquisite, but even that oft used word seemed trite when confronted with the reality of her presence. Like her brother, Sarah had the black Barrett hair and Milly's blue eyes. But where MJ's eyes were a bright, almost startling blue, Sarah's were hauntingly dark. This evening her hair was combed back from her face and held with two diamond clips. Her coloring contrasted elegantly with a dress of white silk, cut to accentuate her slim waist and full breasts. No wonder Milly had mistaken her daughter for a movie star that day at the Elvis.

"Darling," she said to Fletcher, "this is Mr. and Mrs. Michael Reo."

Fletcher touched Vicky's hand and shook mine. "Mrs. Reo. Mr. Reo."

"Michael, please," I insisted. "My father is Mr. Reo. I remember a skinny girl in pigtails bearing no resemblance to this lovely creature."

Sarah laughed, the sound drawing the attention of those milling around us. "And I remember a couple who kept gossip columnists in business and were the talk of the Club."

"We still are, my dear, we still are."

"Your father was my mentor, Mrs. Reo, in spirit if not in fact," Stephen Fletcher said. He was tall, thin, and looked one directly in the eyes when he spoke. MJ had called him distinguished and he was. He was also the only man in the room wearing a blazer as opposed to a suit. If this was a statement of his independence, it worked.

"He would be proud to know it," Vicky answered.

"Mother told you we've bought a home here," Sarah said.

"The old Beaumont house," Vicky replied. "It's the

talk of the town. Will it be your home base, or will you be snowbirds and flee at the end of the season?"

"The West Coast will remain our permanent address," Fletcher said. "Like you two, we're citizens of the world. East Hampton is my wife's passion and I must say I've fallen in love with the area. It's more New England than New England."

"Sarah's passion is East Hampton's good fortune. Best of luck to you both." There were people behind us, waiting to be introduced, and I thought we had taken up enough of their time, but Fletcher would not be hurried.

"What does your future hold, now that Mr. Kirkpatrick is no longer with us?" he asked. Sarah raised an eyebrow at her husband's bluntness, then shrugged in resignation.

I took a deep breath. "It's not for publication, but Vicky and I are erecting a tollbooth on the bridge to the twenty-first century camouflaged as a production company. If I said more I'd be giving too much away."

Fletcher grinned his approval. "It's my domain, Michael, and one I know well. I hope you'll keep me informed."

"If I knew I could call on you for help, I'd feel more confident."

"Then do. Please do," Stephen Fletcher said.

"A tollbooth?" Vicky whispered as we made our retreat.

"Sounded impressive, didn't it?"

"You amaze me, Michael."

"Sometimes I amaze myself."

Having done our duty, we went to the bar for our reward and mingled with those we mingled with most days of the week. Vicky, with little inducement, accompanied a friend to the patio just as I spotted Milly taking a break from her hostess chores.

"*La guerre est fini,* indeed," I said, sneaking up behind her.

"I thought it was rather clever."

"Does your husband know?"

"We had an awful row, Michael."

"Over Sarah?"

"No. MJ."

"He told his father."

She nodded. "I knew, Michael. I've known for a long time. I visit the family in Boston and MJ was at school up there and—well—he's not discreet, my son. There were rumors and I heard them. But I never thought he would get so vocal about it."

"They all do these days, and I wish them well."

"He's going to stay here and practice law," Milly said. "He's not going to run off to New York and hide. I think that's made Mark madder than anything else."

"Good for MJ," I told her.

"That's what I said, and of course it was the proverbial straw for my marriage and amen to that. I'm proud of my son, Michael. I'm so proud of both my children."

"You have every reason to be, Milly. When are you off to Italy?"

"September, the latest. I hope you and Vicky will visit." Her smile told me she didn't miss the humor in this more inclusive invitation. I could have kissed her for her tact. "Vicky and I have been set free," she went on. "I'm flying the coop, but Vicky looks more inclined to feather her nest."

"Not if your husband has anything to say about it."

"It's up to you to make sure he doesn't."

The party was at its height and the din in the room successfully challenged the tinkling keys of the Steinway for the right to be heard. Milly would have to start circulating and oversee the kitchen for the buffet supper to follow, but her last remark caused me to put a restraining hand on her arm and say, "Galen Miller."

"Who, Michael?"

"Galen Miller. The boy whose mother once worked for you. He's been trying to see Mark. Do you know why?"

She looked thoughtful. "I remember, weeks back, that he called the office several times and even the house. But I have no idea why. What is it, Michael?"

I gave the matter a moment's thought and decided that it was time I shared my secret. Milly's former involvement with the boy's mother and Mark's mysterious connection with him made Milly a likely ally. "I'll tell you, Milly, but now is not the time or place. I'll call you tomorrow."

"You look worried, Michael."

"I am, Milly."

A waitress thrust a tray of caviar on toast points between us. A couple paused in their meandering to help themselves, and our twosome became a foursome. A moment later Milly made her excuses and was gone.

Mark Barrett and I played cat and mouse all evening. This only made it more difficult for us to keep our eyes off each other as we circled the room, shaking hands, kissing powdered cheeks, and smiling until our jaws ached. I feared even a polite hello would lead to a confrontation, and I was in Barrett House to support Milly, not embarrass her. In retrospect, a very wise move.

I didn't notice if he had been attentive to Vicky but did observe that he gave as wide a berth to his daughter and son-in-law as he did to me. Mark Barrett was not about to condone or condemn this union publicly until he knew which way the wind was blowing from the direction of the Club. Then he would join the bandwagon. The bastard.

I had started in search of Vicky, when the din of the emergency siren invaded the party via the open terrace doors. I was reminded of New Year's Eve, when it had sounded for Kirk. I had no idea what the various blasts meant, only that they all reminded me of the wail of an ocean liner. From the insistence of tonight's baying this was a major call to arms.

I spotted MJ at the bar in the library and joined him for a refill. "So, where's your date?" I asked.

"I didn't want to distract the gawkers from Sarah and Stephen. One scandal per party is my motto."

"Your mother tells me you've made some serious decisions."

"So has she. A divorce, a mixed marriage, and a fag, all in one season. There hasn't been this much movement in the Barrett clan since George the Third divvied up Long Island and sent us here to collect the spoils."

"For a lawyer you talk just like a stand-up comic." I put my hand on his shoulder and added, "Milly is proud of you and so am I. If you ever need—"

Someone wrenched my hand from MJ's shoulder. "Keep your hands off my son," Mark Barrett stage-whispered loud enough for everyone in the room to hear.

"Keep your hands off my wife," I whispered louder.

In a blind rage he gripped my throat with both hands. I heard a woman scream. MJ tugged frantically at his father's arm. I saw Vicky come in from the terrace, then Milly rushing toward us followed by everyone in the great room tripping over each other to get into the library. Behind them came Annie, her serving cap askew, her arms flailing in the air, her cry turning the polite scuffle into a stampede.

"FIRE, MRS. BARRETT, FIRE! IT'S THE OLD BEAUMONT HOUSE—IT'S IN FLAMES!"

Mark Barrett relaxed his grip on my throat.

Thirty-Six

From the *East Hampton Star*—August 14

FIRE DESTROYS BEAUMONT MANSION:
BLAZE CLAIMS ONE VICTIM

Four chimneys and an unobstructed view of Gardiners Bay were all that remained on the site of the Beaumont mansion after a fire gutted the stately residence last Saturday evening. The fire was reported to the Town police by a man aboard his pleasure boat, enjoying a late-night sail on the bay. Mr. Thomas Innis described the scene as "an inferno. It lit up the sky and water like high noon."

The East Hampton Fire Department received a call at 11 p.m. from the Town police. The thirty-room manor is owned by Mr. and Mrs. Stephen Fletcher of Los Angeles, California. Mr. Fletcher is a television producer and hotel owner. Fire Chief Bruce Stoner reported that the blaze was out of control when the first fire truck arrived on the scene ten minutes after the call was received.

Twenty-seven fire trucks from East Hampton, Bridgehampton, Amagansett, Springs, and Montauk fought the blaze.

Body Discovered

At dawn, sifting through the rubble, firefighters uncovered the charred body of a man later identified as Lester Miller of Cedar Point, East Hampton. Mr. Miller, a landscaper, had a long history of DWIs and drunk and disorderly charges filed against him by both Village and Town police. His truck bearing the logo Les & Son was found less than a mile from the Beaumont mansion. It is not known if Mr. Miller died in an attempt to fight the fire or if he was on the property prior to its outbreak. His son, Galen Miller, 19, refused to talk to our reporter. He told the police, however, he had no idea what his father was doing at the site.

Investigation Under Way

Town police, the Town fire marshal, and the county arson squad have opened an investigation. Fire Marshal Richard DiCosta said that as of yesterday there were no leads in the case. Arson is strongly suspected, but the house is undergoing a massive renovation and exposed wiring and careless workers are also being considered factors. Town Police Chief Frank Zimbalist refused to comment at this time as to the involvement of Lester Miller in the conflagration. "Our investigation has just begun. We have proof of nothing at this time."

House a Landmark

The house, an East Hampton landmark, was built in 1902 by Henry Beaumont, a self-made millionaire, and became the scene of elaborate parties often attended by stars of the silent screen. His son, also Henry, continued the tradition until his death in 1977. Spectacular Fourth of July parties were a hallmark of Henry junior's fetes.

Recent Purchase

After Henry Beaumont's death, the family left East Hampton and the house remained unoccupied until it was purchased by Mr. Fletcher early this year. His wife, Sarah Barrett Fletcher, is the daughter of Mr. and Mrs. Mark Barrett of Main Street, East Hampton. Mr. Fletcher was in the process of renovating the mansion and he and Mrs. Fletcher had not as yet occupied their new home. The house was devoid of furnishings.

No Immediate Plans

Mr. Fletcher has no immediate plans for rebuilding, his lawyer told the *Star* by phone from Los Angeles. The lawyer also stated that Mr. Fletcher did not know Lester Miller.

From the *East Hampton Star*—August 14

RECEPTION ENDS IN TRAGEDY

A reception was held Saturday evening, August 9, in honor of Mr. and Mrs. Stephen Fletcher. Mrs. Fletcher is the former Sarah Barrett of East Hampton. Her husband is the television producer and entrepreneur with worldwide interests in hotels, casinos, and cruise ships. Mrs. Fletcher returned to East Hampton this summer after a long stay in California, where she met and married Stephen Fletcher. The Fletchers purchased the landmark Beaumont mansion and surrounding acreage overlooking Gardiners Bay earlier in the year and, after a major renovation to the manor house, planned to summer in East Hampton in the future. The Beaumont mansion was gutted by a fire the night of the reception for the Fletchers. (A full report of the fire appears on page 1.)

Gala Affair

The reception was given by Mrs. Fletcher's parents, Mark and Millicent Barrett, in their home, Barrett House, Main Street, East Hampton. One guest described the event as "very elegant indeed." Our informant stated that over fifty close friends of the Barretts gathered to be presented to the Fletchers. The Barrett mansion was adorned with fresh flowers, and background music was provided by a cocktail pianist. Guests were indulged with two serving bars, waitresses proffering exotic finger food, and a groaning board offering caviar and other delicacies.

Buffet Supper Aborted

News of the fire reached Barrett House as the caterers began laying out a sumptuous late-night buffet. "It was horrible," our source said. "And chaotic. If I didn't know better I would have thought Barrett House was on fire the way everyone fled to their cars and headed for the Beaumont place."

Sightseers Obstruct Firefighters

The police cordoned a wide area around the Fletcher property to prevent cars and those on foot from impeding the firefighters' efforts to put the blaze under control. Fire Chief Bruce Stoner stated that gridlocked traffic and pedestrians posed a threat not only to his men but to the bystanders as well. He denied that an altercation had taken place between the police and Mr. Fletcher when the latter was denied entrance to the property. The house was demolished in a fire that claimed one victim.

Thirty-Seven

The season was winding down and everyone was playing as fast and as hard as wallets allowed. Golfers golfed, swimmers swam, sailors sailed, and gossips gossiped—about the Beaumont mansion fire and the Barrett House fisticuffs.

It was rumored that traces of gasoline were found in the back of Les Miller's truck. Not unusual for a vehicle that toted gasoline-powered lawn mowers, and why would the old sot want to burn down the house? Maybe he didn't like a black man owning the Beaumont mansion—and maybe others shared this sentiment.

Another story had it that Les Miller had gone to the house in search of liquor. Too drunk to realize that it was uninhabited due to a renovation in progress and believing he would find a well-stocked bar, Les broke in and managed to interfere with exposed wiring, setting off an electrical fire. People liked this version because it absolved the community of even a hint of malicious prejudice, and what better scapegoat than a dead one? The only problems were that it could not be determined whether the fire was caused by faulty wiring and—perhaps more significant—Les Miller had no history of plundering vacant homes.

Stephen and Sarah Fletcher left East Hampton for their New York apartment. MJ told me that Fletcher was pulling political strings, locally and in Washington. He wanted the New York Fire Department to investigate the Beaumont mansion blaze. This not only questioned the competence of the Suffolk County arson experts and the East Hampton firefighters, but also put their willingness to learn the truth in dispute. On the federal level, Fletcher was seeking help on the grounds of a possible civil rights violation. The East Hampton politicos were not feeling too kindly toward Fletcher and wanted nothing more than for the whole business to disappear.

To date, the only things to disappear are the Beaumont mansion and Les Miller's wife. Coincidence?

Milly has gone to New York to be with her daughter and this move conveniently dovetails with the theory that Mark Barrett attacked me because of my attention to Milly. True, in the weeks since Kirk's death, when I was licking my wounds and Vicky was tied up with her lawyer, Milly and I often lunched at the Club tête-à-tête, without any idea that we were the season's ongoing soap opera. This we learned not from our so-called friends, who act as if the aborted face-off between Barrett and me never occurred, but from Maddy, who gets it from her cohorts and takes great delight in passing it on to Vicky. The servants' grapevine is swift and tenacious.

Note, it never occurred to this crowd that a Barrett was acting unprofessionally with his client, who was also my wife.

On the positive side, Vicky is furious with Barrett. She abhors violence and learned at her father's knee that propriety is next to godliness. Vicky mercifully stopped paying regular visits to the office of Barrett and Barrett. Mark Barrett called several times on the pretense of unfinished business, but Vicky didn't take the bait. The fact that he offered neither an explanation nor an apology for his inane behavior didn't help his cause with my wife. Still, she was finding it hard to believe that Mark attacked me because I was offering his son a bit of solace and affection.

"He's homophobic and a racist," I announced, still nursing my bruised throat. "The bastard wanted to kill me."

"We've known him for years," Vicky said. "And until now he has never been anything but a perfect gentleman."

"A gentleman would not propose marriage to another man's rich wife when he's looking for a supply of ready cash."

The tension between MJ and his father has reached the stage where MJ avoids Barrett House and sees his father only in the office.

"They've all abandoned Mark since the fire," Vicky observed, perhaps not without a tinge of guilt.

"Maybe they don't like watching him gloat."

Too often, Vicky's only response was to shake her head and light another cigarette. Once again I could feel her withdrawing, more confused and uncertain than ever. If I lost her a second time I feared it might be for good. "Labor Day will be here before you know it," I reminded her. "We've got to start organizing for our move back to town and planning Kirk's memorial. Let's get on with it, Vicky."

"Mark drew up an invitation list for the service," she put in—timidly, to be sure.

"Did you ever hear the story of old Mrs. Astor's ballroom?"

Vicky looked perplexed. "You mean the ballroom that could hold four hundred people."

"Exactly," I said. "Since her ballroom could hold no more than four hundred people, an arrogant ass called Ward McAllister said there were only four hundred people in New York society who qualified for admission, and proceeded to make up a guest list for Mrs. Astor's ball. The old dowager took one look at the list of four hundred, crossed off Ward McAllister's name, and three hundred and ninety-nine people attended the party. Tell Barrett to send me his list."

Like the other night at Gordon's, I made my wife laugh as if she meant it. Well, it was a start.

I had some ideas of my own regarding the leveling of the Beaumont place. How many coincidences does it take to hatch a plot? The Barrett-Miller connection seemed to have more than was necessary, and I had the knowledge, or thought I did, to break the code.

Only a hero or a fool would taunt a murderer and I, Michael Anthony Reo, am neither, I thought as I drove the Land Rover down Further Lane, recalling the day I had taken the same route in MJ's silver convertible. Then why was I doing this? I didn't look for an answer, because if I did I might regain my sanity and drive past my destination.

I got lucky when someone pulled out of a parking space, which the Land Rover immediately filled. I removed my sneakers in the car and, wearing shorts and a T-shirt, made my way around a mound of sand dotted with sea grass that acts as a buffer between the parking lot and the beach. A turn to the left and I found myself among as large an amalgamation of influential gay and lesbian trendsetters as you were likely to find anyplace on the planet. Gayhampton at Two Mile Hollow.

From the arts to Wall Street, from computers to medicine, from Seventh Avenue to Madison Avenue—here they gathered to see and be seen, and extremes of both were in evidence this lovely summer day. Some of the women were topless, none of the men were bottomless, but if the bodies on parade could be deemed indicative, gymnasiums, exercise machines, and health foods were experiencing an unprecedented boom.

This is the Hamptons that does not appear in gossip columns, magazine articles, novels, and films, and the denizens of Two Mile Hollow like it that way. It gives them elbow room and those that otherwise do appear regularly in gossip columns, magazine articles, and films don't have to worry about overexposure.

Two Mile Hollow is sandwiched between the Club to the west and Amagansett's family beach to the east. Oceanfront homes and picturesque dunes form a chain linking all three. Strolling from one locale to the other is permissible but not encouraged.

I spotted the volleyball net and went right for my mark: he was there. Galen Miller. I felt neither pleasure nor disappointment, only fear. As I watched this near-perfect specimen of American boyhood at play I wondered, again, why he had so brutally murdered his lover. His stepmother. Did their bizarre relationship unhinge him? Had she threatened to expose him to his father? Murder is an act of insanity or desperation, and judging from the aggressiveness of his game, desperation was Galen Miller's driving force.

The players were male and female. The audience, perhaps a dozen of us, was all male. Galen had some formidable competition, if indeed they were that. The sweating bodies, washboard abs and muscled limbs, all in motion, could have been buyers or sellers. One needed a program. As players left the sand court, others took their place. I waited patiently and was rewarded for my perseverance when Galen stepped out of the competition and headed for a small cache piled in the sand. Towel, shirt, sneakers, and as I watched, a bottle of designer water was lifted from the heap. He unscrewed the cap and drank.

I feared someone would get to him first, and seeing the number of heads that turned from the action to follow the blonde in the white trunks, my anxiety was not without reason. Not knowing the proper etiquette, I approached and opened with, "Hot."

He responded by taking another swig from the bottle.

"Did you ever get to see Mr. Barrett?"

He lowered the bottle and studied my face. "The guy on the bike," he said accusingly.

"Did you ever get to see Mark Barrett?" I repeated. I looked for a trace of fear in those blue eyes. What I saw was defiance. This was not going well.

"Who wants to know?" he asked.

"I do. And if you meet me tonight, I'll tell you why."

"I'm booked." He tossed the bottle to the ground and picked up the towel. He used it to mop his face.

A commotion on the volleyball court broke our verbal stride. One of the female players had turned an ankle and was being carried off by two young men. "Galen," someone shouted, "we need you."

Galen twirled the towel lengthwise and wrapped it around his neck. His blond hair was plastered to his forehead and a stream of sweat ran from his throat to his navel. As I had surmised through my binoculars, his chest was hairless, but at close range I could see that his forearms and legs weren't. Galen Miller was all man and strutted his stuff like a day laborer on holiday, which accounted for his popularity with the denizens of Two Mile Hollow.

"Unbook," I said. Would I have had the nerve to speak this way if we were alone on a dark street? But we were on a crowded beach, the incongruity of our dialogue accentuated by the panorama of sea and sky, surf and sun. "There's a local bar in Amagansett. Not the Talkhouse—"

"Fuck off."

"Be there at nine tonight."

He spat into the sand and turned to leave.

"If you're not there I'll ask the police to meet me at a pond off Two Holes of Water Road—with their dredging equipment."

He froze, gripping the towel until his arm muscles bulged. He started to turn, but before he completed the move I was gone.

Thirty-Eight

If Mark Barrett's family had deserted him, it wasn't for lack of just cause. Even if he couldn't be held directly responsible for Mr. Miller's death, he should have known better than to encourage a man whose mind was pickled in alcohol to play with matches. Mark Barrett was solely responsible for Les Miller's death and I saw no reason why I shouldn't plea-bargain with the victim's son to hold Barrett accountable. It wasn't stretching the truth beyond reason that if Mark Barrett had kept his nose out of the Miller family's business, two lives would not have been foolishly wasted.

The boy told me everything. What choice did he have? I held all the cards.

The brash young volleyball player I had deserted on the beach in the afternoon arrived at the pub in Amagansett that same evening a cowering, frightened adolescent. I almost felt sorry for him, but not sorry enough to abort my mission. As I sipped my scotch and soda, surrounded by native sons talking shop and a few weekenders who didn't know any better, I was still not convinced that I could go through with it. When he arrived, ten minutes early, the fear he couldn't hide went a long way toward bolstering my courage.

He sauntered into the bar, trying for a show of indifference, but when he ordered a beer the bartender laughed in his face, causing major damage to his act. "And don't try to pass off any phony ID on me, Galen," the bartender exclaimed, then added, "Sorry about your father." The sympathy didn't make up for the put-down. How often had Galen Miller suffered such indignation? I picked up my drink and motioned for him to follow. There were a few tables in the rear, all empty, and I commandeered one in a dark corner. I told him to sit and returned to the bar, ordering a scotch and beer chaser. I carried both to our table, gave my soda a double dose, and placed the beer in front of him. He didn't thank me.

"How do you know?" he asked.

"It doesn't make any difference how I know what I know. What matters is, I know. Now tell me why you did it and you had better be convincing."

Surprisingly, he did just that.

Barrett had made his offer to buy the Miller farm a few days before Christmas. The next time Galen saw the lawyer was a week ago, when he hired Les Miller to torch the Beaumont mansion. Barrett never followed up on the farm offer because, with the death of Joseph Kirkpatrick, land deals no longer interested the speculator. My rich wife did. This was something Galen couldn't possibly know.

What Barrett couldn't know was that his bid—strictly a fishing expedition, I'm sure—would have a domino effect from East Hampton to Florida and back. If the boy was telling the truth, and I saw no reason for him to lie, the woman called Betty had married Les to get her hands on Barrett's phantom million. Then she betrayed Galen to ensure she wouldn't have to divide the kitty. Did Betty get what she deserved? And what would I get for my meddling? I'd soon know—if I didn't end up keeping Betty company.

I got him another beer, leaving a tip on the bar large enough to pay for the bartender's disinterest in the occupants of a corner table. If confession is good for the soul, you couldn't prove it by Galen Miller. By the time he finished his tale, he looked like he was going to be sick all over our little table. The cigarettes he kept puffing on without inhaling and pounding out into a tiny ashtray didn't help his upset stomach. I sent him to the men's room to put some cold water on his face, and he obeyed like a child being told to wash before dinner. Seeing this reaction made me think that Galen was more embarrassed by the fact that I had seen him in his tattered underpants than that I had witnessed his crime.

"How do you know?" he asked again when he returned, not looking any better for his trouble. He was obsessed with this thought. "You were hiding in the woods, right?"

"I wasn't hiding. I was on a path off Two Holes of Water Road."

"There's no entrance to the pond from Two Holes of Water."

"Not to the pond," I explained. "But a narrow path leads to the rise above the hole of water. I came upon it by accident."

"Why didn't you go to the police?" Fear did not intrude upon his power to detect my vulnerability and pounce on it.

"I couldn't prove anything. If they couldn't find you, I was the patsy."

"You still can't prove anything."

"But thanks to the local press, I now know who she is and where to find you. She never went into the city every Wednesday to see a show or for any other reason. My guess is she got off the bus someplace and doubled back. The police have probably already figured that out. And if she did go to a lawyer regarding the deed to the farm, he must have gotten in touch with the police as soon as he read of her plight. You're the missing link and, like I said, I know where to find you."

"You waited a long time to nail me—why?"

Again, the keen observer. No reason to tell him I didn't read the *Star* and only recently learned the facts when, at the same time, I discovered his passion to contact Mark Barrett. That I was more interested in Barrett than in his crime would soon be apparent. "That's my business," was as much as he was entitled to.

"What do you want from me?"

Shrewd. If I were intent upon seeing justice done I would have gone to the police; if I was standing him beers in a local pub on Main Street, Amagansett, I wanted a favor. I'm sure the word blackmail must have crossed his mind. Good. It saved a lot of time and small talk. It also took the edge off his tension. He put out his cigarette but didn't immediately reach for another. Instead, he leaned back in his chair and stretched his legs across the floor, seductively. It was his first miscalculation.

"Tell me again, slowly, about Mark Barrett's last visit with your father."

Barrett arrived at the Miller house on the Tuesday before the fire and said nothing about buying the farm. He chatted awhile, then asked Galen to leave. When Galen returned his father had money. How much? Galen didn't know. Twenties. Maybe a thousand dollars in twenties. He thought it was another down payment on the property, but his father told him it was for a job he was going to do for Mr. Barrett. What job? His father wouldn't say. The next day Les Miller bought four five-gallon gasoline tanks and had them filled. He gave Galen some money, but still wasn't talking. Galen was out of the house Saturday night and didn't see his father leave in the truck. He heard about the fire and drove to the Beaumont house along with half of East Hampton to see the blaze. He didn't know his father was in the house, dead, until the next morning when he was notified by the police.

"Then Mr. Barrett came to see me. He paid for the funeral. It costs a lot to die, you know. The coffin. Open the grave. They put Les on top of my mother. She was his doormat in life and now she's his mattress. Some deal, eh? When I get the money I'm digging him up and tossing him out."

Under other circumstances I could grow to like Galen Miller. The son I never had. "What money, Galen?"

"The sale of the farm. It's mine now."

And it took two deaths to put you in the driver's seat, I thought. "Barrett again? Of course. How much did he promise you, Galen?"

"A hundred thousand."

"My, my, the bottom has fallen out of the real estate market. From a million to a hundred thousand. And you believe him?"

"Why shouldn't I?"

"Why should you! He promised you a million and you never saw him again until he needed a favor that killed your father. Now it's a hundred thousand, not for the farm but to keep your mouth shut. Doesn't it bother you that Mark Barrett had a black man's home burned for no other reason than the color of the man's skin and that he killed your father in the bargain?"

He leaned across the small table, expressing amazement at the stupidity of my question. "The only thing that bothers me, mister, is pushing a lawn mower for less money than it takes to put bread on the table and getting my dick licked for the extras. My father was a drunk and a bastard and Mr. Barrett is offering me a way out of my misery, so what's to be upset about?"

"If Barrett promised to bail you out, why are you still selling your tail at Two Mile Hollow?"

He glared at me. "I don't take it up the ass, mister."

"It's a figure of speech, not a sexual preference. Why are you still at whatever you do?"

He shrugged. "Mr. Barrett told me not to jump the gun. You know what I mean? Everything as usual. It wouldn't look good . . ."

"If you came into money too soon after your father's demise?" I questioned. "There's nothing illegal about buying property."

"It's what Mr. Barrett said."

Mr. Barrett. After all that had gone on between them, it was still *Mr.* Barrett. The feudal system is alive and kicking on the East End of Long Island. "Did it ever occur to you that he doesn't have the money to pay you off?"

He scoffed at this bit of nonsense. "Them? They have millions."

Had millions, I wanted to say, but it would have been wasted on a boy who grew up believing the name Barrett was synonymous with great wealth. "Rich or poor," I said, "he's not going to buy the farm."

Galen didn't like my forecast and let me know it. "I don't care what you think, mister, and if you just tell me why you got me here I'll be on my way. You're beginning to be a colossal pain in the ass."

Unfortunate choice of metaphor considering the subject matter of a few minutes ago. "Mark Barrett is not going to buy the farm, Galen, because you're going to the police to tell them that he hired your father to torch the Beaumont house."

"Fuck you."

"You have no choice, remember? You do what I tell you to do or I go to the police and tell them where they can find your stepmother."

"I can be off this island before you get to the station house."

I shook my head. "Think, Galen, think. You don't have a penny. Where would you go and what would you do? A fugitive's life is not an easy one, especially a poor fugitive. And, you'd be leaving behind your only asset. The land. Barrett won't buy it but someone else might. No, you have no choice."

"They'd never believe me," he cried. "A Miller against a Barrett. Forget it."

"Did you ever hear of David and Goliath?"

"Gregory Peck, *David and Bathsheba,* Peck kills the giant. It's in the Bible." He spoke by rote, like a schoolboy rattling off historic dates. Galen Miller was a film buff. I was amazed. A film buff. Of course. Every time I conjured up the scene of the crime, I felt as if I had seen it all before. And I had. In a film. An inconvenient woman conveniently falling out of a rowboat. The name of the film would come to me, but now all I could think was, poor Galen, not an original bone in his handsome body.

"Listen carefully," I began. "Call Barrett. Tell him you need a quick injection of ready cash." He waved his arms in annoyance. "Don't worry, he'll listen. If he gives you a hard time, tell him the police are bugging you about your father's involvement in the fire. You need the money to get away for a while. He'll be more than happy to comply. He's to bring the money to the farm. I'm sure he won't want you to come to his office. When the date is set, go to the police and tell them what you know about the fire. Then tell them when Mark Barrett is coming to your home with the money. They'll take it from there."

He was quiet for a long time, playing with the pack of cigarettes on the table. His second beer was long gone but I didn't offer him another. Our meeting was coming to a close and he knew it. Finally he gave me a great big grin. "We're gonna fuck Mr. Barrett real good." If you can't beat 'em, join 'em. The kid was as subtle as a stick of dynamite. "How much is it worth to you to see Mark Barrett get his?"

I could have slapped his face. Instead I smiled. "Galen, my boy, I've stretched my conscience as far as it will go. Be thankful you're walking away with your life." I rose. "One more thing. If the police give you a hard time, tell them you'll take your story to Stephen Fletcher. That should keep them honest."

Eddy Evans

Thirty-Nine

The Barretts' party was in progress and there was nothing for me to do but patrol the grounds, slip into the kitchen for an occasional taste of the elegant pickings, and watch the catering service prepare turkey, ham, and fillet of beef for the midnight buffet. Say what you want about the rich, they know how to eat.

They also knew how to give a party. The guests drove right up to the front door, where three car jockeys waited to park their vehicles on the back lawn. With nothing to do until the party ended, the three boys settled down to foraging in the kitchen and eating their loot, picnic fashion, on the front lawn. Bored, I walked down the long driveway to Main Street and found it lined with cars parked on both sides of the highway, thanks to the Community Theater's current hit at the John Drew Theater. I could see the lights and imagine the pedestrian traffic a few blocks away in the heart of the business district, and wondered if Helen was busy in Main Street Video.

Helen had refused to see me for two days after her strange reaction to Galen's overdue tape. This made me certain that more was troubling her than a film Galen forgot to return. When we finally did get together again, she pretended she didn't know what I was talking about when I asked for an explanation of the episode. To my way of thinking, this proved that something was very wrong and—taking her position as a warning—I refrained from pursuing the subject.

My stance and her reluctance to share took its toll on our courtship. It didn't exactly go into a nosedive, but it didn't go anywhere either. Her silence on the subject of Galen Miller and my desire to know the reason for that silence created a tension between us that refused to dwindle with time. Like the stifling humidity of a summer day, the strain this standoff caused was acutely felt but not seen.

We went from a couple about to announce our engagement to strangers walking on eggs. I was afraid to speak the name Galen Miller, fearing it would put her in a snit. She was afraid to say anything that might bring Galen into our conversation. She picked at her food, making our dinner dates an expensive farce, so we gave up eating out in favor of sitting home in silence.

I took my problem to Jan, who was overjoyed at my predicament. Short of saying, "I told you so," she advised, "She's a child, Eddy. A child. You must give her space to grow."

"It's that film Galen rented," I told Jan. "Sounds crazy, I know, but this all started the moment her father brought up Galen's delinquent account on his computer screen."

"What was the film, Eddy?"

I couldn't remember. I was so taken with Helen's reaction that I doubt I even heard the name of the film. And what difference did that make?

"All the difference in the world," Jan pointed out. "I think it's a love story. A very poignant love story or, knowing children, a very saccharine love story. They had watched it together. It was 'their film.' You know, the way couples have 'their song' this was 'their film.' She discovers he—Galen is it?—has rented it unbeknownst to her. Why? Why else? To view it with another girl, of course. If he got what he wanted from one girl with this method, why not try it on another? Or several if you consider that he's kept it all summer." She closed this reassuring tirade with her toothpaste smile.

I need Jan Solinsky like I need another Galen Miller.

I was walking back up the driveway when the alarm sounded. Four blasts. A major blaze someplace and the weather was on the side of the enemy—warm and breezy. The full moon and twinkling stars made it an evening for lovers, not firefighters. By the time I reached the front door of Barrett House, four more blasts drowned the sounds of the party coming from within the house. An urgent call to arms. A few minutes later I heard, ever so faintly, the sirens of the fire cars moving out of their berth on Cedar Street.

Later, I would be questioned in great detail about what happened next. As best I can remember, the man who attends the grounds of Barrett House came running round from the side of the house where the kitchen is located, waving his beeper. "I just got a call," he shouted as he passed me. "The Beaumont mansion is on fire! Annie is telling the Barretts." He ran toward the garage, stopped, turned, and shouted at the car jockeys, who were huddled in a group. "Move those cars. Move those damn cars. I'm a marshal. I've got to get my car out of that fucking garage."

Before they had a chance to react, the front door

opened and the partygoers began filing out of Barrett House as if it, not the Beaumont place, was on fire. After this I wouldn't swear to anything until I spotted Stephen Fletcher coming out of the house. He was a head taller than any of the guests and the woman with him was the most beautiful woman I had ever seen. The men and women who had come out before Mr. and Mrs. Fletcher ran for their cars and my polite pleading to let the jockeys do their job fell on deaf ears. The cars, perhaps thirty in all, were parked in three rows and the poor jockeys tried, without success, to direct the flow of traffic toward the single-lane driveway. The result was gridlock in its purest form.

Did I know anything about the fight that took place in Barrett House before the mass exodus? Absolutely not. Did Mark Barrett join the caravan to the fire? I honestly didn't know. When I saw Stephen Fletcher and the woman I guessed was his wife, Sarah Barrett, I went directly to him, identified myself, and told him I had a patrol car parked on Main Street.

"You are a gentleman, sir," Stephen Fletcher said, casting doubt on the status of the men who ignored him in favor of rushing off to see his house burn.

We reached Main Street, by foot, before a single car made it down the driveway. I helped them into the backseat. Mrs. Fletcher had diamond clips in her hair that sparkled in the yellow light of the streetlamps. The John Drew was emptying out for intermission just as cars started creeping out of the Barretts' driveway, trying in vain to merge with the usual Saturday night traffic. Unable to hit the gas pedal, drivers took out their frustrations on their car horns. Drawn by the noise, strollers began moving down Main Street toward Barrett House. All of East Hampton was on a treadmill.

I set my roof light in motion, turned up my siren, and pulled away from the curb. I got as much respect as the traffic jam would allow, but at least I was moving.

"Is this to prevent me from strangling you?" Stephen Fletcher asked, tapping on the metal grate that divided the back and front seats of the patrol car.

Some sense of humor for a guy on the way to watch five million of his bucks going up in smoke.

We could see and smell the blaze long before we were able to reach it. The sky over the bay glowed, obliterating the moon and stars. Cinders, some smoldering, descended on us as we approached. Fire cars, sirens screaming, kept arriving from every hamlet in the area, their progress obstructed by the monumental traffic jam. Uniformed police, none of whom I recognized in the harsh glare of headlights, managed to get me to the front gate of the Beaumont house—or what was left of it. A good half-mile up the drive we could see four chimneys rising above a bed of fire the size of a football field.

The Chief appeared out of a crowd of people in and out of uniform. I lowered the car window as he neared. "No civilians past this point," he shouted at my passengers.

"Chief, this is—"

"I know who it is and I repeat, Evans, no civilians past this point. Now pull over to the shoulder and stay there."

"I understand," Fletcher said, from behind me. "Please do as the officer advises, Mr. Evans."

And that was the extent of the "altercation" that took place between Stephen Fletcher and the East Hampton police, as reported in the *Star.*

When I pulled off the road I asked Fletcher if he kept a security crew at the house.

"No." Mrs. Fletcher spoke for the first time. "There are no people in the house."

She was wrong.

Forty

Les Miller is dead. Trapped in the fire he started. Crazy fool. I was in the station house when the news came through. I went straight to Main Street Video, but was too late.

"A customer came in a while ago, Eddy, and broke the news," Mr. Weaver told me. "Helen took it real bad. She and Galen go back a long ways, you know. Truth is, until you came along I thought she and Gay would . . ." He shrugged, sheepishly. "Just as well, bad blood in that family."

"Where is she?" I asked.

"Home, Eddy. I sent her home. Go see what you can do, son. She doesn't look well. Her mother's been after her about the way she's been sulking around the house. Now this. Talk to her, Eddy. She listens to you."

You couldn't prove it by me, I thought as I made for the door. The only good news was that she hadn't gone running off to see Galen—I hoped.

Mrs. Weaver let me in the house. If it's true that daughters age like their mothers, Helen wouldn't have to worry about losing her looks and figure with her youth. Mrs. Weaver is a good-looking woman, slim and agile as a teenager. Today, her usually pleasant greeting was over-shadowed by her worried frown. "What do you know, Eddy?" she asked before I was through the doorway. "Rumors all over town."

"I know Les is dead and I suspect he torched the house."

"But why?" Mrs. Weaver questioned.

"Looking for booze, is my guess. How is Helen?"

"Awful. She won't talk and she won't cry. Just stares into space and jumps down my throat when I say good morning. And it's not just today, I mean because of Les. She's been this way for days and days."

"I know. But she won't talk to me either. Where is she now?"

"In her room. Go on up, Eddy. Talk to her." When I looked hesitant, she added, "Straight ahead at the top of the stairs. It faces the back. And don't be shy with her, Eddy. She needs a hand, but don't wrap it in a velvet glove."

I had never been in Helen's room or even on the sec-ond floor of the Weaver house, and I didn't know what to expect. Pink walls and glossy photos of teenage movie stars? Her door was open and to my relief she was stand-ing by a window, not stretched out on her bed. But that would be very unlike Helen, as would the pink walls and pictures of movie stars. The room was done in a pretty flowered paper and the artwork, what there was of it, was watercolor renditions of East Hampton landmarks.

She didn't turn when I entered, and before I had a chance to speak she said, "Did he do it, Eddy?"

"It looks that way," I answered.

"How do you know?"

"His truck tells the story. They found it, half hidden, in

a copse off the road, not far from the entrance to the Beaumont place. With all the cars converging on the area last night, he would have had to fly his truck in to park it there after the alarm sounded. He was there before the fire started."

She turned to face me. I could see a tall blue spruce framed by the window. Her eyes were red and puffy. Helen obviously cried in private. "Suppose he was the first to spot the blaze and—"

"Hid his truck a half-mile from the house and ran back to put out the fire?"

She walked the short distance to her bed and sat. It was a double bed, covered in a yellow quilt that matched the flowers in the wallpaper. I looked around the room. A rocker, two chests of drawers, a closet door; all neat and modest, it gave away nothing about its resident, except for the room's prevailing scent—jasmine. It was Helen's scent and I could see the small pear-shaped vial on her dresser that was its source. I felt like a giant in a doll-house. One wrong move and I'd knock it all to pieces.

"He didn't go there looking for liquor," Helen continued, squashing the rumors and the police department's prime theory. "The house was being rebuilt. We all knew that. It contained nothing but tools and building supplies."

"Les didn't know that."

She looked at me as if pitying my ignorance, her gray eyes bright with defiance. "Les Miller was a drunk," she began, "and maybe a little crazy, but he wasn't stupid, Eddy. The only place that line of thinking will get you is up the garden path."

"What's your theory?"

"I don't have one, and why don't you sit down. You

look like a little boy who has to use the bathroom but is too ashamed to go."

Helen could always say it all in twenty-five words or less. "Will that rocker hold me?"

She smiled and patted the space next to her. "Here. I don't bite."

I accepted the invitation very cautiously. "We're sharing a bed, Helen."

"If we get married, Eddy, we'll do this lying down."

"Are we? Going to get married?"

"Are you reneging on your offer?"

"I'm waiting for an answer."

She withdrew, silently, her mind closing like a door in my face. The tension between us was suddenly so great I couldn't resist gripping her elbow to keep her from fleeing. "When is the funeral?" she asked.

"From wedding bells to funerals. You're a barrel of laughs, Helen."

She turned and looked hard into my eyes. "We stopped laughing when Les married that woman. It all goes back to that."

"Sorry, Watson, but you're wrong. It all goes back to that million Mark Barrett offered Les for the farm. Do you think he was serious?"

"What I think doesn't matter, does it? Les and Galen believed him and now Les is dead."

"And the lady is missing."

Helen shook herself free of my hand and rose, returning to the window and the blue spruce. "Dead. Missing. What's happened to all of us, Eddy?"

"Only what we've allowed to happen."

She made a noise that could have been a giggle or a

snort. "Jan told me you have a platitude for all the important questions of our age."

"I can think of worse things."

"Name one."

"Being miserable and not allowing someone who loves you very much to help ease the pain."

I could see her shoulders stiffen. "I love you, Eddy."

I wanted to jump up and down on the bed. Instead, I went to her and touched her shoulder. She didn't move. "When is the funeral?" she asked again.

"They identified Les this morning. It should be in a few days, unless the coroner has other ideas. If not, it's up to Galen." When she didn't answer, I said, "You don't have to go, Helen."

"But I do, Eddy. I'm all the family Galen has."

Les's body was released two days after he was found in the ashes and the funeral was held two days after that. The weather cooperated, with gray skies, the threat of rain at any moment, and a breeze that toppled one of the floral arrangements. On his last day above ground, Les Miller was surrounded by those who had surrounded him all his life. Most of the Bonacker families were represented as well as Les's drinking companions, or the few that hadn't succumbed to AA or cirrhosis, and a good number of town and village policemen—the boys in blue wondering, no doubt, who was going to relieve the monotony of the long winter months in East Hampton now that Les had been forced into retirement. Thanks to Les's sensational finale, his funeral also drew two men I suspected were FBI or private investigators in the employ of Stephen Fletcher. Our two newspapers, the *East Hamp-*

ton Star and the *Independent,* each sent a photographer and a reporter.

Like extras in a film, the curious appeared in great numbers, and among them I spotted the lawyer Mark Barrett, the man whose daughter and son-in-law had lost their home thanks to Les. Curious how the guy, in flesh or spirit, kept weaving in and out of the Betty Zabriskie Miller saga. In light of events to follow, I could give Helen's psychic a run for her money.

We gathered at Cedar Lawn Cemetery shortly before noon. Situated a short distance from the heart of town, Cedar Lawn is an oasis of green grass and tombstones in the midst of a middle-class neighborhood with pretensions. Helen looked very grown-up in a navy blue dress with white collar and cuffs, dark stockings, and high-heeled shoes. I was so used to seeing her in T-shirt, shorts, and sneakers, the change was remarkable. The kid was a very pretty young lady.

Galen, who had got himself up in tie and jacket, was at the grave site when we arrived. Helen went directly to him and he bent his head to receive her sisterly kiss, which was the extent of his acknowledging her presence. As always, I was struck by Galen's good looks. His golden hair and blue eyes shone in sharp contrast to the gloomy day, and if I had any doubt that most of the spectators had their eyes on Galen, all I had to do was turn my head to know that this was true.

Why did he so attract and repel me? Was it his nerve or stupidity that triggered these responses? Here, with Helen standing between us and a coffin before us, I admitted shamelessly that I had won her because Galen Miller didn't want her. It was a bitter dose of truth, but Helen's hand tightly gripping mine made it go down like honey.

The minister from the Amagansett Presbyterian Church performed the graveside service. Thankfully, he didn't eulogize the deceased but spoke instead of the brevity of the here and now, and the longevity of a piece of Cedar Lawn real estate. Throughout the short sermon Helen held my hand and Galen, perfectly rigid, seemed to hold his breath, fearing even a ripple of air would upset the applecart. Three people had a stake in Barrett's million-dollar offer. One of them was dead and the other had vanished. You could appreciate the boy's anxiety.

When the service was over Helen invited Galen back to the house for lunch. She accepted his refusal without even a polite try at coaxing him to come with us. This falling-out between the two should have pleased me; instead it only had me scratching my head over its cause. Galen had stayed clear of Helen for weeks and she seemed to accept this until the day Mr. Weaver discovered the overdue tape. Then she turned moody and now it was clear Helen was keeping her distance.

It made no sense to me, but then why should it? I was the intruder and very aware of how little I knew of her relationship with Galen Miller before I came along. "They go back a long ways," Mr. Weaver had said, and what they had shared would always belong to them and no one else. That's as it should be, I guess, but parting as they now did, especially under the circumstances, was not. Because he had shared "their movie" with another girl? Baloney.

The minister closed his book. The rain had held off. And the leaves on the tall maples were beginning to color. The summer was over.

I received a warm thank-you for my appearance when I shook Galen's hand. The guy didn't hold a grudge, I'll say that for him. As we departed and the crowd dispersed, I noticed Mark Barrett standing his ground as if waiting for someone. Who could it be but Galen? Interesting.

When we got in my car I turned to Helen and said, "You did your duty and I'm proud that you did."

She burst into tears and cried all the way back to the Weaver house. Was she crying for Les? Galen? Herself? Or some long-cherished memory she had left at Cedar Lawn Cemetery along with Les & Son?

Forty-One

Alpha and omega, as the poets say. A few days before the Fourth of July weekend Les Miller walked into the station house, not handcuffed and more or less sober, to report his wife missing. Now, just before the Labor Day weekend, Galen Miller paid us a visit and asked to see me. I honestly thought that the mystery of Betty Zabriskie was about to be solved. I led him into the interview room, closed the door, and invited him to sit. Then I listened to a story so astounding I withheld even a courteous nod of the head before I ran into the Chief's office.

"The kid is crazy," the Chief bellowed, looking for something on his desk to straighten or realign. A manila folder, a pen caddy and an ashtray filled with paper clips were chosen.

"I think you should listen to what he has to say," I advised.

"That family is all nuts, Evans. What's Galen trying to do, shift the blame from his father to . . ." He didn't want to think it, let alone say it aloud. Tiny beads of perspiration suddenly appeared on the Chief's smooth forehead, or was it the way the shaft of light from the window played on his oily complexion?

"He said he was thinking of going to Stephen Fletcher but decided to come to us first, seeing as this is a local case. I think he was dead serious, Chief."

It was definitely sweat. Heavy-duty sweat.

"I'll bring him in here," I offered.

"No." The Chief jumped out of his swivel chair with as much speed as his newly acquired bulk would allow. "No sense in starting tongues wagging out there for no reason. I'll follow you out and then pop into the interview room."

The fact that everyone in the house started speculating about Galen's appearance the minute he walked into the station house, I didn't tell the Chief. I had no desire to see heavy-duty sweat turn to blood. Galen's stepmother's disappearance and his father's death and implication in the Beaumont Blaze—as it had been labeled—made it obvious that one or the other was the reason for this call. Which one, not what, was the question.

"If you're bullshitting, kid, I'm going to make your life miserable from today until the day you join your old man." Tact was not the Chief's long suit.

"I'm telling you what I know," Galen said.

"Why?" the Chief shot back.

"Because they're saying my father was crazy. A psycho. That he was drunk and looking to raid the liquor closet in an empty house. *That's* the bullshit. He was there doing a job and getting well paid for it. Seems Barrett didn't want fancy niggers snapping up prime real estate, especially one married to his daughter."

The Chief banged his hand on the table that separated us from Galen and winced with pain. "Shut up, you little— Just shut up with that kind of talk. Did you happen to notice the color of some of the people working out there?" The Chief jerked a thumb over his shoulder.

"Hey man, I'm no racist. I'm just quoting the lawyer and if you don't want to hear it"—he gripped the arms of his chair as if about to rise—"I'm outta here."

"What proof do you have?" the Chief asked.

Galen produced a wad of twenties from the pocket of his jeans and placed them on the table.

"I counted it. There's seven hundred and twenty dollars there," I told the Chief. "Galen said his father had spent some and so did he. He thinks there was a thousand in all."

"Why would he go looking for liquor in an empty house when he could buy enough to drown in?" Galen put in.

"You call this proof? How do I know where it came from or when you got it? If you can't do better than that, beat it and take your lousy money with you."

"Chief . . ." I put a hand on his shoulder and motioned for Galen to stay seated. "Tell the Chief what happened yesterday, Galen."

"The Chief doesn't seem to like what I have to say, so if you'll excuse me I'll find my way out and take my lousy money with me."

This was madness. "Stay where you are, Gay." I turned to the Chief. "Barrett offered Galen a hundred thousand for the farm. Galen called Barrett yesterday and told him he wanted a fat advance now, in cash, so he could get away from the police and their questions about Les and the fire. Barrett is bringing the money to the farm tomorrow, sometime before noon." For good measure I added, "You don't conduct legal business that way."

The Chief called our arson liaison in Riverhead. He

told the Chief to keep Galen under lock and key along with the other officer who had witnessed the story. Quote, full quarantine. I don't want either of 'em near another human being with ears and a mouth, unquote.

Then the Chief called the town supervisor.

The four of us sat in the interview room as tension mounted outside. We sent out for pizza and ate slices in silence. When Galen announced that he had to pee, we all went with him. The men and women on duty stared at us as we filed past and into the men's room, then again as we filed out and back into the interview room. One of the officers caught my eye, pointed at Galen, and drew a finger across his throat. So, they thought we had arrested Galen for the murder of Betty Zabriskie. Better that than the truth.

The Miller house was wired. Just like in the movies. Galen must have loved that. Then Galen was instructed by the team from Riverhead on what to say to Mark Barrett, after which he was placed in a cell where he spent the night in the company of one of the Riverhead crew. I was barred from leaving the station house. It seems only the Chief and the supervisor were trusted to keep their mouths shut. Rank has its privileges.

The trap was set and Mark Barrett walked into the Miller house carrying five thousand bucks in cash in an envelope; he came out empty-handed and into the arms of the law. The rest is history.

Galen must have played his part well. So well Mark Barrett pleaded guilty with cause, whatever that means, and is awaiting a hearing and sentencing. Where he's waiting, I don't know, but not in East Hampton or in New York with his wife, who it's rumored has left him. His son, called MJ—for Mark junior, I guess—refused to comment on his father's conviction but released a brief statement to the *Star*. "The Barretts have been in East Hampton for three hundred years and practicing law for one hundred. I see no change in the foreseeable future. The firm of Barrett and Barrett will enter the new millennium with a Barrett in charge."

I received a letter from Stephen Fletcher, extending an invitation for two to spend two weeks at his luxury hotel in Las Vegas, all expenses paid and a thousand dollars' worth of chips to parlay into a million. Would I be allowed to accept it? I said nothing to the Chief or Helen. Las Vegas? Not a bad place for a honeymoon.

We were parked at Indian Wells Beach in Amagansett. It was dusk. Our favorite spot at our favorite time of day. Before us was a stretch of sand that the seagulls were busy reclaiming as their own and the Atlantic Ocean, looking ice-cold in the fading light. Labor Day had come and gone and so had the second-home owners, the renters, and the day-trippers.

"Why do you think Galen turned on Mr. Barrett?" Helen asked.

"Why do you?"

She shook her head, setting her hair in motion. I put my hand around her shoulders. "I don't know," she answered, not resting her head against my chest as she often did when we sat here.

"You want the truth?" I asked.

"It's time for the truth, Eddy, isn't it?"

"Overdue I would say." I took a deep breath and began. "I can't imagine Galen Miller rejecting the hundred thousand in favor of justice. Can you?"

Again, she shook her head but didn't answer.

"I think someone was holding a knife to his throat."
Helen started. "It's just an expression, Helen. I mean it
was to his advantage to give up the money and tell what
he knew about the fire. Galen is a con artist. We both
know that. He uses people to his advantage. This time,
someone used him, but I don't know why."

"And you think I do?" Her voice was so low I could
just make out the words.

"I think you know something, Helen, and if we don't
have it out I don't know what's going to happen between
us. You can't take much more, and frankly, neither can I."

She stared at the ocean as if trying to see what was on
the other side. Half a moon, white as fine talc, appeared
on the horizon. What she said was so unexpected, spoken
so softly, I had to bend my head toward her to catch every
word.

"Galen arrived in the first grade with a lunch box. His
mother bought it for him a few weeks before she died. It
was his most prized possession. Maybe his only possession, except for the clothes he wore and I don't think he
owned more than one change of shirt and pants. He
gripped the handle of his lunch box so tight his knuckles
turned white. He never tossed it to the ground in the
schoolyard in favor of a game of tag or left it in the cloak-
room during class, but kept it under his chair, embracing
it with his ankles. It was his membership card into the fraternity of first-graders.

"I was the only one who knew Galen's lunch box was
always empty. He begged me never to tell. I shared my
lunch with him every day—and I never told, Eddy, I
never told."

She talked and I watched Galen Miller grow up. The
son of the town drunk. I saw him discover the hole of

water. Watched him swim and strut, naked as a jaybird, king of his domain. I saw him there with Helen and closed my eyes; I didn't want to see that. I saw them watching the film Galen had rented and never returned. I heard their conversation:

"You don't have the nerve."

· "Don't I?"

Helen was crying, her tears soaking my shirt. "He was afraid Betty was going to do him out of his place in the sun, like poor George Eastman in the film. I told him it wasn't his farm to sell, but he wouldn't listen. Then I told him to befriend his stepmother to see what she was up to, and after that I almost never saw him." Her voice was pitched a shade too high for comfort. She was getting hysterical. I held her as tight as I could, stroking her back and pleading with her not to go on. Not now. When she was calmer.

"I went there," she almost screamed. "To the pond."

"Why? Why didn't you tell me?"

"I wanted to be sure, Eddy."

"And are you?"

"I don't know. The boat is gone but—but there's nothing floating . . ." She shuddered in my arms. "Maybe somebody took the boat. It's possible, Eddy, isn't it?"

It's also possible that he sank the boat, and if he did, and it came to rest over the body, Betty was locked in a watery coffin. Now *I* shuddered.

I waited until Helen quieted before I said, "You know what I have to do, Helen."

"I know."

We sat for a long time, saying nothing, just watching the sky grow dark and the moon turn yellow. I was going to have one hell of a day tomorrow.

"Eddy?"

"Yeah, Helen."

"Galen has been trying to fill that lunch box all his life."

Galen Miller

Forty-Two

Nobody in their right mind is going to buy this place. I've been to every real estate agency in town. They'll list it, but that's all. No ads. So how are people going to know it's for sale? A few of the agencies put signs out front, but who the fuck ever rides past this place?

And I need money. Fast. They took all the money Barrett laid on Les and the five grand Barrett was going to give me. My mouth watered when I saw it. Now Mark Barrett is my enemy. Will he put a contract out for me? Fuck, I don't know. I just don't know.

The phone.

Midnight and the phone is ringing. Who would call at this time? Trouble, that's who. Maybe it's the guy who put the screws on me. I don't even know his name. He had me so fucked up I never thought about it until after he was gone. I don't even know his name. He can put me in the electric chair and I don't even know his name.

I won't answer.

The phone is in the kitchen. I was going to get an extension for my room with Barrett's money. Now I got dick. Who's calling? Why? Four rings. Five rings. Fuck.

I go downstairs. Maybe it'll stop before I get there. Nine rings. Ten rings. Trouble. It has to be trouble.

"Hello."

"Galen. It's Helen. Listen. Just listen . . ."

Epilogue

"An intriguing title, 'The Hampton Affair,' and a story to match." Stephen Fletcher placed the bound film treatment on the desk. "Congratulations, Michael. If the film plays as well as the script reads, I foresee a winner with your first venture."

Michael Anthony Reo reached for the script and drew it toward him. "I wanted you to see it before we went into production. A libel action, I don't need on my first time out. Of course, all the names have been changed to protect the guilty."

Fletcher laughed. "You'll get no flak from me. The fire is in the past and I never dwell on memories. Bad for business. And a phoenix is already beginning to rear its lovely head above the ashes."

"So I've heard. We'll make the Dunemere Lane house our headquarters during the shooting. All the exteriors will be authentic. Not even Hollywood magic could duplicate East Hampton in July and August. You'll be at Barrett House while waiting for the phoenix to rise?"

"If my brother-in-law invites us. He plans to spend some of the summer in Italy with his mother."

"So Milly wrote us. When *The Hampton Affair* is in the can—that is the expression, Stephen, 'in the can'?"

"Yes, Michael. In the can. Finished. Done. Over. The rest is up to God and the *New York Times* film reviewer. They work as a team."

"When it's in the can, Vicky and I hope to visit with Milly for a deserved rest."

"I understand the Kirkpatrick Foundation has announced its intention to save libraries and promote literacy. Good for Vicky. But tell me, Michael, aside from the fiery finale, the boy and the dead woman, what is fact and what is fiction in *The Hampton Affair?*"

Michael shrugged. "From the time the body was raised from the pond, MJ sent me all the clippings from the *Star* relating to the story and telephoned all the rumors. I filled in the blanks with my vivid imagination and turned it all over to the best screenwriter in the business." He picked up the script. "This is the result."

"The hero—if he can be called that—who witnesses the murder and forces the exposure of the arsonist and the villain is of course a creation of your vivid imagination."

Michael nodded in agreement. "To be sure. And he most certainly can be called a hero. If I were younger, I'd play the role."

"The policeman acted on a tip from a girl who used to rendezvous with the boy you call Guy. This is fact?"

"Oh yes. It was in the newspaper."

"And you think she fingered Guy and then tipped him off?"

"Why else would he disappear the day they dragged the pond? I mean, who else knew the police were going to act that morning? Only the police themselves, and I don't think they tipped him. Besides, Stephen, it makes a great love story."

"And they've never found him," Stephen Fletcher said.

"And neither have we. I mean the actor to play the role of Guy. None of the current Hollywood brats will do. I'm going to put on a search for the actor to play Guy, Stephen, that will make the search for Scarlett O'Hara look like a yawn."

"I like your style, Michael." Fletcher rose to leave. "And your digs. One of the few towers that has a view of both rivers. I'm jealous."

Michael rose along with his visitor. "It was my father-in-law's office, I'm sure you know. I'm filling it, but not his shoes," he added modestly.

"Your own shoes appear more than sufficient." The two men shook hands and Stephen Fletcher went to the door. He opened it, paused, and turned back to face Michael. "Suppose the real Guy turns up to claim the role. What would you do?"

"He wouldn't have the nerve," Michael answered.

"Wouldn't he?"